She stared at him, bathed in silver, still touching her. "What are *you* doing out here?" She kept her tone as casual as possible.

"Checking my mare." He inclined his head toward the barn. "She's due to drop a foal any day now."

"Ah." She really *wanted* to believe him. His thumbs traced warm circles against her bare arms, sending shockwaves of longing straight to her core. Her breath caught. "Um . . . how is she?"

"Beautiful."

"The mare?"

"You."

Was it her imagination, or had he stepped closer? His breath was warm against her cheek. Definitely closer. "What are you doing, Ty?" she asked, barely able to breathe, let alone speak.

His grip tightened, then eased as he slid his open palms to her back. "Something I've wanted to do since I stopped to change your tire."

Beth's heart slammed mercilessly into her ribs and she met him halfway. "I'm probably going to regret this, but the feeling is mutual," she whispered. Without hesitation, she draped her hands behind his neck.

Just a taste, she promised herself as he leaned toward her. *Just a taste . . .*

The Gift

DEB STOVER

LOVE SPELL   NEW YORK CITY

LOVE SPELL®

November 2009

Published by

Dorchester Publishing Co., Inc.
200 Madison Avenue
New York, NY 10016

ISBN 10: 0-505-52606-9
ISBN 13: 978-0-505-52606-9
E-ISBN: 978-1-4285-0768-5

The name "Love Spell" and its logo are trademarks of Dorchester Publishing Co., Inc.

Printed in the United States of America.

10 9 8 7 6 5 4 3 2 1

Visit us online at www.dorchesterpub.com.

In memory of David Allen Stover:
husband, father, hero.
April 21, 1955–May 14, 2005.

And welcome to our first grandchild,
Annabella Debra Carr, born May 22, 2009. She is a
true Gift and adorable evidence that the circle of life
and love really are eternal.

With much love and gratitude to Johnny Andrew
Jackson (AKA my dad and the best one ever born); my
critique partners, Paula Gill, Maureen McKade, Mary
Chase, Carol Duncan, and Peg McCool; and to a man
with great patience and much love, Martin Yaslowitz.
They all have more faith in me than I have in myself,
and probably far more than I deserve.

Special thanks to Annelise Robey and Alicia Condon
for patience *far* above and beyond the call of duty.

The Gift

PROLOGUE

Blood. Crashing rivers of it erupted from the corners of her mind.

The shimmering steel blade ripped and retreated again and again. Crimson waves of pain pierced her. Dripping life's blood . . .

Death tugged at her, greedy and demanding, dragging her into the victim's world, toward the cold, the dark.

Not yet . . . She had to see the face. The killer's face.

A voice rose, taunting, but she couldn't see, couldn't understand the muffled words. Then a moment of clarity, just before death claimed its victim. Thank God. The monster came closer, hovered over her. His name formed in her mind and she filed it away in the part of her brain that was still sane. Still hers. He laughed as he wiped his bloodied blade across his victim's blouse. Arrogant bastard. A moment later he shoved it into his pocket before he walked away. The door squeaked open, clicked shut.

The pain in her skull became unbearable. There wasn't room inside her for them both. *No more. No more.* She couldn't do this anymore.

A silent scream tore through her. *Go away,* she pleaded. *Release me. You're finished now. I'm dying, too.*

Blinding light flashed as a tunnel formed. The pressure eased as the spirit gradually moved beyond her and into the light.

CHAPTER ONE

Three years later . . .

Life could be a real bastard sometimes, but Beth Dearborn worked overtime to stay one step ahead of the damage. That night on Lakeshore Drive, she'd decided to slam-dunk her career as a homicide detective into the toilet and flush. Sobriety was the brass ring now, and so far, she had it firmly in her grasp.

She damned well planned to keep it that way.

But this assignment worried her. Up until now, her career as an insurance investigator had proved safe, but this was her first case of possible life-insurance fraud. The evidence gave her no reason to believe there might be any . . . problems. Still, this was the closest she'd come in over three years to the life she'd left behind.

One day at a time, Dearborn.

A sudden *pop*, followed by a kick-ass tug on the steering wheel and an ominous *thump thump thump* meant trouble. She aimed her ancient Honda toward the shoulder, braked, and rested her forehead against the steering wheel. "Damn." Less than a mile from Brubaker, Tennessee, and she had a flat.

"My life story in frigging rubber," she muttered.

Beth unfolded her nearly six-foot frame from the cramped car and headed for the trunk just as an oversized Dodge pickup rolled to a stop behind her. Shading her eyes, she made out the shape of a straw cowboy hat through the windshield.

Oh, great—a good old boy to my rescue.

Beth Dearborn was *not* helpless. Lonely, yes. A failure, yes. Helpless, no. And these Southern gentlemen just couldn't seem to grasp the concept of a woman who didn't require rescuing on a semiregular basis. With a sigh, she opened her trunk and lifted her spare tire from its bed beneath the trunk floor. She wrestled it onto the hot pavement, then reached for the jack and lug wrench.

"Afternoon, ma'am," a deep drawl rumbled. "Appears you got some trouble here."

"No trouble at all." Beth rolled the tire toward the rear passenger side. "Nothing this spare won't fix, anyway."

"Here, let me give you a hand with that." He reached down. His large hand covered hers on top of the tire.

Beth's breath came out in a rush of exasperation. *Don't piss off the locals before you even get to town*, she reminded herself. Of course, for all she knew this guy was just passing through. She silently counted to ten, then glanced sideways at her unwelcome Sir Galahad.

Tall, dark, and handsome didn't begin to describe her Good Samaritan. He wore a pair of sunglasses beneath the brim of his straw cowboy hat, and the open collar of his chambray shirt revealed just enough tanned chest to give Beth an enticing glimpse of curling black hair.

All right, change of plans. Watching this guy change her tire might be a nice diversion, after all. She stepped back and wiped her suddenly sweaty palms on her jeans. "Uh, thanks."

He flashed her a devastating grin as he set to work, muscles rippling beneath his rolled-up sleeves. When he stooped to slide the car's jack into place, she tilted her head to admire the fit of his jeans, worn nearly white in all the right places. Very, very nice.

Since she kept emotional entanglements to a minimum by choice, her sexual encounters were way too few and even farther between. Sex was strictly for fun—she had a "no strings" policy. But a girl could look.

"You live around here?" she asked, hoping the small talk might help her recover from that sudden jolt of sexual awareness. Even so, she didn't pick up strangers for one-night stands. She hadn't sunk that low, and she sure as hell wasn't that stupid. Walking a beat on the streets of Chicago before making detective had seen to that.

He glanced back over his shoulder and nodded, then made quick work of releasing the lug nuts on the flat tire. "Got a farm east of town."

Sexy farmer. Beth almost chuckled at herself. He was probably married and had a brood of kids on that farm of his. Besides, she was here on business. With that reminder, she drew a deep breath and took another step back. Her gaze drifted to the ring finger of his left hand. Naked ring finger . . . An unwelcome and uncharacteristic warmth—was that relief?—settled over her, but she shook it off and cleared her throat.

A few minutes later, he had secured her spare tire, lowered the car, removed the jack, and placed the flat in her trunk. Beth thanked him and handed him a bottle of water from her cooler. He removed his sunglasses and dropped them into his shirt pocket, revealing piercing blue-green eyes.

Holy . . . "I—I'd better be going," she said, her throat doing an imitation of a desert.

"Thanks for the drink. You'll find Gooch's Garage on the edge of town. They can either fix your tire or replace it."

"Yeah, thanks." Beth cleared her throat. "Let me pay you for your—"

"No thanks, ma'am." He slammed her trunk. "Drive safely."

An odd expression crossed his face, and for a second she thought he was going to say something else. Instead, he shook his head and replaced his sunglasses. Without another word, he strode back to his truck, climbed inside, started the engine, and drove away.

"Whew!" She fanned herself and sank into her car, wondering if all the men in Brubaker were like that one. All Southern jokes aside, if that guy was an example of inbreeding, she was in favor of it.

Back to reality, Dearborn. She dropped the Honda into gear and allowed the sound of passing cars to bring her back to reality. Eventually, she merged back into the traffic's easy flow. The passing scenery around Brubaker made her want to slow down and take in the natural beauty—something she rarely did. All right, something she *never* did.

The Great Smoky Mountains ringed the valley on three sides like purple smudges against the vast sky. Easy to understand why agriculture was big in the area, since everything was green and lush as far as she could see. Rainfall was obviously plentiful, and she crossed numerous bridges over brooks and streams on her way into town.

But Beth didn't have time to slow down and admire the scenery. She had a job to do.

After a brief stop at Gooch's Garage, where a slack-jawed yokel promised her a new tire by next week and tacitly assured her of the variety in the local gene pool, she headed toward the center of town. Once there, she couldn't help staring.

When was the last time she'd seen a town square, except in the movies? There was even a clock tower in the center of a picturesque little park. Brubaker, Tennessee, proved small-town America was alive and well.

The sooner she got out of here, the better. She parked and exited her car, then stretched the kinks out of her legs and spine. At her height, she needed a roomier vehicle, but she could worry about new wheels later. The engine sputtered and gave a mighty shudder before falling silent, as if reminding her of its advanced age.

"Nice car," she said, patting the hood and crossing her fingers. "Have a good rest." The last thing she needed was to end up stranded here in Bumpkin-ville. That would mean paying for car repairs and charging a rental to her employer. The flat was more than enough trouble for one day.

She worked cheap, which put her in the good graces of her boss. Avery Mutual was reputable—for an insurance company—but it kept investigators on a short leash and an even shorter budget.

Her mission was simple—make sure claims were legit. She slung the strap of her backpack over one shoulder and retrieved her bag from the trunk. Then she headed toward the old hotel across the square.

The Brubaker Arms was a sweet three-story brick Victorian, complete with turrets and gingerbread. She grimaced. Just looking at it gave her a toothache. But Beth didn't care as long as the bed was decent and she had her own bathroom. She'd hit bottom and was still on the low rung, but not low enough to share the john with strangers.

As she strolled across the quaint little park, she had the feeling of being watched. She looked from side to side, counting several gazes focused solely on her. She chuckled and rolled her eyes toward the brilliant blue sky. These people must be bored stiff to waste their time staring at a gangly newcomer. Of course, if they knew everything about her, they would be even more likely to stare.

Or run for the hills.

This ex–homicide detective and recovering drunk used to relive murders on a routine basis, folks. And thank God she didn't have to do that anymore. Beth barely suppressed a shudder as memories threatened to emerge from the vault she kept sealed at the back of her mind. Carefully, she slammed the door shut again and turned the key.

She was a stranger here, she reminded herself as she crossed the narrow cobblestone street to the hotel. She'd been in the South for almost three years now and was well versed on the significance of being a Yankee in God's country.

Focus on the job, Dearborn.

She was here to either prove or disprove that Lorilee Brubaker-Malone—hometown girl for sure—was alive and well. Somewhere. In this case, the seven-figure policy alone was enough to raise suspicions, but the lack of a body screamed insurance fraud as far as Avery Mutual was concerned.

Beth preferred to think of her assignment as a fact-finding mission, but she couldn't deny the bottom line. Insurance companies preferred not to pay claims. She uncovered the facts and left the rest to her employer. What happened afterward was none of her business. She did her job, did it well, and moved on to the next assignment.

Easy. Simple. The way she liked things. The way she liked life . . .

She pushed open the front door of the hotel and strolled through the lobby. Blanche DuBois and Minnie Pearl would be right at home here.

Beth paused at the front desk and looked around. Waiting. Anytime she entered an old building she had to stop and consider if anyone had ever died a violent death there. And if they had, was their spirit still in residence? She couldn't place herself at risk, even if it meant moving to the dumpy motel she'd passed on the edge of town.

Avoidance of spirits who'd died violently had given Beth three peaceful, *sober* years. Like an unused muscle, her gift—her curse—was wasting away. That was the plan, anyway, and so far it seemed to be working. She couldn't be happier. Her cousin Sam insisted that someday she would regret the loss of her empathic gift.

That'll be the day.

She drew deep, even breaths. Nothing. The place was deserted, apparently by both the living and the dead. Sometimes even she had to admit a pang of loneliness after a lifetime of encountering spirits on a semiregular basis.

No, don't go there, Dearborn.

The living weren't any speedier than the dead in this place. After a few minutes, she tapped the bell on the counter, wincing as the metallic ringing echoed off the high ceilings and polished woodwork.

A short, bald man appeared in front of her as if by magic. "May I help you?"

"Elizabeth Dearborn," she said, noting the tiny twitch in the man's jaw at her decidedly Yankee accent. "I have a reservation. Avery Mutual made it."

The man keyed her name into his computer terminal and nodded. "Yes, ma'am, I have it right here, and this here says third-party billing." One woolly eyebrow arched almost imperceptibly. "We'll need a credit card for incidentals, of course."

This was always a problem. She hadn't qualified for a company credit card. Managing not to groan, she flashed the man the best Southern-belle smile she could muster, and even batted her lashes for good measure. Scanning his name tag, she said, "I don't do incidentals, Mr. Wilson, so that won't be necessary."

Perspiration popped from every pore on the man's shiny head. Obviously taken aback, he asked, "You don't intend to make any phone calls during your stay, ma'am?"

"The only calls I'll make are for business, and my employer covers those, too."

The first thing a drunk loses is her credit. She couldn't

rent a car, reserve a hotel room, or even place an order from the J. C. Penney catalog without a credit card. Life as she'd known it had come to a screeching halt, but she was rebounding. Thank God Avery Mutual covered all her expenses. "If you require a cash deposit, we can call Memphis and get one authorized." She batted her lashes again and didn't bother to inform the man she had a company cell phone in her backpack. It was none of his damned business.

He looked at his computer monitor again, his face reddening. "My apologies, ma'am. The reservation does indicate that Avery Mutual will cover everything."

"Good." She smiled and shifted her weight. "This room has a private bath, right?"

"Of course." Mr. Wilson slid a form and a key across the counter. "Sign here, please. Do you require the bellman, Miss Dearborn?"

"*Ms.* Dearborn." She scribbled her signature on the hotel registration, then returned it to the red-faced man. "I travel light." She reached for the key. "Bellman gets a break."

"Very well, ma'am." He obviously didn't intend to address her by name again. "Enjoy your stay."

Beth turned to leave, then remembered something she would need. "Is there a local directory in my room?"

"Yes, ma'am." If Wilson lifted his chin any higher, he'd be staring at the ceiling. "And just dial the front desk if you require anything."

"No charge for that?" She winked again and held up her hand. "Just kidding, Wilson. Chill."

"Of course, ma'am."

"By the way, do you know a family named Malone?" She waited, knowing damned good and well he knew.

"Ty Malone is well-known in Brubaker, ma'am." Wilson's brow furrowed and his eyes developed a suspicious glint.

"Yeah, that's the name. Tyrone Malone." Of course, Beth already had all the particulars—name, address, birth date, marriage date, number of children—so she was fishing more for reaction than anything. "Man's parents should've been shot for sticking a kid with a rhyming name," she added under her breath, then headed for the staircase with her typical long-legged stride. She'd learned years ago to flaunt her height. In her line of work a woman couldn't think petite, even if she was. And Beth wasn't. "Is the local library close?"

"Just across the square, ma'am."

"Thanks. That's where I'm heading after I unpack. Catch you later, Wilson." She waved and jogged up the stairs, hoping her stay would prove very brief.

On a hunch, she paused at the top of the curved staircase and glanced back at old Wilson. Of course he was on the phone. She knew without overhearing that he was either calling Avery headquarters about her incidentals or alerting Malone that some "damn Yankee" was snooping around.

Good. That was precisely why she'd made sure to mention where she was going this afternoon. The sooner all the principal players came out of the wood-work—especially Lorilee herself—the sooner Beth could vacate this backwater.

And leave *y'all* behind.

* * *

Ty Malone swung the final bale of hay onto the truck bed and gave the driver a thumbs-up. The engine rumbled to life, and the flatbed took off across the field toward the hay barn.

The whirring blades of Rick Heppel's chopper filled the sky moments before the metal bird rose above the hedgerow to the south. Ty shaded his eyes and watched, wondering what his quirky neighbor was up to now. The Vietnam vet kept mostly to himself unless one of the neighbors hired him to herd stray cattle or drive away deer with his chopper. After hovering for another minute, the helicopter rose higher and headed east.

Ty stretched, his thoughts drifting back to the woman he'd met on the highway earlier. Her tall, athletic build had awakened his hibernating libido, even though she wasn't his usual type—petite and blonde. She had a head full of dark thick curly hair long enough to drape over a man in the heat of passion.

He groaned inwardly.

It didn't matter anyway. She was probably halfway to North Carolina by now, tormenting some other poor sucker with those eyes. His housekeeper, Pearl, would call them haunting or brooding or something else straight out of one of those gothic novels she loved. Ty wasn't even sure what color the woman's eyes were, but he'd never forget the expression in them when she'd met his gaze.

She'd looked at him with interest. No denying that. But he'd seen something else there he couldn't forget. Something . . . wounded. Guarded. Like a stray dog who wanted to make friends, but wasn't sure if it would be fed or kicked.

Crying shame for a woman who looked like that to feel insecure about anything. He straightened and scanned the clouds on the horizon. On the other hand, she'd had an edge. He grinned, remembering. On the exterior, she'd come across as tough and aloof. He'd be willing to bet she had no idea her eyes gave away so much.

Besides, her problems were none of his damned business. Hell, he didn't even know her name. He'd much rather remember her legs. A man could spend a lot of time dreaming about having those long, lean legs wrapped around his—

Whoa. Down, Malone. He swallowed hard. Sweat trickled down his face, pooling in his collar. Damn. His reaction to the woman was one more bit of proof that he was starting to feel human again. He owed the sexy stranded motorist a debt of gratitude for that, if nothing else. In record time, she'd managed to give him a boner harder than a two-by-four. He had to grin. Amazing, considering how long it had been since—

"Hey, boss, got a phone call." Cecil Montgomery passed Ty the cell phone.

"What happened to the days when we were safe from this crap out here?" With a sigh, Ty brought the phone to his ear, secretly grateful for the distraction. "Yeah, Ty Malone here."

"Mr. Malone, this here's J. D. Wilson from the Brubaker Arms."

What the devil did that old fart want? Probably money for some cause or another. "Yeah?" Hell, it was the middle of the day, and they still had another field of alfalfa to haul before it rained. He was already running late from that errand. And from helping the mystery lady with her flat.

"Well, sir, a guest just checked in I thought you might want to know about."

"I'm not expecting anyone." Ty wished the man would get down to business. "Why should it concern me?"

"I'm sure I don't know, sir," Wilson continued, "but she asked about you by name."

"And . . . ?" Ty mopped sweat from his forehead and tugged his hat lower over his eyes. "Who is she?"

The sound of a clicking keyboard filled the line, then Wilson said, "Name's Elizabeth Dearborn."

"Don't know anybody by that name, Wilson, but thanks any—"

"She's from an insurance company, Mr. Malone."

Ty's blood turned to ice, despite the soaring afternoon temperature. "Avery Mutual?"

"Yes, that's it." Silence stretched between them. "Well, sir, I just thought you might want to know. In case it's important, she did mention she's going to the library this afternoon."

"Yeah, thanks." With a thick knot in his gut, Ty disconnected the call and handed the phone back to Cecil. "I guess Avery Mutual didn't want me to know when they were coming."

"Lorilee's insurance company?" Cecil wiped his brow with the back of his hand. "Well, you knew this was gonna happen."

"I suppose." Ty studied his old friend's dark, weathered face. "Sooner or later."

"If you're serious about goin' through with—"

"I am." Ty clenched his teeth and looked across the field.

"What'd Wilson say?"

"Just that a woman checked in who works for Avery Mutual, and she asked about me by name." Ty wished it didn't matter. But it did. Damn.

He stared out across the fields. The Smokies created a bold backdrop to the valley, and puffy white clouds dotted the June sky. Even so, rain would come and he had hay to haul. "We'd best get back to work."

"I started haulin' hay when I was nine," Cecil said, rubbing his chin. "That was forty-two years ago . . . *boy*."

"You bucking for a raise, Cecil?"

The man shook his head. "I reckon I could use one, but that ain't my point."

"What is?" Ty narrowed his eyes, trying to pay attention to his old friend and mentor, though his thoughts strayed to his conversation with Wilson.

"You get your ass into town and talk to that insurance lady." Cecil propped both fists on his hips. "I can take care of these fields in my sleep, and you dang well know it."

Ty chuckled, though dread oozed through him. He didn't want to face the investigator, but it would be better to end this quickly. "All right, Cecil."

"You're kiddin' me. Ty Malone givin' up without an argument?" Cecil rolled his eyes heavenward and slapped his palm against his chest. "Lord, ain't this a *glorious* day?"

"Watch it, old man." Ty knew his warning would be greeted with good humor, and Cecil's chuckle confirmed that. "No reason for us to beat around the bush here. We both know why that investigator's here." He swallowed hard. "Damn." That seemed to be his word of the hour.

Cecil's expression softened and he patted Ty's shoulder. "Man's gotta do what he's gotta do."

"Yeah." Ty drew a deep breath and nodded. "All right, you take over and I'll go to town."

Cecil arched a salt-and-pepper eyebrow. "And once this is over, I expect you to get on with your life." He sighed again. "Can't wait forever, son."

Ty closed his eyes for a moment and nodded. Then he met Cecil's sympathetic gaze. "All right, I'm going. That's a start."

"Great, I'll just tell the boys it's quittin' time, and we'll head to town for a beer."

Ty knew Cecil was kidding, but he didn't have the heart to play along. "Thanks, old man. For everything."

Cecil gave a solemn nod and ambled away, leaving Ty alone with his memories. "Damn." Definitely the word of the hour.

He jerked open the door of his pickup and climbed into the cab. Time to end this nightmare once and for all. Seven years was a hell of a long time to wait for someone to come home.

CHAPTER TWO

As planned, Beth headed for the local library to pore over old newspapers dating from around the time of Lorilee's disappearance. The first few articles reflected the town's certainty that foul play had been involved, but the tone gradually changed over subsequent weeks.

And that was putting it lightly. The town of Brubaker had turned on Lorilee like a mob of Puritans on a suspected witch.

Letters to the editor suggested she'd run away with a handsome stranger, and others hinted at drug use, prostitution, and alcoholism—just Beth's luck. Of course, the articles had remained vague about Lorilee's continuing absence, but the editor's willingness to run that kind of defamation at all intrigued Beth. The catalyst for the attacks was, apparently, an article about a typewritten letter received by Lorilee's father, postmarked London—allegedly from Lorilee herself. In the letter, she claimed to have left voluntarily to start a new life. After that, the town decided she was a hussy.

Right. As if no small-town wife had ever strayed from her husband.

Beth rolled her tight shoulders. Her mental picture of Lorilee Brubaker-Malone was confusing at best. She ran another search on her name and came up with earlier articles about Lorilee's contributions to the community over the years.

Interesting . . .

Leaning closer to the monitor, Beth tucked a wayward curl behind her ear and squinted. An article published two months prior to Lorilee's disappearance called her "Brubaker's guardian angel." Beth leaned back, crossing her denim-clad legs and rubbing her chin.

"Who are you, Lorilee?" she whispered.

"Were. Past tense," a strong male voice corrected from behind her. "Who *were* you, Lorilee?"

Beth sucked in a breath and snapped her head around to face the intruder. A familiar intruder. Tall, dark, handsome, and blue-green eyed, her Good Samaritan from the highway stood there with one eyebrow arched, thumbs hooked through his belt loops, the kind of rugged tanned features that made most women drool.

Even though Beth wasn't most women, she still had to admit he was a fine male specimen. She swallowed hard, poised to stand. "You know Lorilee Brubaker-Malone?"

"*Knew* her." He shifted his weight and lifted his chin a notch. "Past tense."

Of course. Her knight in shining armor had to be none other than Ty Malone—the dearly departed's beneficiary. Small world. Beth rose and thrust out her hand. "I'm Beth Dearborn. Avery Mutual sent me. And you are . . . ?" She feigned ignorance.

"Ty Malone." He eyed her hand for a moment, then took it in a firm but brief handshake. "You're the woman with the flat tire."

Beth nodded. His straightforward manner and strong handshake surprised her. Most Southern men took her hand like a snotty lace hanky. She sometimes used her height to intimidate people, but Malone stood a full head taller. Not many men made her feel small, let alone insignificant, and she wasn't about to let this one get to her, even if he did pack one hell of a sexual wallop.

"Thanks again. I ordered a new tire at Gooch's."

He hesitated a beat, his expression wary. Suspicious. "I guess you're here about the claim."

"Yes, I'm the investigator assigned to the case. I'll bet you wish now you hadn't changed my tire."

His expression softened. "Look, I just want this nightmare over with. It's time to let Lorilee rest in peace."

"We want a resolution, too, Mr. Malone," she said with complete sincerity. "But when we have a claim this large and no body or witness to the alleged death, we have to investigate." She shrugged. "It's standard procedure. You aren't being singled out for any reason."

He narrowed his gaze, then gave an emphatic nod. "Fair enough. Guess I'd be curious, too, given the circumstances."

"Since we all want this over with, I'm sure you won't have any objections to answering a few questions."

One corner of his sensuous mouth slanted upward. "What do you want to know?" he asked, his voice smooth and rough at the same time.

A shiver skated along the surface of her skin. Beth remembered the sexual heat that had erupted between them out on the highway. It had *not* been one-sided. She glanced at her watch. "Is there somewhere else we can talk?"

"Diner down the street," he said, inclining his head toward the door.

A man of few words. That suited Beth, since she was eager to settle this case and leave town. She crossed her arms and smiled. "I have a better idea."

"Oh?"

"We both want to resolve this investigation quickly, Mr. Malone," she said steadily. "Let's just cut to the chase."

"By all means."

"Avery Mutual's records indicate you still live at the same address you did at the time of your wife's disappearance."

"True." He folded his arms across his abdomen, and Beth wondered if he realized he was mimicking her. "And?"

She dropped her arms to her sides. "I need to look around your house, since that's the last place anyone saw Mrs. Malone."

Furrows appeared on his brow. "I don't want the kids upset by this." He removed his straw cowboy hat. "They've already lost their mother. That's bad enough."

Beth glanced at her watch again. "What time do they come home?"

"Not until four today."

"That gives us most of the afternoon." Beth grabbed her notes and backpack from the table. "Lead the way."

A grin split his handsome face and her breath hitched. The transformation from cynic to charmer caught her off guard. Mr. Sex Appeal from the highway had returned with some to spare. She had to struggle for her composure. This guy had more mood swings than Jekyll and Hyde. She had to watch more than her back around him.

"Does that grin mean yes?" she finally asked.

He nodded and swung toward the door. "Let's get on with this."

"Good. We're on the same side here." Beth followed him down the staircase and outside. The sky had turned a leaden shade.

He paused on the stone steps leading to the sidewalk and faced her. "That remains to be seen, Miss Dearborn."

"*Ms.* Dearborn, or just Dearborn." She flashed a smug smile. "We both want the truth. Right?"

He pinned her with a steely stare. "Yep."

"Then we're on the same side."

"My truck's right there." He jabbed his thumb over his shoulder. "Let's go."

Normally she preferred the independence driving her own car afforded, but the way it had been running—and without a spare—she didn't want to risk it. Beth followed him down the steps and opened the passenger door, amazed to find a Southern man who didn't race ahead to do it for her. Should she be insulted?

Get a grip, Dearborn.

The powerful engine rumbled to life and he backed out of the parking space. "I don't know what you expect to find at the house," he said quietly, tugging the brim of his hat lower over his brow. "Sheriff never found anything."

"Maybe nothing." Beth gazed at the passing countryside. "Then again, maybe he missed something."

"It's been seven years." He shot her a sidelong glance. "We've cleaned a time or two."

He's nervous. Beth made a mental note to keep an eye on Ty Malone. Actually, it was damned hard *not* to keep an eye on him. He looked good enough to eat.

Too long without some good, old-fashioned, bone-crunching sex. She let her gaze drift downward to where his belt buckle rested above slim hips and other very male equipment. *Yep, and long is the operative word here.* Heat flashed through regions of her body that should have been disengaged during business hours. Beth drew a deep breath and dragged her gaze away from the rippling muscles in his forearms as he steered the truck away from town.

She needed to maintain her perspective, and his good looks were distracting. "Why are you so convinced your wife is dead, Mr. Malone?"

He peered at her again from beneath the brim of his hat. "I *know* she's dead."

"Ah, yes, that's right." Beth remembered his comments when he'd first confronted her. "You believe she's dead. *Why?*"

"Like I said, I don't *believe* she's dead." He kept his gaze straight ahead. "I *know* she's dead."

"You saw her die?"

He cleared his throat. "No."

"Then why do you insist your wife is dead?"

He slowed the truck, turned onto a dirt road, and

stopped. Draping both large hands over the steering wheel, he half turned to face her. With the tip of his finger, he tilted his hat back off his brow, again revealing those incredible eyes. "I know, because Lorilee never would've left her babies. Anyone who really knew her will tell you that."

"Anyone?" From what she'd read in the newspaper, Beth wasn't so sure. She made a few more mental notes about Malone. Stubborn as hell. However, she had to admire his conviction. Or was it acting? "Without proof, it's still just your belief, Mr. Malone," she said steadily. "What we need are facts."

Or a body . . .

"Facts like that bogus letter her father got?"

"Now that you mention it." Beth smothered her grin. He'd played right into that one.

"Lorilee didn't write that letter." Malone's voice was flat.

"Who did?"

"I don't know." He faced her, and his expression seemed sincere. "But I do know this—"

"What?"

"Whoever wrote that letter knows what happened to my wife."

Beth held his gaze for several seconds. He was either completely convinced his wife was dead, or a damned good actor.

"Did you have her signature analyzed?"

A muscle twitched in his jaw. "No."

"Why wasn't it analyzed by the authorities?"

Malone remained silent for several moments. "Her father wanted to let it drop. The letter was mailed to him. Not me."

"Where's the letter now?" Beth asked, determined to have a look at that crucial piece of evidence.

"Sheriff has it."

"Then he must've had it analyzed."

He snorted. "Don't be so sure."

Convincing. She wished the man weren't so attractive, and especially that she hadn't reacted to him so carnally earlier today. Of course, she hadn't known who he was then. Still . . .

He dropped the truck into gear again and drove. "The house is just over yonder."

"Good." They crested the hill and Beth held her breath. The house was pristine white against a backdrop of green so lush it looked as if an artist had painted the setting. "Nice."

Malone pointed toward the house as he continued to steer the truck closer. "Lorilee's great-great-grandfather built it after the War Between the States."

Beth rolled her eyes. No true Southerner would ever refer to it as the Civil War. More often than not, she heard it called the War of Northern Aggression. Sheesh.

"It's beautiful."

"Her grandfather built a more modern home over that ridge, and that's where her father and step-mother still live." Malone's sigh drew Beth's gaze back to his impressive profile. "Lorilee wanted to live here, so we bought the place from her father. Lord, it was a dump when we first got married."

Making more mental notes, Beth tried to concentrate on information, rather than the man himself—not an easy task. "So you and your wife fixed it up?"

"Right, though it was a lot more *fix* than *up* at first."

His expression hardened again as he brought the truck to a stop in front of the house. "She called it . . ."

"What, Mr. Malone?" Beth watched that same muscle in his jaw clench and release several times as he stared at the house. "What did she call it?"

He opened the door and climbed out; Beth did the same. Staring at her from over the hood, he said, "She called it her castle."

His pain was clear, but that didn't prove anything. Even the guilty could feel and show genuine pain. "Well, let's open the drawbridge and have a look around."

After a curt nod, he headed for the massive wrap-around porch and turned the knob. The door swung open easily.

Another old building. Full of lingering memories, lingering . . . spirits?

A ball of lead settled in her gut, and her palms turned clammy. The world was full of old buildings. She had a job to do.

Buck up, Dearborn. She braced herself and followed him to the door.

Something stopped her at the threshold. Her belly churned and this morning's egg-and-muffin sandwich turned on her. That would teach her to skip lunch and live on coffee all day—a bad habit remaining from her detective days.

"Come on in and look your fill," Malone invited.

Beth gritted her teeth and stepped through the door. A powerful sensation gripped her. Fear. Gut-wrenching terror. Her throat tightened. Sweat trickled between her breasts. She couldn't breathe. She had to get away. They were hurting her.

They who? What the hell? She'd felt this before. Was it happening again? No, it couldn't be. Her gift was gone. It had to be. She was safe now. But then an icy chill swept through her. She'd let down her guard—grown too confident and allowed this crack in her armor. She wouldn't let it come back.

A moment later, the creepy sensation vanished completely. Had it been her imagination? Maybe it really was nothing more than an empty stomach compounded by the long drive, and that would be the end of it.

"Where do you want to start?" He dropped his hat on a table near the door.

Beth shook her head and walked slowly through the entryway. The sensation she'd detected at the door returned for a fleeting moment, then passed. It definitely hadn't been strong enough for her to call it one of her empathic experiences. She breathed a tentative sigh of relief, though niggling doubts still lurked in the back of her mind. Sucking in her breath, she faced Ty Malone, pinning him with her gaze.

"What is it?" He took a step toward her, his expression a tentative blend of wariness and concern. "You look kinda puny."

"Mr. Malone . . . ," Beth began, hoping her worries were unfounded. "Has anyone ever . . . died in this house?"

The investigator swayed and Ty reached out to grab her arm. All the color had drained from her face. "You okay?"

"No. I'm not." Beth Dearborn shivered and looked up to meet his gaze, her expressive hazel eyes wide.

Pleading. "Just answer me. Please? Has anyone ever died in this house?"

The woman looked downright terrified. "It's an old house." He shrugged, struggling to remember this woman wasn't an ordinary damsel in distress. She was—could be—the enemy. "No telling what happened here in the hundred years before we got here."

She shook her head and drew a deep breath, her efforts to regain control visible in her eyes and the set of her mouth. "It's gone."

It? "What's gone?"

She managed a weak smile and shrugged off his supporting hand, then shoved hers through her thick mane of dark curls, freeing them completely from the elastic band that had tried and failed to restrain them. "Nothing." Swinging toward a painting near the archway that led to the parlor, Dearborn made it clear the subject was closed.

What the hell? This woman's problems were none of his business. All he cared about was putting an end to a nightmare that had festered far too long.

"Nice painting."

"Lorilee's work." Ty stepped closer to the watercolor his wife had painted of this house and the valley surrounding it. "She liked to paint."

"It's good." Dearborn tilted her head to one side as if memorizing the texture and colors of the painting. After a moment, she removed a pad and pencil from her backpack and scratched a few lines.

Ty studied the woman's profile. What the hell was she thinking now? "Something wrong with the fact that Lorilee liked to paint?" What significance could an insurance investigator find in a simple watercolor a woman had painted of a home she'd loved?

"Wrong?" The investigator shoved her hair back from her face again, the expression in her eyes unreadable. "Just making notes, Malone. Investigating. It's my job. Remember?"

"How could I forget?" At least she was back to her normal prickly self now. He released a slow breath. "Where do you want to start?"

"One room at a time." She paused, then jabbed her pencil toward the back of the house. "Kitchen that way?"

"Yeah." The back door slammed, and he inclined his head toward the sound. "But based on that, I suspect Pearl's in there and fixin' supper."

"Pearl?"

"Housekeeper, nanny, cook, lifesaver."

"Ah." Beth smiled—really smiled—and the transformation from suspicious hard-ass to open beauty was like a sharp right hook. *Damn. Don't notice, Malone. Insurance investigators aren't supposed to be pretty.*

The kitchen door swung open. "Cecil James Montgomery, if that's your sorry hide sneakin' back here for another one of them quickies, I've got a news bulletin for—"

Pearl froze, her short plump body framed in the doorway, her mouth gaping in a perfect circle. "Ty, well . . ." She patted her kinky white hair and groaned. "And you have company, too. Now, don't that just beat all? Pardon me, ma'am."

Beth stepped forward and thrust out her hand. "Beth Dearborn. Avery Mutual."

Pearl's momentary embarrassment fled as rapidly

as it had appeared. "You're from the insurance company about Lorilee." It wasn't a question. She shook Beth's hand, but it was a halfhearted effort at best. Her dark gaze met Ty's over Beth's shoulder. "And . . . ?"

"Ms. Dearborn is here to investigate Lorilee's death," Ty explained. "She wanted to see the last place anyone saw her alive."

"Well, I reckon that would be here." Pearl took a step back and lifted her chin, her expression fierce. "My Lorilee didn't run off, Ms. Dearborn. She's dead, pure and simple as that. And it's time—way past time—for her to rest in peace."

Several seconds of silence stretched between the two women. They were testing each other. One thing Ty knew for sure, these two were more-than-worthy adversaries.

Maybe—just maybe—between them, they would learn what happened to Lorilee once and for all. Why he believed an insurance investigator might bother with the details of his wife's death, he didn't know. Foolishness, maybe. But his gut said otherwise.

"My job is to find the truth, Mrs. . . . ?" Beth broke the silence first.

"Montgomery. Pearl Montgomery."

"Mrs. Montgomery." Beth's pencil scribbled more notes across her pad of paper. "How long have you worked for the Malones?"

Pearl's full lips pulled into a tight, thin line. "I've been with Lorilee's family since before she was born."

Ty moved close to Pearl and placed a supportive hand on the African-American woman's shoulder. "Pearl raised Lorilee after her mother died."

Pearl sighed and looked up at him. "She was like

the daughter I never had." She covered Ty's hand with her own. "And when she married this fine man, I came here to work, and so did that ornery foreman of yours."

"He couldn't let you out of his sight."

Pearl swatted him playfully with her dish towel. "He'd better mind his manners if he knows what's good for him."

"So you've known Lorilee all her life?" Beth interrupted, still writing.

"Knew," Ty corrected. "Past tense."

"Yes, so you said before."

"And I'll keep saying."

The greenish cast in Beth's hazel eyes sparked to life when she met and held his gaze. He caught his breath. This woman was like a chameleon, constantly changing. He couldn't read her, and that worried him.

Even knowing who and what she was, he still wanted her as much now as he had back when she'd been nothing more than a sexy, stranded motorist.

Maybe more.

Beth was in deep shit. First, the possible spirit encounter, and now the reminder of her attraction to this man. Between her raw emotions and her rioting hormones, she couldn't think straight. She mentally shook herself and squared her shoulders, then dragged a hand through her hair.

Back to business, Dearborn. Breathe in, breathe out. Easy does it.

"Would it be possible for you to make some time to talk with me about Lorilee, Mrs. Montgomery?" she asked. "Since you know—knew—her so well?"

She quirked her lips at Ty's arched brow when she changed her tense. *Humor them. Whatever it takes.*

"Yes, of course." Pearl glanced nervously in Ty's direction.

Beth noted Ty's nod of approval. Pearl might have practically raised Lorilee, but she was still an employee asking permission to speak to the enemy.

"Thanks. I appreciate that. Right now, though, I'd just like to look around the house, if that's okay."

"Sure. Fine." Pearl twisted the dish towel in her hands. "I'll just get back to my chores."

"Thanks, Pearl." Ty kissed the older woman's cheek. "What's for supper?"

She rolled her eyes. "Chicken and dumplings."

"Mmm."

"Men." Chuckling, she returned to the kitchen.

Beth tried not to admire the way Ty had handled Pearl Montgomery, but she couldn't help it. He'd known exactly how to soothe her, exactly how to defuse an awkward situation. Or maybe all this had been staged for the expected insurance investigator. Sooner or later the truth would surface. It always did.

She just hoped that eerie feeling she'd had when they first arrived had been nothing but a long day and a sour stomach. She blew out a long breath and faced Malone.

"Let's save the kitchen for another time," she suggested. "I've terrorized Pearl enough for today."

"Fair enough." Ty's lips curved and his eyes twinkled. "Thanks."

"No problem." Damn. Why'd he have to be nice *and* good looking?

"Parlor's this way." A clock chimed twice. "Kids'll be home in two hours."

"This won't take long." Beth admired his commitment to his children, though all of this could be an act. Lorilee could be waiting for them all to join her in some tropical paradise right now.

Along with her seven-figure insurance settlement.

Beth planned to follow up on the painting angle. Was Lorilee pursuing her interest in art somewhere? Perhaps even selling her work? Could she be traced that way? Beth made a note to contact an art expert she'd worked with a few times back in Chicago.

Antiques coexisted with contemporary comfort in the parlor. She ran her fingertip along the polished cherry of the rolltop desk near the archway. "Nice."

"Lorilee spent years collecting these pieces," Malone explained. He stood in the center of the room, thumbs hooked through his belt loops. "We spent a lot of weekends at antique and estate sales."

Beth waited for him to face her again before she spoke. She wanted—no, needed—to see the expression on his face. Holding her breath, she counted. *One, two, three, four . . .*

Finally, he turned, but his expression was bland. Not tortured. He didn't look like a man still madly in love with his dead wife—or with a wife who could still be alive, for that matter.

And why the hell did knowing that make relief ease through Beth? No, she should consider this evidence. *Get with the program, Dearborn.* He wasn't tortured, because he knew his wife was safe and sound somewhere else. Right?

She licked her suddenly dry lips and tried to ignore the quickening of her pulse. There was another possibility she had to consider—one the former homicide detective in her couldn't completely discount.

Was it possible that Ty Malone wasn't worried about his wife's fate because he knew exactly what had happened to her?

CHAPTER THREE

Ty didn't know whether to stand his ground or to escape while he still could. One minute she was polite and friendly, the next she pissed him off by insinuating Lorilee had abandoned her family. Of course, the fact that Beth's sex appeal had pushed him to the brink of self-control didn't ease back any on his confusion meter.

"Anything in particular you'd like to see in here?" He deliberately glanced at the clock again. "*Before* the kids get home from school?"

"I'll be out of here before four o'clock, as promised."

She flashed him another of those smiles that transformed her whole face. He caught his breath. Hell, he'd be better off if she'd just stick to hard-ass investigator and leave the sex kitten persona for some other poor sucker. He shoved his hands into his pockets, reminding himself that his hormones had probably translated her common courtesy into more than she'd intended.

Seven years of living like a damned monk could do that to a man.

"Is this Lorilee's desk or yours?" she asked, still touching the wood.

"It *was* Lorilee's desk," Ty corrected.

Dearborn rolled her eyes. "Was. Sorry. Momentary lapse." She started to raise the top. "Er, may I?"

"Looks like you already are." He grinned. "Be my guest." Ty folded his arms and watched the investigator's wild curls spiral down her back to her waist. He'd never seen so much hair on one human head. Almost as if she sensed the direction of his thoughts, she pulled the same elastic band from her pocket, swept the mass onto the top of her head, and secured it again.

She had a pretty neck—long and slender. He licked his lips, imagining how sensitive and soft the skin there would be.

Damn. He cleared his throat and released a long, slow breath. "Anything in particular you expect to find in there?" His voice sounded gruff and thick. A lot like he felt right now . . .

"I'll know it when I see it." She shot him a quick glance, then pulled open drawers, leafed through appointment books, looked through Lorilee's Rolodex. "Would you mind giving me a list of your wife's closest friends? I'd like to chat with them while I'm in town, too." She held up the Rolodex. "Will I find their contact info in here?"

Ty inclined his head. "I expect."

"You aren't sure?"

"I never use Lorilee's desk." He swallowed the sudden lump that formed in his throat. What he didn't say was that taking or moving her things had always seemed too final.

"You mean you haven't touched anything in this desk since your wife left, Mr. Malone?" Dearborn arched a dark eyebrow. "I find that hard to believe."

Ty shrugged. "Believe it or not, I haven't touched anything in that desk since my wife *died*. It's a fact."

"It's not dusty in here, Malone."

"I said *I* don't touch it. Pearl cleans everything, and the kids use the supplies for homework."

Her expression wavered and she gave an emphatic nod. "Okay. If you say so." She turned her attention to the side drawers. "Does that mean you've left everything else of Lorilee's alone, too?"

"I reckon."

"Well, in that case, I'll examine things more closely." She passed a pad of yellow paper to him and a pencil from the Mardi Gras cup that had sat on Lorilee's desk for as long as Ty could remember. "Would you jot down the names of those friends for me, please?"

"Sure." His hand brushed against hers as he took the pad, and the sudden urge to grab hold and tug her up against him slammed into him like a gut punch. A film of perspiration coated his skin.

"Mr. Malone?"

The sound of her voice jarred him back to reality. Holy shit. He was in pitiful shape. They were talking about his dead wife, and he was attracted to another woman. That made him lower than a snake. "Sorry. I was just . . ." Just what? It wasn't as if he could tell the truth.

"Not a problem." Dearborn turned her attention to the drawers on the far side of the desk. She rose from the chair and bent over, denim hugging her curves like a lover's caress.

Definitely a problem.

Ty mopped sweat from his forehead with the back

of his sleeve, then walked to the window on the far wall and raised it. A cool spring breeze tinged with the scent of rain drifted through the window, drying the perspiration from his skin.

He had to regain his self-control. The only reason this woman had such an effect on him was because he hadn't been around any women near his own age lately. They'd all either been a lot older or younger or married.

So . . . maybe she was married. That would cool his desire in a hurry. He needed to know. Dammit.

She straightened after a moment and stretched. The action pushed her breasts forward, straining against her blue T-shirt. *Please be married.* He drew a deep breath and said, "Must be hard on your family, you gallivantin' around the country all the time like this."

She froze midstretch and blinked, clearly oblivious to the effect her pose had on Ty's deprived—and depraved—state. "Pardon?"

He walked toward her, thankful when she finally straightened and relaxed her shoulders enough to stop aiming her nipples at him. "Your family. Don't they mind you traveling so much on business?"

"Oh, I'm not married." She placed Lorilee's Rolodex in her backpack. "Thanks for letting me borrow this. I promise to return it unharmed."

Not married. Ty managed not to sigh, and he refused to acknowledge the cheering section between his legs. "What . . ." He shook himself and managed to form a complete sentence. "What would you like to see next?"

"Did Lorilee have a computer? An office other than this desk? A studio where she painted?" The investigator tapped her chin, then snapped her fingers. "Oh, did she keep a diary?"

The woman's enthusiasm stunned him. Her attitude had changed drastically since entering his home. Why? Was it the prospect of snooping? It didn't matter. All he knew was that he actually *liked* this side of her. "Yes to most of the above," he finally answered. "It's a big house."

"I can see that now." She smiled again. "Thanks for being so cooperative. I, uh, get a little carried away with investigative work sometimes. I guess it shows."

"You must love your job."

Her smile vanished as quickly as it had appeared, and the haunted expression returned to her eyes. "Not exactly." She looked away, the moment lost. "I used to have a job I loved," she added, her voice soft.

Her vulnerability tugged at him. His chest tightened and his breath caught. She didn't seem as tall now, either.

"But that's not important," she continued, her mask of indifference in place again. "What matters is finding out what happened to Lorilee."

Again Ty realized this woman just might be the one to finally learn the truth, if he only kept his hormones under control and his head screwed on straight. "Yes, that's what matters."

"Good, then we really are on the same side, Malone." She faced him again, but now she was all business.

"Could be." He nodded slowly, wanting to actually believe that, hoping his gut was right. "I'm afraid it's going to take you more than one afternoon to look through all of Lorilee's things, though."

She nodded and chewed her lower lip. "Do you mind if I spend time here while your children are at school?" She peered at him from beneath her lashes. "I promise to return things as I found them, and I won't take anything off the premises without your explicit permission. Like the Rolodex." She patted her backpack.

"Do I have a choice?" Ty arched his brows and waited.

A sly smile curved her full lips. "There's always a choice, Malone."

"All right."

"Thanks for trusting me with your wife's things," she said, her tone sincere. "Maybe I'll find something that will give us both answers."

Except that Ty's reaction to this woman had triggered an entirely new set of questions.

Ty Malone was easily the greatest temptation Beth had encountered since her college days at Northwestern. And she was one hell of a lot older and wiser now.

This is business, Dearborn. Get with the program.

"Where are Lorilee's office and studio?"

Malone took a step nearer just as the clock chimed the half hour. "We converted the attic into one big multipurpose room. Added windows and skylights." He rubbed his chin. "She moaned and groaned at first that skylights didn't complement the historical integrity of the house, but she got over it once she saw how much more light she had."

"I'll bet she did." Beth drew a deep breath. Malone even smelled nice, and not a damned thing like the way she'd expected a farmer to smell. Soap, fresh air, sunshine, a hint of leather, and just enough sweat to make him all man.

Where was the stench of dirt and manure when she needed it most? That would dampen her libido in a hurry.

"Mind if we take a quick look up there now?" She had to concentrate. Get the job done. "Then I'll come back tomorrow morning for a longer look."

"Okay." He motioned for her to follow him across the parlor and through an archway, where a curving staircase led to the second floor. "The attic stairs are at the end of the hall."

Beth gave a silent prayer of thanks that they weren't going through the foyer again just yet. She wasn't ready to face whatever—or whoever—had greeted her when she'd first arrived. Maybe she never would be. It would be better that way. She needed to talk to her cousin Sam. He'd know how to handle this situation. Maybe she could even convince him to come down after the semester ended. Let *him* contact the something or someone in the foyer. And if it had been nothing more than her imagination and indigestion, then it would give that uptight college-professor cousin of hers an excuse to get away from Chicago for a few days. Yes, she'd definitely give him a call as soon as she returned to the hotel.

On the second floor, they walked past open bedrooms, some scattered with toys, one with a poster of Hannah Montana on the wall, and another that was obviously the master bedroom. A huge four-poster covered by a colorful quilt occupied most of the room.

Warmth oozed through Beth at the thought of spending the afternoon in that bed with the man leading her down the hall.

Malone stopped before a short, narrow door and grabbed the cut-glass doorknob, then froze, his chin lowered. After a moment, he looked back over his shoulder. "I haven't been up here since . . ."

"Not at all?" Beth blinked several times. Was this part of the act, or genuine grief at work? "In all this time?"

He shook his head slowly and swallowed, his Adam's apple traveling the long length of his throat. "Pearl cleans up here, and the kids come up occasionally to find things they need for school projects, but . . ."

"Not you. Just like the desk downstairs?"

"Now that you mention it."

Beth chewed her lower lip. "Look, I can go up alone if you'd rather."

He seemed to consider her offer, but finally shook his head. "No, it's time." He released a weary sigh. "Past time."

Dramatic. Very impressive. Lorilee was—is—a lucky woman.

"Let's have a look then, Malone."

He opened the door and flipped on a light switch, then headed up the newly illuminated steep, narrow staircase.

A girl could be in worse places than following this sexy farmer in tight jeans up the stairs. What a view.

"If you're going to be around here a lot," he said without looking back, "I expect you ought to call me Ty. Everybody does."

It didn't seem professional, but if it made him

more comfortable, so be it. After all, she'd been ogling his buns. That seemed grounds for being on a first-name basis, though she'd ogled more than her share of anonymous buns in her day. "All right. Ty it is, then. I'm Beth."

At the top of the stairs, he looked over his shoulder and grinned. "Not Dearborn anymore?"

Beth's cheeks warmed. Damn. It had been years since she'd blushed. "Only if you prefer it."

"Beth'll do."

They emerged into a light-filled open space. "Nice." Against one wall stood a desk with a computer that belonged in a museum, and against the other was an easel and a table filled with paints and brushes. A spattered drop cloth covered the floor around the area; a half-finished watercolor leaned against the easel.

This didn't look like a place anyone had planned to leave. Wouldn't an artist have taken her unfinished painting with her? Or finished it first? Then again, leaving it this way may have been part of the plan—a well-choreographed, deliberate, and ingenious plot to make Lorilee's disappearance seem sudden and unplanned.

Against the wall opposite the stairs, three tall bureaus and a cedar chest were shoved beneath the eaves. "What's in these?" she asked, stepping around Ty and heading toward them.

"Photo albums. Stuff like that. You name it."

Beth opened one drawer and whistled low. "It's going to take a while to go through all this." She'd have to read every piece of paper, each document, everything.

"I want the truth."

Beth closed the drawer and spun around to face the man again. "That's why I'm here. Avery Mutual wants the truth, too."

Raindrops spattered against the skylights overhead. Ty glanced upward with a scowl.

"Problem?" Beth asked.

"Weather and farming are either great friends or great enemies." He appeared resigned. "I hope Cecil got that last field hauled."

"Speak English, please?" She shrugged. "City girl, born and bred."

He aimed his thumb toward the sky. "We were hauling hay today when I heard you . . ."

"Ah." Beth nodded. "Let me guess. You heard some damn Yankee was in town asking questions about Lorilee?"

His lips twitched. "Something like that."

She grinned and waggled her eyebrows. " 'Good,' said the spider to the fly."

"You . . ." Ty threw his head back and laughed, surprising her. "You set me up."

Beth didn't bother to hide her grin. "Something like that." She held her hands out to her sides, palms up in mock innocence. "Hey, I figured the sooner we got this show on the road, the sooner we'd get to the truth."

His expression grew solemn again. "Fair enough."

Their gazes met and locked. Something Beth didn't dare try to define passed between them. She looked away first, breaking the spell, and walked slowly toward the easel. She needed physical distance between herself and Ty. Not only was she sexually attracted to the man, but she found something else about him compelling as well. Just her rotten luck. If only she knew what the hell it was that drew her to the man . . .

Focus.

Dust coated Lorilee's unfinished painting. Beth mentally anchored herself in the half-finished scene, looked out the long window directly behind the easel, then back at the canvas. "Landscape?"

"Looks like." Ty walked to her side and touched the corner of the canvas. "Lorilee loved this place. This farm. This house. And especially her kids. She didn't run away, Beth. She had no reason to."

Beth half turned to face him. He'd left out one very telling piece of the perfect family scenario. "And how about you and Lorilee? Was your marriage solid? Strong? Fulfilling? Happy?"

His lips pressed into a thin line and a muscle in his jaw twitched. Ah, so maybe everything wasn't perfect in paradise. Her homicide-detective persona scratched at the door of her brain, asking for free rein. But Beth wasn't ready to grant that just yet.

"Lorilee and I loved each other very much," he said gruffly. His eyes snapped, but he continued to hold Beth's gaze. "She would never have left me, either. We both said, 'Until death do us part,' and meant it."

Whose death? The hairs on the back of Beth's neck stood on end and a chill chased itself down her spine. As appealing as Ty Malone was, she had to remember that *if* his wife was dead, he might have been responsible.

Silence stretched between them again, and despite her commonsense warnings, Beth found herself pulled toward him in more than just a physical way now. She *wanted* to believe him, and that was dangerous. She couldn't afford to let herself become emotional about her work. *Facts, Dearborn. Evidence. Truth.*

"Let's find the truth, then," she said quietly.

"That's what I want."

"No matter what it is?"

Again, he swallowed audibly. "No matter what it is."

"Okay." Beth walked to the nearest window and stared through the drizzle at the fields below. A stream meandered through the green valley. Cottonwood and hickory trees followed its banks. Mountains ringed the entire area, and she felt as if she'd arrived in a fairy-tale land.

At least she hadn't experienced any other close encounters of the eerie kind since leaving the entryway. "Mr. Malone—er, Ty?" She turned to face him. "Is there another way into the house and up the stairs to this room?"

He furrowed his brow and angled his head, his expression curious. "Sure. Why?"

Beth rubbed her arms. This was awkward. How could she explain that she was *afraid* to use the front door again? "I think it might be less disruptive to the household if I come and go through the back door. That's all."

He didn't seem convinced, but he shrugged and said, "Suit yourself. We'll leave that way, and I'll let Pearl know you'll be back in the morning."

"Thanks."

Ty handed her the list of names he'd written. "These women were in Lorilee's women's group at church, PTA at school, and most of them knew her from childhood."

Beth scanned the list. "What about Rick Heppel?"

Ty chuckled. "Half-crazy Vietnam vet who lives next farm to the east. Rick's a good old boy, but missing a few screws since Nam. Lorilee was nice to him after he first inherited his grandpa's farm and moved down here. After that he was like her self-proclaimed protector."

"Interesting." Beth circled Heppel's name on the list. She'd pay him a visit first. Maybe Lorilee and Rick Heppel were more than just friends.

She glanced at Ty through veiled lashes.

Did that leave Ty in the role of jealous husband?

CHAPTER FOUR

Beth stood in front of the Brubaker Arms and watched Ty drive away. The moment his truck turned the corner, she spun on her heel and headed across the town square toward her Honda. Even without a spare, she was driving out to Rick Heppel's farm.

She glanced at her watch, then at the sky. She had about two hours of daylight left if she was lucky. The rain had stopped, and patches of blue broke through heavy clouds, though she'd heard on the radio that they were under a tornado watch. Having grown up in Illinois, she had a healthy respect for violent spring weather.

Unfortunately, it also made her restless as hell. She had to keep busy tonight. This would be one of *those* nights. A vulnerable one. A night when comfort sounded like the clink of ice against glass and smelled like the acrid aroma of bourbon. No matter what happened, she couldn't give in to weakness.

Ty had said Heppel's place was due east of his. She should be able to find that. Shouldn't she?

Okay, so she'd stop at Gooch's to see when her new spare would be ready, and ask for directions. No testosterone on board to prevent her from a simple safeguard like that. The wisdom to ask directions was one of the virtues of womanhood, in her humble opinion.

She drove the short distance to Gooch's Garage, where she found the father instead of the son in charge this time. Lester Gooch was easily the skinniest man Beth had ever seen. She figured the reason he wore overalls was probably because he couldn't find jeans small enough to stay put around his scrawny hips.

"My boy told you earlier the tire would take a couple weeks to get in, li'l lady," he drawled, shifting an unlit cigar from one side of his mouth to the other.

Little lady? Beth bit her tongue.

The guy's bald head glowed in the fading afternoon sun as he looped his thumbs through the bib of his overalls. "Month at the outside."

Month my ass. She'd be long gone before then, and she definitely knew bullshit when she smelled it. Gooch's excuses reeked. "Thanks, Mr. Gooch, but—"

"Just Gooch, ma'am."

"Just Dearborn, Gooch." She flashed him her belle smile and batted her lashes.

The man threw his head back and guffawed, his cigar falling to the pavement. "All right, Dearborn. What can I do for you, since your tire ain't here yet?"

"I need directions to Rick Heppel's farm." Beth watched with interest as a scowl replaced Gooch's grin. "You know where it is?"

He stooped to retrieve his cigar stub, wiped it on his overalls, and shoved it back between his teeth. "Yep." He swung around to face her again. "What in tarnation you wanna go see that no-account for?"

"Business." She lifted a shoulder. "I'm investigating the disappearance of Lorilee Brubaker-Malone."

"Ah." Gooch stroked the gray whiskers on his chin, which far outnumbered the hairs on his head. "Disappearance, is it?" He snorted.

One of those.

"I'd appreciate directions to Heppel's farm, if you don't mind," Beth urged. She wanted to take advantage of the remaining daylight. "I figured you would know everything there is to know, so you're the first person I asked."

Gooch puffed up a little at that and finally gave her the damned directions. Beth thanked him and left before he could launch into his opinion of what had really happened to Lorilee. His snort had given her a pretty fair impression of that already, and now she was even more curious about Rick Heppel than ever.

Heppel's house sat near the creek that bordered the Malone farm—the property line, more or less. She parked her car next to a metal barn easily more than twice the size of the house.

It was little more than a cabin. The porch sagged, the roof had been patched with tar paper, and heavy plastic covered two of the windows. Beth glanced back at the high-tech metal building. Interesting.

A black and tan hound scurried out from beneath the porch and barked a warning. His tail wagged furiously, though, so she figured the mongrel was more friend than foe. "Hey, fella," she said. The old dog stopped barking and melted against her leg, tail still wagging. She couldn't resist scratching him behind the ears.

The front door of the cabin squeaked open and the largest, hairiest man she'd ever seen materialized on the threshold. He could easily have passed a screen test for Sasquatch.

The overall-clad monster stepped out onto the porch and stared. Wiry gray hair hung to his shoulders, and a bushy beard fell halfway down his barrel chest. "Yeah?" He folded his arms and kept staring.

"Rick Heppel?" Beth straightened from petting the dog.

The man didn't move. "Depends who's asking."

Oh, goody. "Beth Dearborn." She approached him, her right hand outstretched. When he didn't reach for it, she dropped it to her side. Well, no Southern gentleman here, or risk of being treated like a little lady. "I'd like to ask you a few questions about Lorilee Brubaker-Malone."

His eyes widened, then narrowed to dark slits. "Why? What's your interest in Lorilee?"

"I'm an insurance investigator." No point in hiding that fact. "The Malones want Lorilee declared legally dead."

Heppel chewed his lower lip for several seconds and stroked his beard. "What's that got to do with me?"

"Did you know Lorilee?"

He blinked once. Twice. Moisture collected at the corners of his brown eyes, and he looked beyond her at something she suspected only he could see. Then he drew a deep breath and met her gaze, all evidence of emotion carefully masked. "Everybody around here knew Lorilee."

He's hedging. "Some better than others."

His beard twitched as one corner of his mouth lifted upward. "Lorilee treated me decent."

"How decent?"

He narrowed his eyes again and set his lips in a hard line. "I won't stand here and listen to you bad-mouth a fine lady like Lorilee." He turned toward his house.

Thunder rumbled in the distance. "I'm sorry. I didn't mean to insult you or Lorilee." That much was true,. though her suspicions about the relationship between Heppel and Lorilee had just escalated ten-fold. "Her family and Avery Mutual are looking for the truth. Maybe you can help us find it."

He stood with his broad back to her for several seconds. His head lowered, then he sighed and turned to face her again, lifting his chin to meet her gaze. "I was in the middle of fixin' supper." He looked the length of her. "You don't appear vegan to me."

And you do? Beth blinked, biting back the smart-ass comments that came to mind. "I'm more the burger-and-fries type." She lifted a shoulder. "Guilty."

"If you expect me to answer questions about Lori-lee, you won't be eating flesh tonight."

She grimaced and shook her head. "Well, that's a . . . graphic way to put it."

A sad smile split his beard. "That's a fact."

Eating dinner alone with this odd man didn't rate high on her list of wise ways to spend her first eve-ning in Brubaker, but she needed to hear about Lori-lee. "Thanks for the invitation."

Without speaking, he motioned for her to follow, then turned and lumbered into his house.

Beth glanced down at the hound and whispered,

"If I'm not out of there in one hour, run for the sheriff, Lassie."

The dog licked her hand and ambled back to the porch, circled three times, then dropped with a contented sigh.

Beth stepped over the hound on her way to the screen door. "Big help you're gonna be."

The inside of Heppel's cabin came as a surprise. It was immaculate, first of all, and furnished with bent-willow and log furniture. Some of the tables had intricate carving, and after a few minutes, she realized all the pieces were handmade—not the type found on a showroom floor.

She brushed her hand along the back of a rocker with a gorgeous grapevine motif. "You make all these?"

"Keeps me off the street." He flashed her a sheepish grin that had "gentle giant" written all over it.

This guy is a pussycat. And an artist. "It's beautiful. I hope you charge a fortune for it."

"I get lucky now and then." He pulled out a chair at the table.

"Can I help?"

"Set the table if you want. Plates are in there." He pointed to a cabinet near one of the plastic-covered windows. Beth didn't ask the questions that sprang to mind—at least, not yet.

Rick Heppel was a walking, breathing contradiction. The scents of onions, garlic, and ginger filled the room as he stood stir-frying vegetables and spices in a hot wok at the small stove.

They sat down to eat a spicy mixture of wild rice, greens, seeds, and sprouts that made Beth's mouth water. She took one bite and moaned. "This is delicious, even without meat." She refused to say flesh. "Wow. You make furniture, you cook, and this place is neat as a pin. You'd make someone a great wife." She grinned, hoping to soften him up a little.

Rick's expression grew solemn as he ate his food and sipped his herbal tea. "You might as well know I was in love with Lorilee," he said at last.

Beth coughed. She'd suspected something, but having him come right out and say it shocked the hell out of her. "I . . . see." She took a sip of herbal tea, though she was more the black-coffee type, and mentally patted herself on the back for trusting her instincts enough to drive out here this evening. It would be dark before she headed back to town, but she was a big girl.

"So . . . does Lorilee return your feelings?"

Rick took a long drink of his tea before answering. His soft brown eyes held a wealth of sadness. Why? Unrequited love? Or had they been lovers, and Lorilee had left him, too?

"Oh, Lorilee loved me all right," he finally said. His smile was sad, distant. "She *did*—like a brother." He sighed. "Ty was the only man for her."

"Ah." A tangle of emotions warred within Beth. Disappointment. Relief. Jealousy? She couldn't quite define them, but they all irritated her, and that pissed her off.

Time to get back to work, Dearborn. "Do you know where Lorilee is, Mr. Heppel?" she asked.

His fork clattered to the table, making Beth jump. His dark eyes glowered at her. "Lorilee is *dead*. Period. End of discussion."

Beth swallowed the glob of stir-fry stuck in her

throat, washed it down with tea. Yep, a walking contradiction. Gentle one minute, almost violent the next. He outweighed her by at least a hundred pounds, but her martial-arts training would help even the odds. Theoretically . . .

Not to mention the knife in her boot and the Glock in her backpack. She nudged the bag with her foot, where it rested on the floor beneath the table.

Calmly, she rested her hands in her lap and kept her expression bland. "No, Mr. Heppel, it isn't the end of the discussion. Lorilee's family wants, needs, and deserves answers." She drew a deep, steadying breath. "And from a practical standpoint, I have a job to do. An insurance claim has been filed. A large one. And there's no proof that Lorilee is really dead. An investigation is standard procedure. That's all there is to this. Really."

His shoulders relaxed, dropping at least two inches as he shook his head. "I—I'm sorry." His cheeks reddened and he ran his beefy fingers through his long, gray hair. "I just get so all-fired pissed off when somebody speaks ill of Lorilee."

Beth took another sip of the flower-and-twigs brew to hide the relief that oozed through her. He didn't have to know she'd almost peed her pants when he dropped that fork and yelled at her. Detective training or not—Glock or not—she was a woman alone with a giant of a man, a long way from anything remotely resembling backup.

"I stopped at the library today." *Proceed with caution, Dearborn.* "I read some of the nasty things people wrote after she dis—"

"Lies. All lies." He seemed more disgusted now than angry.

"I was surprised by how quickly the townspeople turned on Lorilee." Beth paused, leaned forward, hoping to encourage him. "Just a few months before her disappearance, an article called her the town's 'guardian angel,' or something like that."

"Nothin' but a bunch of damn hypocrites."

"Seems like." Beth took another bite of stir-fry. Time to change the subject. "I'd love to have this recipe, if you have it written down." Keep him off guard, mellow, friendly . . . "I had no idea vegetarian meals could be so tasty, Mr. Heppel."

He smiled—really smiled. "Call me Rick. We broke bread together, after all." He passed her the basket of muffins to punctuate his point. "These are made from flax meal."

"All right. I'm Beth." She took a muffin, broke it open, drizzled molasses over it. She'd already been informed that vegans didn't eat honey, since it came from bugs. "So, Rick, I know you believe Lorilee's dead. We've established that." She peered at him from beneath her lowered lashes, noting that he still seemed mellow enough. "What do you think happened to her? Really." She took a bite of muffin, letting the warm, chewy sweetness fill her mouth and soothe her.

Rick steepled his fingers on the table in front of him and drew a deep breath. "I honestly believe Lorilee was murdered."

Beth stiffened, her homicide-detective antennae on alert. Ty hadn't actually used that term to describe his wife's fate. Why? Or maybe, Why not? was the right question. Did he know something he didn't want Beth to know?

"Murder is a strong word, Rick." Beth pushed her

empty plate aside and took another sip of tea. "Why do you believe that?"

"She would never leave her babies."

Those words echoed, verbatim, what Ty had said. "Yet . . . we both know there are others in Brubaker who believe Lorilee abandoned her family."

Renewed anger flashed in Rick's eyes. "I told you, they're *wrong*." He rose and started clearing the table.

Beth followed, carrying her empty plate and cup to the sink. "What about that letter from England?"

Rick didn't look at her, and his words were barely audible. "Find the bastard who sent that letter, and he'll lead you to Lorilee's killer."

Ty had said, *Whoever wrote that letter knows what happened to my wife*. Again, he echoed Ty's opinion, though the word *killer* had never left Ty's lips.

Why did that omission disturb her?

Beth shoved the thought aside. Right now she needed facts, not speculation about Ty Malone's guilt or innocence. Beth had been in this business too damned long not to trust her hunches, and she had a hunch Rick Heppel knew things about Lorilee her husband might not.

She needed to stay in Heppel's good graces. Somehow.

Make nice.

"Dinner was great, Rick. It was really nice of you to invite me."

"It really is about damned time someone found out what happened to Lorilee," he said. "Past time."

His words sounded genuine. Beth nodded. "Let me help wash these dishes."

"Nah, it'll only take me a minute." Thunder

boomed outside, and lightning flashed outside the window. "You oughta head back before the storm."

A chill swept through her. "I hate storms."

"Storms are in my blood. I'm from Kansas," he said through a grin. "But I can't fly in weather like this, so I hate 'em, too."

"Fly?"

"Chopper pilot."

"Oh, so that's what's in the metal building."

"Yep." He grinned again. "Truth is, I earn a lot more money hauling water and hay with my chopper than I do selling my furniture and carvings."

"That's a shame." She glanced around the cabin again. "Because this stuff is gorgeous."

He blushed above his gray beard. "Thanks." His tone softened. "Lorilee thought so, too. You know she was an artist—a painter?"

"I saw some of her work at the house." Beth saw genuine grief in this man's eyes, but he still seemed more than a little unstable. "Guess it takes an artist to know one."

He muttered something unintelligible, and lightning flashed again. "You'd best get goin'."

Beth wished she could stay longer, draw him out more. But there was a storm coming, and she sensed that if she pushed too hard too fast, this man could very well withdraw completely. She needed his trust and cooperation. One step at a time.

"I'd like to meet—have met—Lorilee," Beth said.

Rick nodded. "She had her . . . problems, but she sort of took me under her wing after I got here, encouraged me to keep up my craft, even though I'm quite a bit older than she was."

"Artist to artist?"

"Exactly."

"So you're from Kansas, huh?"

"Still a damn Yankee to these folks." He walked her to the door. "And they don't approve of my so-called hippie lifestyle either. Stir-fried sprouts are sinner's food."

Beth chuckled. "Even so, you're a sprout-eating veteran."

Rick stiffened. "Who told you that?"

She studied his expression for a few seconds. "Ty must have mentioned it."

Rick's gaze dropped to the floor, and he shook his head before looking up at her again. "I reckon Lori-lee told him."

"Why don't you want people to know?"

His nostrils flared slightly, and she heard him swallow. "I try not to think about Nam. The only good thing the army taught me was how to fly a chopper."

"I won't mention it." It was hard not to like this guy. She could easily see how he and Lorilee had become good friends. "Here's my card with my cell number, and I'm staying at the Brubaker Arms. If you think of anything I should know that might help solve Lorilee's case, give me a call."

"Will do." He tucked her card in his bib pocket, then opened the squeaky screen door and held it. The wind picked up, and lightning flashed in the dark sky. "I don't think you're gonna beat that storm back to town."

Beth drew a shaky breath. "Won't be the worst thing that's ever happened to me."

* * *

Country dark and city dark were two entirely different beasts. Once she'd left the comforting glow of the security light on Rick's hangar, Beth drove through black ink, broken only by intermittent flashes of lightning.

"Great, Dearborn." She tightened her grip on the steering wheel. "Just dandy."

Her first day in Brubaker had turned into a marathon that would end in hell. And another thing—stir-fried sprouts didn't mix well with violent weather.

Clenching her teeth, she steered her car along the curvy dirt road that led back to the highway. At least it had led *from* the highway *to* Heppel's house. Somehow, it hadn't seemed as far driving in the other direction in calm weather and daylight.

The road meandered along the creek, ducking into and out of the trees. Lightning flashed, transforming the blackness into a photographer's negative. Blinded, she slammed on her brakes. Her heart thumped against her ribs, and she licked her dry lips.

It's just a storm, you wimp.

"Just a storm," she repeated aloud. Of course, they were never *just storms* for her. It had something to do with her freaky gift—something she'd failed to suppress, unlike her empathy with murder victims, because she couldn't avoid Mother Nature the way she could crime scenes. Electrical storms affected her, sometimes violently. She *felt* them—either with a giddy sense of power, an overwhelming fear, or an almost sexual lust that reverberated through her until she thought she'd go insane waiting for the storm to pass.

Tonight, terror crept along the fringes of her sanity. The lightning flashes came more frequently, and the wind whipped the trees into a frenzy. Small twigs and leaves scraped across her windshield on their way to Oz.

"Where the hell is the yellow-brick road when you frigging need it?"

Finally, Beth found the highway, squeezed her eyes closed for a moment, and breathed a sigh of relief. She turned on her blinker, preparing to turn left onto the two-lane highway just as her cell phone played a few notes of theme song from *Twilight Zone.*

"Shit." Beth grabbed her cell out of her backpack. "Dearborn here." *Sitting in a tin can during an electrical storm in the middle of nowhere, like an idiot, talking on a frigging cell phone.*

"This is Sarah Malone," a young woman said.

Whoa! Ty and Lorilee's kid? "Yes? What can I do for you?" Ty didn't want her to speak to the children, but Beth couldn't very well stop them from contacting her. Could she?

"I—I heard you're here to solve my momma's murder."

Oh, boy. There's that word again. "Sarah, who told you that?"

"No one. You're an investigator," the girl said, the tremor in her voice audible even though the signal was breaking. "I just thought . . ."

"How did you get this number?"

"I found your card on my dad's desk."

More static garbled the line, and Beth glanced at her dashboard. Eight o'clock wasn't late. "Then you know I work for an insurance company."

"Y-yes."

"Does your dad know you called me?"

"No. He went to town this evening. I'm the one who asked him to find out what happened to Momma."

Suddenly, Beth had to talk to this girl. Tonight. "How old are you, Sarah?"

"Sixteen."

Not an adult, but not a baby, either. Ty would have a fit. Lighting struck the ground somewhere nearby. Too near. Beth could *smell* it. Feel it. Hear it in her bones.

"I'm not far away from your place now." Beth might regret those words, but she pressed onward. "Is it too late for us to talk?"

"No." The girl sounded eager. "Come now. I'm babysitting my little brother and sister. They just went to bed."

Common sense told Beth to turn left and head back to the hotel. Gut instinct told her to turn right and cross the bridge, turn right again, and return to the Malones' house for the second time today.

"I'll be there in about ten minutes."

Beth disconnected and headed in that direction, mentally kicking herself as she made the necessary turns. The kicking didn't help. She still had to risk this.

Fat raindrops pelted her windshield, and the storm rocked her tiny car. Lightning transformed the inky landscape to pseudowinter. Raindrops sparkled like eerie ice shards in the flash, then reverted to watery missiles landing on the hood of her car.

Beth clutched her steering wheel. A fierce blast of wind slammed into the vehicle, and she swerved on the graded gravel road leading to the Malones' Victorian farmhouse. And shelter.

She hit the brake and stopped the car, pressed the heel of her hand against her breastbone. Her heart hammered frantically against it. "Easy. It's only a storm."

She could handle this. If only she weren't so alone. If only it weren't so damned dark. In town, it wouldn't be so dark. The storm wouldn't seem so . . . eerie. So otherworldly. But she knew better.

Tiny pellets of hail scurried against her windshield. "Drive, Dearborn. Drive, damn you." She eased her foot off the brake and pressed on the gas. The car inched forward through the deluge. Her wipers barely cleared the glass enough to enable her to see the path illuminated by her headlights and Mother Nature's electrical show.

She crested the final hill and envisioned the valley floor the way she'd seen it this afternoon from Lorilee's studio window. Pastoral. Picturesque. Amazing what a difference a few hours, a little pitch-blackness, and Mother Nature's ire could make.

She squinted into the darkness, spotted the comforting lights of the farmhouse and the outbuildings in the distance. The rain and wind increased, but the hail stopped. Lightning and thunder followed one another in rapid succession now, matching the staccato rhythm of her pulse.

Sweat rolled down her neck and dampened her bra. She didn't dare release the steering wheel to adjust the temperature on the defroster. Her palms slipped and she tightened her grip even more. Lightning struck the ground nearby, and a whimper escaped her lips. The hairs on the back of her neck stood on end; she smelled something burning. Too close. Too dangerous. "Show-off."

Her bravado didn't help.

The wind whistled around her closed doors as she pulled to a stop in front of the big white house at last. It looked more like the haunted house at an amusement park than the pastoral scene she'd viewed earlier today. She swallowed the lump lodged in her throat, but that didn't stop the tremor that had taken hold. She shook like a human vibrator from head to toe, and she knew it wouldn't stop until the storm had passed.

Lightning flashed again. Again. Again. The hot, burning stench filled her nostrils. Panic swarmed around her. Raindrops pummeled her car, sounding like a semiautomatic battering a metal coffin. Terror and heat crowded the cramped interior. She released the clutch while the car was still in gear and it lurched forward, sputtered, and died. She groped in the dark for the door handle and wrenched it open, but the seat belt held her captive.

Like an animal caught in a steel trap, she struggled to free herself. An inhuman sound rumbled from somewhere deep inside her until, finally, she broke loose and bolted for the front door. The house was dark now. Damn!

Rain soaked her within two steps of her car. By the time she lurched onto the porch she was drenched.

Terror ripped at her. Shelter. She had to escape. Hide. Run. She pounded and clawed at the front door, pounded again. It swung open and she stumbled. Beth plunged forward into the Malones' foyer.

Her screwup registered just as a new kind of fear closed in on her.

Please don't hit me again.

Crushing pain slammed into her face before she fell with a sickening thud.

Don't hit—

Then blessed blackness saved her ass.

CHAPTER FIVE

Pearl pulled open the back door and slipped into the Malones' mud room. Sarah would still be awake, of course, but Mark and Grace should be in bed by now. Ty had insisted that Sarah could handle the children, but this storm was a humdinger.

All right, she was really here to ease her own worries. "Might as well 'fess up, Pearl, old girl," she muttered as she removed her hooded raincoat and hung it from a peg. She shivered and rubbed the goose bumps on her arms. She'd just sit with the kids a spell until the storm passed, then head back home and listen to Cecil gloat, "I told you they'd be fine."

But she couldn't help herself. With Lorilee gone, worrying about this family was her job, and she always took pride in a job well done.

Ty hardly ever went out in the evening, but tomorrow was Mark's twelfth birthday, and he had to pick up the gift he'd ordered from Robey's. The least Pearl could do was check on the youngsters.

If you asked her, which nobody ever did, that young man needed to get out more, meet a nice woman, fall in love again . . . Pearl paused just inside the kitchen and drew a deep breath.

Lordy, Lorilee, but we sure miss you, child.

The lights flickered as a fierce blast of wind struck the house. "Please, no twisters." She gazed upward and mouthed a silent prayer. Just in case.

Sarah came down the back staircase into the kitchen, her eyes widening when she spotted her. "Pearl? You aren't supposed to—"

"I remembered how much that last storm scared your li'l sister." She narrowed her eyes, tilting her head to study Sarah. "Don't tell me you're scared, too."

"No, of course not." Sarah licked her lips, and her gaze darted toward the door leading to the foyer. "It's just that—"

The lights flickered once, twice, then died completely. Pearl sighed. She'd expected this.

"If your brother didn't get his hands on it, the flashlight should be in this drawer right here." She felt her way past the now-silent refrigerator to the second drawer, fumbled around, and flipped on the flashlight. "Fetch that oil lamp from the pantry. Better save these batteries. No tellin' how long the power might be out."

Pearl shone the light in the pantry while Sarah collected the lamp and a box of matches. Once the girl carried the items to the drop-leaf table beneath the window, Pearl passed her the flashlight. "Here, hold this steady."

She struck a match and touched the flame to the wick. The golden flame cast eerie shadows along the walls and ceiling. "There, that's better."

Sure it is, Pearl.

She studied Sarah's expression for several seconds. Pearl's heart constricted. "You remind me so much of your momma when she was your age." She reached out and cupped Sarah's cheek, detecting a faint tremor. "What is it, child? The storm?"

Sarah released a long, slow breath as a gust of wind shook the house and the lights flickered again, only teasing. They remained in darkness. Wind sifted in beneath the swinging door that separated the kitchen from the foyer.

"Hmm. Do you suppose your ornery brother left the parlor window open again? Let's check. Then we'll peek in on him and Grace." She took Sarah's hand and gave it a squeeze. "Nothin' to be afraid of now, honey. Pearl's here."

They pushed through the swinging door together. The front door stood wide open, transforming the foyer into a wind tunnel. A wet one.

"I do believe the devil has come a callin'," Pearl muttered.

"The wind must have blown it open."

"This floor is slicker than greased piglets, but we've gotta get that door shut." Pearl released Sarah's hand and trod carefully along the glistening wood. She held the oil lamp higher to flood the foyer with light.

Sarah gasped from behind her, and Pearl almost dropped the oil lamp. "What . . . ? Who . . . ? Lord have mercy!"

A woman lay flat on her face right inside the front door in a puddle of rainwater. Pearl handed the lamp to Sarah and hurried to the woman's side.

Rain and wind slashed through the open door. "Sarah, shut the door," Pearl shouted over the racket. "She's either sick or hurt. Reckon I'd best see which."

Sarah eased past them and closed the heavy front door. Without being told, the girl grabbed towels from the kitchen and sopped up the rain from the wood floor, then brought more dry ones to Pearl.

"Do—do you know who she is?" the girl asked.

Pearl nodded. "The insurance investigator who was here earlier, talkin' to your daddy." She gave the woman a gentle shake. "Ms. Dearling, or something like that."

"Dearborn." Sarah blinked when Pearl glanced up at her. "I saw her card on Dad's desk."

"That's right." Pearl shook the woman's shoulder again. "Ms. Dearborn? Can you hear me, ma'am? Are you hurt?"

"Help . . . me," she whispered, though it sounded more like a groan. "Don't . . . hit me."

"Nobody's hittin' you, child." Pearl stroked the woman's damp hair and patted her back maternally. She couldn't help herself—that was her way. Cecil swore she was forever bringing in strays, and this one had come right in the front door.

She leaned down and sniffed. At least the woman didn't smell like liquor, so she couldn't blame her condition on that. She winced inwardly as another memory surfaced—one she tried not to think of often. Her sweet Lorilee had sometimes drunk in secret.

Don't think about that, old woman. Not now.

Someone had obviously hurt Ms. Dearborn, and she needed some good, old-fashioned TLC. Pearl knew just the person to give it to her.

"Sounds like the storm is blowing over," Sarah whispered.

"Good. Maybe the power'll come back on soon. Now let's see to our patient here. I don't think anything's broken." Even so, she hesitated to move Ms.

Dearborn. It would be best if she could stand up on her own. "Can you get up, honey? We'll move you into the parlor."

Ms. Dearborn opened her eyes, her expression frantic. "Out of here. Away from . . . door."

"You got it, but first you stand up for Pearl." She put one arm around the woman's waist, and her shoulder braced under her armpit as she rose. Ms. Dearborn was considerably taller than Pearl, but on the slender side. The lights flickered twice more, then finally stayed on. "Let there be light. Now if only they'll stay on for good." She squeezed her eyes closed for a second. *Amen.*

"Sarah, grab a quilt from the linen closet. She's shakin' like a sinner on Judgment Day. But we're gonna have to put ice on that goose egg bloomin' on her forehead, and I'm afraid that's gonna make her shake even more."

Thunder rattled the house again. "After we get her settled, you'd best check on your brother and sister. Make sure the storm didn't scare the bejeebers outta them."

Once they had the woman settled on the sofa with a quilt wrapped around her and a pouch of frozen peas on her forehead, she looked half-alive again. The color returned to her cheeks, that desperate hunted expression disappeared from her eyes, and her shivering slowed.

Assured that Mark and Grace had—amazingly— slept through the raging storm, Pearl sent Sarah to the kitchen again, this time for hot cocoa to counter- act the chill from the frozen peas.

"What brings you back out here at this hour, Ms. Dearborn?" If the woman wasn't injured, Pearl would be *demanding* an answer to her questions. The investigator wasn't supposed to return until tomorrow morning. "And in this god-awful weather?"

"Well . . ." The woman glanced toward the doorway where Sarah had gone. "I was nearby when the storm broke, and I think—"

"I called her," Sarah announced as she returned. She placed a tray bearing cups of steaming cocoa with floating marshmallows on the coffee table.

"Oh. I see." Pearl knew full well how Ty felt about the children being touched by this investigation. "You put Ms. Dearborn in a nasty spot, girl." *Not just the storm, but your daddy's temper, too.*

"I—I'm sorry." Sarah handed a cup of cocoa to the investigator.

"I'm a big girl." No longer trembling, Ms. Dearborn took a long drink. "Mmm. Besides, anyone who brings me chocolate this rich receives instant forgiveness."

Pearl chuckled. "Ain't that the truth? Old family recipe, passed down from Lorilee's great-granny." She reached for a cup. "Creole from New Orleans, she was."

"So Lorilee's family wasn't from here originally?" The investigator watched them over the rim of her cup as she took another sip.

"Oh, her daddy's family founded Brubaker, but her momma's side came from Louisiana."

Pearl turned her attention to Sarah, who kept shooting nervous glances at the grandfather clock against the far wall. "Why'd you call Ms. Dearborn out in this storm tonight, Sarah?"

"I . . ."

"Really, I was already out," Ms. Dearborn said.

"But Sarah must've had a reason for callin' you," Pearl said. "And she knows her daddy's feelings on the subject. So . . . why?"

The clock's ticking filled the strained silence for several seconds. Then someone cleared his throat from across the room. Their heads turned toward the foyer, where Ty leaned against the doorframe as if he'd been there for quite a spell. Listening.

"Yes, Sarah. Why?"

Ty felt as if he'd been rode hard and put up wet.

And now this. What was Beth Dearborn doing here at this hour? And hadn't Pearl gone home hours ago? What could Sarah have said to Beth? What the *hell* was going on here?

"Well?" He gritted his teeth and counted silently to ten. Again. "Sarah, I'm waiting. You put Ms. Dearborn in danger. She—and I—deserve an explanation."

Tears welled in his daughter's eyes and trickled down her cheeks. Strands of blonde hair, so much like her mother's, clung to the dampness. She shoved them back and sniffled. "I—I'm sorry." Her lower lip trembled.

"I know that, honey, but you still haven't told us why." Damn, but he hated it when she cried. Reminded him that Lorilee wasn't here to pick up the broken pieces of their little girl's life. Reminded him the buck stopped with him. Reminded him he was alone in this parenting deal . . .

"I saw her card on your desk." Sarah cleared her throat and squared her shoulders. The girl had the Malone stubborn streak a mile wide. "I thought . . ." Her face crumpled.

Ah, shit. Ty walked across the room and gathered his daughter in his arms. "Shh." He tucked her head under his chin and held her while she cried. That was one thing he'd grown to excel at in the past seven years. "Sorry, darlin'. I dang near had to swim home, and I'm getting you all wet."

She giggled a little at that. "I don't care." Her voice sounded muffled against his chest.

Ty turned his attention to Beth Dearborn. She looked even worse than he felt. Her upper lip and nose were swollen as if she'd taken a blow to the face, and she had a bag of frozen peas plastered to her forehead.

"What happened?" He eased Sarah slightly away from him and turned her to face Beth as well. His daughter was, at least indirectly, responsible for this. "Were you in an accident, Beth?"

Crimson crept upward along her neck, from the opening of the tightly clutched quilt. Holy crap! Was she naked under there? He glanced down and saw her damp jeans beneath the quilt, putting an end to that speculation. Remembering his manners, he dragged his gaze back to her flushed face and waited for an answer. Come to think of it, Sarah still owed him an answer as well.

"We aren't sure what happened," Pearl said after several awkward moments. "We found her passed out on the floor by the front door with that goose egg on her forehead."

Ty raked a hand through his damp hair, keeping his gaze fixed on Beth, who set the now-sweating bag of peas on a towel, then turned her attention to spinning her empty cup in her saucer. Anything but risk making eye contact?

The quilt slipped from her shoulders, and her damp T-shirt clung to her like shrink-wrap. Shit. He swallowed hard, and a thin film of sweat coated his brow.

She had nice breasts. Firm, full, though smaller than average. Still . . . nice. And her nipples . . . Well, he'd noticed those earlier today, and he'd thought about them all damned—

Criminy, Malone. Get a grip.

Yeah, he'd like to get a grip all right. On her. Vaguely aware of Pearl and Sarah talking to each other, he drew a deep breath and looked up at Beth's face again. Of course, *now* she would look at him—just in time to catch him ogling her nipples.

She wasn't blushing now. She arched an eyebrow, tilted her head slightly to the right, parted her lips ever so slightly in a knowing smile . . .

And winked.

Ty choked, and Sarah stepped away to pat him on the back. "You really are wet, Daddy. What happened?"

He coughed for a minute, trying not to bust out laughing at Beth Dearborn's audacity. The woman was perplexing as hell. Finally, he shook his head and ended his fake coughing spell, mustered the sternest expression he could, and faced his daughter.

"I'm not answering your question until you answer mine."

She ducked her chin. "Oh."

"Thought you women could change the subject on me." He nodded and crossed his arms over his abdomen. "Not this time. I want to know why you called Ms. Dearborn this evening." He swung his head toward Beth. "Then I want to know how you got hurt."

"Okay." Sarah sat on the end of the couch and rested her chin in her hands. "I heard you and Pearl talking after dinner, and you said you thought maybe Ms. Dearborn was the one who would finally find the truth."

Damn. Ty wasn't sure how he felt about Beth hearing that. "That still doesn't explain why you called her, Sarah."

"I—I'm not sure." The girl looked anxiously from Beth to Ty to Pearl, then back to Ty. "I just needed to talk to her—to tell her how important it is that we find out what happened to Momma. That we make people stop thinking..." She drew a stuttering breath and brought her hand to her quivering lips.

"Sarah," Beth said gently. "You know I work for an insurance company. Right?"

The girl nodded. "It said so on your business card. Of course I know."

"I *am* here to find the truth." Beth looked up at Ty, her expression open and sincere. "No matter what it is."

"Right. No matter what," Ty repeated, unable to look away.

Pearl rose from her rocking chair near the hearth. "We'll all be glad to know the truth. That's for sure."

"Your turn." Still holding Beth's gaze, Ty arched both eyebrows. "What happened to you? Why did I find your car out front with the lights on and the driver's door standing open?"

She looked down for several seconds, then met his gaze again and held her hands out to her sides, palms upturned. "The big, bad investigator is afraid of thunderstorms. All right?"

This tough-as-nails woman afraid of a little thunder and lightning? He didn't buy it. "If you say so." His tone dripped sarcasm.

"I was at Rick Heppel's when Sarah called, and—"

"Heppel's?"

"He was on the list you gave me. Remember?"

He nodded. Why had she started with the only man on the list? And, more importantly, why was that knowledge eating a hole in Ty's gut? There were plenty of people in town Beth could have talked to this evening, without driving back out into the country. In the dark. During a storm.

Afraid of thunderstorms, my ass.

"So how'd you get the goose egg?"

"I—I'm not sure." She gingerly put her index finger on the purplish bump, puckered her brow, and winced. "Ow, that hurts."

"Some aspirin before bed is a good idea," Pearl said.

"Yeah, I have some." Beth unwrapped her legs from the quilt and looked around. "I probably left my backpack in the car."

"You still didn't tell us how you got the goose egg," Ty reminded her.

"Oh, yeah." The look she gave him said she might have stuck her tongue out at him—or worse—if they'd been alone. "I remember knocking on the front door, but the storm was so loud, no one heard me. I kept pounding on it, and it flew open. I must've been leaning on it when it did, and I stumbled through."

All the color drained from her face and she seemed short of breath.

"You all right, honey?" Pearl felt the side of her

face farthest from her injury. "No fever. Is your tummy upset?"

Beth shook her head. "No, really. I'll just head back to the hotel now. I'll be fine. I'm sorry I've been so much trouble."

"You got no business driving tonight." Pearl had that stubborn set to her jaw that told the world the battle was lost before it began. "Since your tummy's all right, I'll fetch you some aspirin."

"So . . ." He had to keep talking. "You fell through the front door and landed on your forehead?"

"Flat on my face. I think." Beth pressed her lips together, as if trying to remember. "I might have tripped. Or something. Maybe my forehead made contact first."

"You thought someone was hitting you," Sarah said.

"What?" Ty waited for Beth to explain, but she didn't. The expression on her face said more than words. Something or someone had scared the holy crap out of her. Heppel? "Who hit you?"

"No one. I just fell."

"She was out cold, Ty," Pearl said as she handed Beth two aspirin and a glass of water. "Hallucinatin', I think."

Hallucinating? Ty didn't like the sound of that, and he sure as hell didn't like the look on Beth's face. She was hiding something. But what?

Sarah interrupted his thoughts. "It could've been worse." She collected the empty cocoa cups and placed them on the tray. "I'm sorry I brought you over here in the storm."

"It's not your fault. Really, Sarah. I was already out," Beth said.

"I'm still sorry." Sarah looked at Ty. "Honest, Daddy."

"I know you are." Ty had to drop the other shoe—the one he knew about that they didn't. The one that had been tormenting him ever since he saw Beth's car in front of his house when he came home this evening.

She pushed herself up off the couch and grabbed her head. "Whoa, not a good i . . . de . . . a."

Ty caught her before she fell again. "Definitely not." She blinked up at him, completely alert. "Just dizzy. Don't get any ideas, Malone."

He couldn't suppress his chuckle. All his ideas had been born a hell of a lot earlier. "You sure about that, Dearborn?"

Ty remembered Sarah, where he was, what he was doing. Damn. He was losing it. Carefully, he eased Beth back onto the couch, though he liked the feel of her against him. Too much. Way too much.

"Like we said, you got no business driving tonight," Pearl repeated.

"Besides, you wouldn't get very far, unless you're planning to head toward Knoxville instead of Brubaker." Ty barely suppressed a shudder, remembering his harrowing drive home.

"Knoxville's in the opposite direction. Why would I want to do that?" Beth lifted her chin a notch, sensing a challenge. "And I'll have you know I'm an excellent driver."

He held up his hand to silence her. "I'm sure you are, but unless that heap of yours is equipped with a rudder and oars, you won't be driving it to Brubaker tonight."

"Oh, no. The bridge is out again." Pearl moaned.

"Last time we had to drive to Knoxville for groceries for nearly a month, before—"

"A *month*?" Beth started to stand again, but grabbed her head and slumped back onto the couch. "A month? You can't be serious."

"Bridge washed out right behind me. It was too dark to see the water heading toward me. Was only dumb luck that saved me."

"More than dumb luck, Tyrone Malone," Pearl admonished. "And don't you be forgetting it. I'll say an extra prayer of thanks for God bringin' you home safe tonight." She gave him a peck on the cheek. "I'm just gonna go make up the guest room. Sarah, you'd best run along to bed. It's gettin' late."

" 'Night, Daddy. 'Night, Ms. Dearborn. I hope you feel better in the morning." Sarah hugged Ty and Pearl, then headed up the stairs.

"Thanks, Mrs. Montgomery," Beth said. "You've been very kind."

"Pshaw. No bother at all, but no more of this *Mrs. Montgomery* nonsense. Call me Pearl." She patted Beth's arm.

"All right, if you'll call me Beth."

"Beth it is. I'm just glad you were on this side of the bridge when it went out, and not in town. We don't want anything to keep you from findin' the truth 'bout Lorilee. Do we?"

"Good point."

"Now I'll see to the guest room, then I'd best get back home before Cecil comes lookin' for me. Don't want him out at this hour."

Beth seemed to relax and leaned back against the sofa, her expression almost smug. "If I'm going to be stranded, I guess this is the best place for it."

She crossed her arms beneath her shrink-wrapped breasts.

And aimed her nipples right at him again.

His blood supply redirected itself so quickly that now *he* was dizzy.

A month of having Beth Dearborn—and her nipples—in his home full-time? All day? Every day? All night? Every night?

A month?

Hell, he wouldn't survive the first week.

CHAPTER SIX

Silt and sewage from the Chicago River coated the inside of Beth's mouth. She forced down the urge to gag—or worse—and cleared her throat.

Where the hell am I?

She half-opened one eye. Sunlight slammed into her pupil and arrowed straight to a nuclear headache. She closed it again fast.

Think, Dearborn.

My God. Had she fallen off the wagon? The way her head pounded and belly churned were agonizingly familiar. But, no . . . Her mouth would definitely have tasted more like puke than pollution if that horrible nightmare had come to pass.

The storm. Lightning. Thunder. Wind. *Terror.*

A shudder rippled through her, and cold sweat coated her body. Gingerly, she touched her forehead. The golf ball–sized knot she found there explained the headache. Okay, but how the hell had—

The foyer.

She opened both eyes and stared at the ceiling fan rotating slowly overhead. The Malone house.

Don't hit me.

Bile scalded Beth's throat as the memory pierced through her headache with scalpel-like precision.

Again, a presence had confronted her at the Malones' front door. And again, she'd experienced pain. Fear. Now there was no doubt. No more denial.

Shit.

Her so-called "gift" was staging a comeback. Big-time.

Panic launched her heart into hyperspeed, but she willed herself to remain still. To remember more. Whoever the spirit was, it seemed confined to the foyer. The voice had belonged to a woman. Beth seemed safe from her memory here, in this part of the house. But why hadn't she returned to the Brubaker Arms last night? She closed her eyes again, drew deep breaths through her nose, releasing them slowly through her mouth. In. Out. In. Out.

Her bedroom door clicked open, but she deliberately kept her eyes closed. She had no idea where her backpack was, exactly where in the Malone house she was now, or how vulnerable she could still be to the presence inhabiting the foyer. Her old precinct captain would have said she was playing possum. Whatever worked, was Beth's philosophy—then and now.

"Do you think she's dead?" someone whispered. Loudly.

"Nah. She ain't dead. She just looks dead."

"Don't say ain't, or Pearl will wash your mouth out with soap again."

Kids. Damn. Beth opened her eyes to narrow slits and tried to focus on the human forms near the door.

I've landed in Oz and these are the Bumpkin Munchkins. Of course, if that were true, then she was the wicked witch, and Dorothy had dropped a house on *her* head.

"Pearl *ain't* here."

"I'm gonna tell."

"You're such a baby."

They sure as hell weren't whispering now. Beth opened her eyes all the way and checked out the intruders while they bickered back and forth. The smaller of the pair was a brown-eyed blonde who looked like a younger version of Sarah. The boy looked like a miniature of Ty.

"I am not a baby."

"Are so."

"Am not."

"Are so."

"Hey, hey, hey." Beth struggled to a sitting position. "Keep it down to a dull roar, will you?"

"See? Told ya she ain't dead," the miniature Ty said.

Man, kid, you're lucky you're cute, or somebody would've done more than wash your mouth out with soap by now.

Beth sighed and then glanced down. "What the . . . ?" Someone had taken her clothes and dressed her in . . . ruffles. The neckline plunged halfway to China, she could see actual body parts through the filmy fabric, and—worst of all—the thing was *pink*. "Whoa! Somebody snuck in here and dressed me like a freaking Barbie doll."

The little girl giggled. "That's just a nightgown." She came closer to the bed. "What's your name?"

"Apparently, Barbie. Er, Beth. I think." She grimaced and rearranged some of the silly ruffles and lace so at least her nipples were no longer visible. The boy was old enough to at least be curious. "What's yours?"

"I'm Grace, and I'm nine."

"A baby," the boy said.

"Nine is not a baby," Beth interrupted before they could start the yo-yo bickering again. Her headache couldn't take it. "And what's your name, smart man?"

His face and ears turned the shade of a ripe tomato, and his blue-green eyes flashed fire. "I'm Mark, and I'm twelve today."

"Happy birthday, Mark." Beth studied the kids for a few seconds. They seemed healthy and well cared for. With Pearl around, how could they be anything less? Of course, she'd seen Ty's apparent dedication as well. "So . . . do you always spy on guests, or only on your birthday?"

"Sorry." Mark lifted a shoulder. "Didn't mean no harm."

"*Any* harm," Grace corrected. "And I'm sorry, too."

Beth rolled her eyes. "You're forgiven, then."

"You, uh, won't tell our dad." Mark glanced over his shoulder at the half-open door. "Will you?"

"Why shouldn't I?"

"Because he'll be *mad* at us." Grace's eyes grew round and her lower lip quivered.

"Because it's my birthday?" Mark ventured, a dimple appearing in his cheek.

Definitely a lady-killer. Beth cleared her throat and managed not to grin. After all, they had invaded her privacy, and even if she wasn't exactly the maternal type, she knew kids shouldn't be rewarded for that. "Okay, I won't tell your dad *if* . . ."

"Ah, man." Mark snorted in disgust. "I knew there'd be a condition. Grown-ups always got 'em."

Grace blinked and wisely waited in silence.

"You promise never to spy on anyone again. Deal?"

The kids' eyes lit up like downtown Chicago on Christmas Eve. "Sure!" they said in unison.

"And . . ."

"I knew it was too good to be true," Mark muttered.

Beth's lips twitched. She could get to like this kid. "You tell me what I'm doing here and how I ended up dressed in"—she plucked at the pink froth just above her breast—"this . . . this *thing.*"

Grace giggled again. "Haven't you ever worn a nightgown before?"

Beth probably shouldn't tell innocent children she preferred to sleep in the buff. "Maybe when I was too young to decide for myself."

"It *is* kinda silly lookin'," Mark said, though his gaze kept dropping to where Beth had strategically arranged the ruffles to cover her chest.

"Is not," Grace shot back.

"Is too."

"Is not."

"Is too."

"Is—"

"Do you suppose you can stop arguing long enough to tell me why I'm here instead of at my hotel in town?" Beth interrupted. It seemed a little less controversial than gagging both children with bedsheets.

"Sorry." Grace inched closer to the bed. "Daddy said you're going to stay with us until they fix the bridge."

Bridge . . . Last night's events roared through Beth's aching gray matter in a maddening, horrifying flash. Oh, my God. Was she really stranded here with the Malones and the foyer's invisible Welcome Wagon?

She swallowed hard. Her stomach twisted into knots.

"You look kinda green," Mark said from right beside her. "You gonna barf or somethin'?"

"Or something." Beth shoved back the quilt and swung her legs to the floor, drawing long, slow breaths. "Wonder how long it'll take to fix that bridge."

"I dunno, but I wish school was on the *other* side instead of this side." Mark sighed and looked as though he'd just been dosed with castor oil.

"I like school," Grace said.

"That's 'cuz you're teacher's pet," Mark chided.

"Just because I'm smart doesn't make me teacher's pet."

"That's why Andy never wants to sit beside you on the bus."

Grace lifted her chin, thrust out her lower lip. Her eyes glistened, and Beth thought for sure she was about to have a bawling kid in her room, when Grace redeemed herself by doubling up her fist and punching her brother right in the nose. Whoever the unknown Andy was, the kid had definitely motivated Grace to action.

Mark howled as blood spurted from his nose. Beth lunged across the room and grabbed a hand towel from the dressing table, sat Mark down on her bed, and scrambled through her pitiful memory for basic first-aid training from the academy. Tilt his head back or down? Ah, hell. She settled on back and hoped for the best.

"What in blazes is going on in—" Ty stared at Beth, his mouth open in stunned silence.

"I didn't hit him, if that's what you're thinking."

"Hit who?" Ty's Adam's apple traveled the length of his throat, his gaze riveted on her.

Ty had stumbled into the Twilight Zone. Either that or he'd followed a white rabbit down a hole. This gorgeous, soft, feminine creature couldn't be the hard-as-nails insurance investigator who'd driven him to distraction all day yesterday, *and* invaded his dreams.

"Take a picture, Malone. It lasts longer."

Then again . . . "I thought I'd join the party." He looked at his son, then at his daughter, before bringing his gaze back to Beth. "Did you forget to invite me?"

She snorted. Yep, definitely the same Beth. He grinned.

"What are you laughing at? This nightgown wasn't my idea. And where's my backpack?"

"Hold on there." He removed the towel quickly and checked his son's nose. "Grace do that?"

Mark nodded.

"You deserve it?"

Another nod.

"Doesn't look broken to me. Go tell Pearl you need some ice before your party guests get here."

Towel clutched to his face, Mark darted from the room. Ty could have sworn he heard Beth mutter

"Coward" after his son's retreat. Smart was more like it. "I think he'll be all right by party time."

"Birthday party?" Beth asked.

"Yep." Ty knelt in front of Grace. "Haven't we talked about punching your brother's lights out before, honey?"

Grace bobbed her blonde head and shuffled her feet.

"I know Mark's rotten more often than not, but try a little harder to resist the urge to belt him next time. Okay?"

She heaved a long-suffering, Southern-belle sigh that would have made her momma proud. "Okay, Daddy."

"Now go tell your brother you're sorry for breaking his nose."

Grace's eyes widened and her mouth formed a perfect circle. "Really?"

"Well, almost." He gave her a quick hug. "No need to look so proud of yourself for it either."

"Sorry, Daddy." Grace dropped her gaze, but her lips twitched as if struggling not to smile.

"Go tell Mark that. Not me."

"Okay."

Beth applauded as Grace scurried from the room. "You're good, Malone. Damn good."

"It's Ty. Remember?" He straightened to his full height, his gaze raking her. The nightgown must have belonged to Lorilee, though he couldn't remember his wife wearing that specific one. Thank God. Still, it was just the sort of thing she always wore— soft and feminine. "You look nice."

"Heh." Beth folded her arms and tilted her head to one side. "*That's* a matter of opinion."

"Yes. Mine."

She arched an eyebrow and walked toward the window, where sunlight streamed through the lace curtains and flowed around her. The woman clearly had no idea what she was doing. She might as well have been standing in front of a spotlight wearing nothing at all.

Ty's mouth went dry and his blood supply took the direct route straight to his cock. After a few moments, she turned to face him again, hands on her hips.

"So where's my backpack?"

Flustered, he shook his head and dragged in a shaky breath. "It must still be in your car." He wanted to cross the room to get a closer look at, and his hands on, her. But he didn't. He reminded himself who she was and why she was here, and managed to stay put. Barely . . .

"Okay."

She turned sideways, her profile toward the window, outlining her firm breasts for his simultaneous pleasure and torture. Damn.

"Your son reminded me what you said last night about a bridge being washed out between here and town." She shook her head. "I didn't dream that. Did I?"

"Nope. It's all true." Sweat trickled down Ty's neck and into his collar. He swallowed hard and raked his fingers through his hair. It was next to impossible to carry on a conversation with a practically naked woman while sporting an erection hard enough to spade through drought-baked summer soil.

She spun around to face him again and he managed a nod. "Figures," she muttered. "Just my rotten luck. Which bridge was it? The one between your farm and Heppel's place?"

Ty clenched his teeth. Why was she so damned interested in Heppel? What was it about that man? First Lorilee, and now . . .

Knock it off, Malone.

"Earth to Ty Malone." Beth waved her hands in the air. "Earth to Ty Malone. Come in, Malone."

"Ha. Ha." He drew a steadying breath. "No, not that bridge. The big one across the river right outside of town."

Her expression grew sober. "You *were* lucky. You could have been killed, Ty." She licked her lips, her hazel eyes soft for once.

He didn't say a word—he didn't dare. All he could do was stare and concentrate on his breathing. She looked so kissable right now it was all he could do not to cross the room and do just that. Just grab her and do the deed.

Shit.

She met his gaze and arched an eyebrow. One corner of her mouth twitched. "You staring at my breasts again, Malone?"

His breath rushed from his lungs, the spell shattered. Thank God. "Damn straight."

She laughed—actually laughed—out loud. "At least you're honest about it. I've been doing my share of staring at your, uh, package myself." She winked and walked back to the bed and sat on the edge.

"My . . . package?" Ty's voice broke.

"Well, hell, Malone." She glanced pointedly below his waist. "You didn't expect me not to notice *that*. Did you?"

"If that don't beat all."

"What? It's okay for men to ogle women, but not okay for women to ogle men?" She laughed again. "I've got a news flash for you, Ty. Women ogle all the time. Most of us just won't admit it." She bit her lower lip and gave him a sexy smile. "I'm admitting it."

"Shit." He was in bigger trouble than he'd imagined.

"Don't you want to know if I like what I—"

"Stop right there." He held his hand up, palm toward her. "My male ego can't take another word."

She leaned back on her arms, her breasts nicely displayed against the filmy fabric. "Okay, back to business, then. I'm stuck here while the rest of my clothes are at the Brubaker Arms."

I'll say. "Pearl will find you some things."

Beth plucked at the pink froth in her lap. "More like this? I think not." She aimed a thumb at his jeans. "What size are your jeans?"

He lifted one corner of his mouth, and his gaze dipped to her slender hips. "They'd fall off of you."

"I'd rather take my chances with your jeans than Barbie-doll hand-me-downs, if you don't mind." She grimaced and crossed her legs. "Now . . . about my backpack."

"I'm sure it's still in your car. I'll get it." Hell-bent on escape, he crossed the room, pausing with his hand on the knob to look back over his shoulder. "You're welcome to continue your investigation full-time, since you're here, of course."

"Thanks." She grinned. "I fully intend to."

Chuckling, he left the room and closed the door behind him. He glanced down the hall to ensure he was alone, then tugged on his belt to ease the pressure on his "package."

Having Beth Dearborn in such close proximity was going to wreak havoc with his libido. Hell, he'd probably walk around like a sixteen-year-old with a never-ending hard-on.

But he couldn't do that. He drew three deep breaths, reminding himself with each one why Beth was here: to learn the truth about Lorilee at long last—not to fulfill his sexual fantasies.

Sexual fantasies, my ass. Ty Malone wasn't a man who indulged in that crap. Self-disgust slithered through him.

For seven years he'd mourned his wife, raised his kids, and dealt with a town full of gossipmongers. One long-legged insurance investigator wasn't going to change his life, even if she did like his "package."

He paused on the landing and stared out the window at the bright morning. The rain had washed the air and left everything dazzling. Clouds skated along the mountain ridge to the east, but the rest of the sky was clear and bright.

No, Beth Dearborn wasn't going to change his life.

That was what he wanted. Wasn't it? Truth.

No matter what it is, she'd said.

But were they ready to hear it?

Beth waited until the door clicked shut, then flopped back on the mattress with a groan. "Beth, you slut." Why hadn't she just grabbed the man and torn off his clothes when she had the chance?

She had enough to deal with already, without the ramifications of seducing a client. Or was he the subject of an investigation? Lord, she hoped not. Whatever. It all amounted to mixing business with pleasure, any way she looked at it. And that was wrong with a capital *W*.

But—whew!—the way he'd looked at her. Liquid heat swept through her, pooling low in her belly. When she'd walked over to the window, she hadn't thought about the consequences of the sun spilling around her in the flimsy Barbie getup. Until she'd turned around and noticed the look in Ty's eyes and the condition of his anatomy . . .

When she'd realized he could see right through the pink froth, she should have moved away from the window like a good girl. Or draped a sheet around her shoulders to cover herself. Like a lady . . . Yeah, right.

She pushed herself up onto her elbows and glanced down at her dark nipples, clearly visible through the tissue-thin material. "You hussy, you."

No, she hadn't moved away from the light or made any effort to cover herself. Instead, she'd flaunted her attributes right in front of Ty. Advertising.

Beth Dearborn smorgasbord—take what you want and leave what you don't.

Oh, and he'd clearly wanted. A smile curved her lips as she recalled the blatant bulge in his jeans, the dangerous glitter in his eyes. This lusting problem was definitely not one-sided.

So just what the hell were they going to do about it?

She pushed to her feet, her headache and dizziness nothing but a memory, and returned to the window. Ty had the driver's door to her car open and leaned across the front seat to grab her backpack. She always left it in the passenger seat when she drove, so she knew that was where he'd find it.

His jeans stretched nicely across his butt as he leaned into the car. A girl could do worse than a wild fling with a sexy farmer built like Ty Malone.

Resisting temptation, with temptation in her face day in and day out, would be damned near impossible. For both of them.

So maybe they shouldn't resist. Get it over with and move on with the investigation. Was that the answer? Slake their lust and get it out of their systems?

"What the hell are you thinking, Dearborn?"

Of course, she knew damned well what she was thinking. The same thing she'd been thinking ever since he'd stopped to change her tire.

She wanted to have mind-numbing sex with that man. Tyrone Malone. Rhyming name or not. Damn.

She had an itch that demanded to be scratched, and she knew he had the same problem. They were both consenting adults, and—at least for now—they were stuck together under the same roof. Of course, there were the rug rats to consider, but they weren't always underfoot.

Were they? Perish the thought.

Beth chewed the fingernail on her index finger as Ty straightened and slammed her car door. She was so confused—an unusual state for her, which pissed her off even more. Would sex with Ty really be as irresponsible as it sounded?

Probably. With a sigh, she returned to the bed and wrapped a sheet around her to wait for Ty and her backpack. She'd call her cousin Sam in Chicago on her cell phone. He was the only family she had left, and if ever she needed advice, it was today.

Not only was Sam Dearborn the only person close enough to her to confide in about Ty, but he was also the only human on the planet who understood her family gift and why she had worked so hard to suppress it.

Furthermore, he was the only person on the planet she could tell about the spirit in the Malone entryway.

CHAPTER SEVEN

"Where the hell'd I put my glasses?" Sam Dearborn muttered as the phone rang for the third time. He squinted at the caller-ID display on his breakfast bar, then lunged for the cordless handset before voice mail answered. "Shit for timing, as usual, Cuz," he said.

"Great to hear your voice, too, Sammy."

He cringed. "That's Professor to you." He reached up to rake his fingers through his unruly mop, but encountered an obstacle. "Aha, my glasses."

"Wearing them again and forgot?"

He could hear his cousin's laughter across the miles, even after he'd set the phone down on the counter to retrieve his glasses from the top of his head and put them on his face, where they belonged. He picked up the receiver and said, "Let there be clarity."

"Okay, now that you can see, can you also pay attention?" As usual, Beth's tone said light-years more than her words.

"What is it, Beth? And where are you, anyway?" He shoved a pile of books off a bar stool and sat. "Did it ever occur to you that I'd like to know your whereabouts once in a blue moon?"

"You sound like my mother."

Sam's gut clenched. "Perish the thought."

More laughter, but with a note of sadness this time—one Sam recognized far too well. "Come on, Beth. What's up? Something's wrong. I can tell."

"Gee, you psychic or something?"

"Or something, and you damn well know it, smart-ass." He leafed through the papers he'd graded before dawn, then slid them into his portfolio. "So give me a synopsis—I have a lecture at eleven."

"I'm on assignment in Brubaker, Tennessee."

"Where's Brubaker?" Sam glanced at the digital clock on the microwave. He had forty minutes. He'd make it on time or die trying. "Near Memphis?"

"Other side of the state, near Knoxville." She sighed into the phone.

"So, only a few leagues from civilization." He listened to her breathe for a few seconds. "Tell me what's wrong."

"Someone is trying to make contact. You know. To engage me?"

"Aha!" Sam leapt off the bar stool and punched the air with his free hand. "So your gift isn't gone. I *knew* it!"

"Don't sound so frigging happy about this, damn you. I'm sure as hell not."

"So you say," Sam said, though he continued with his now-silent victory dance around his tiny kitchen. "Tell me what happened."

He listened as his cousin described her two empathic encounters in the farmhouse foyer, and how at first she hadn't been sure it was a spirit. "But now you're certain?" he asked.

"Oh, yeah. Positive after last night." She cleared her throat. "There's more."

"I'm listening."

"You always do. That's why I called."

"I know."

"A storm washed out the bridge, and I'm stuck out here until it's repaired."

"Fascinating. Fate steps in once again."

"Fate, my ass."

"Are you sure we're related?"

"Ha. Ha."

Sam rubbed his chin, remembering his cousin's years on the Chicago police force. "Beth, you're one of the best. If a spirit is trying to contact you, that means he or she—"

"She."

"She . . . died violently. I don't have to tell you that." He set his portfolio and backpack by the front door and returned to the kitchen to turn off the lights, glancing again at the clock.

Twenty minutes. Shit. "If you allow her to contact you, her cause of death may be resolved."

"Sam, don't you think I know that? This is exactly what I've been trying to avoid the last three years." Her voice broke. "Sorry. Sorry. This isn't your fault. I'm sorta wrung out."

"I can tell. That storm you mentioned rattled you. Didn't it?"

"Big-time."

He scowled at the clock. He'd never get tenure if he didn't make his classes on time. But this was only one class, and Beth needed him. Besides, she *never* asked for help. Not anymore. Not since she'd stopped drinking. He wasn't about to turn her away when she needed him. Resigned to missing his class, he drew a deep breath and said, "Wait a minute."

He momentarily put her line on hold and switched to text-message his graduate assistant. *Amy—Can't come. U R on.* He returned to Beth. "I'm back." A minute of silence stretched over the line. "Beth?"

"Oh, I'm still here." She gave a nervous—a very un-Beth-like—laugh. "Well, see . . . there's . . . this . . . man . . ."

"Whoa." He slumped against the bar. "No kidding? Wow! That's incredible. It must be serious for you to bother telling m—"

"It isn't serious *that* way, Sam. Serious hormonal overload for both parties, I think." She cleared her throat. "It's serious because it's *wrong*. He's involved in the case."

"Ah, now I understand. Perfect Detective Dearborn mustn't mix business with pleasure." He rolled his eyes, remembering how uptight she'd always been about that. "Let your hair down, Beth. You only live once. When was the last time you met a man who interested you enough to make you even consider taking such a risk?"

"Oh, gee, let me think. Like . . . never?"

"My point." He glanced at the clock. He'd been right to surrender. Amy would do just fine, and she'd been dying to lecture. "And think more about this spirit, too. Will you?"

"Sam . . . Do you think you could fly down here and contact the spirit—find out what she wants and send her away?"

He released his breath very slowly. "Our gifts are different, Beth. You know that. If she's trying to contact *you*, she may not have anything to share with *me*."

"I thought of that, too."

"I see . . ." Suspicion slithered through Sam and he stiffened. "Exactly *how* does this man figure into the case you're investigating? And whose house is it?"

"Give the man a cigar."

"Ah, so it's like that." Maybe good news, maybe bad. Sam needed to check out this guy. "So you're staying in his house?"

"Yep, along with his three darling children and a housekeeper who rules all. Trust me, we're well chaperoned."

"How inconvenient."

"Or maybe it's a good thing."

"I take it he's single, at least."

"Well . . . allegedly."

"What?" Sam shook his head. "You're talking riddles now, Cuz. Either he is or he isn't."

"Well, it depends on whether or not his wife is really dead."

"Oh-*ho*! I get it now. This is the case you're investigating . . . ? Let me guess—he's having his missing wife declared legally dead after all these long years?" Sam *definitely* had to meet this guy.

"Yup."

"You certainly know how to get yourself into messes."

"I do, don't I?"

He bit his lower lip, hating to ask the next question, but it needed to be asked. "So . . . you having any trouble . . . you know?"

"Booze?" Brittle laughter rang over the line. "It's okay to say it, Sam. I promise I am still clean and sober. Thanks for asking. And for caring . . ."

"And . . . can you stay that way while dealing with

the spirit in that house?" He swallowed hard, waiting for her answer.

"Why the hell do you think I asked you to come down here?" Her breathing quickened audibly. "I haven't had to face anything like this in over three years, Sam. It drove me to Bourbonville once. I don't want to go back there."

"Then don't. Just don't."

"Easy for you to say."

Yes, it was easy for him to say, because he wasn't powerless over alcohol. He'd gone through the treatment-program sessions with Beth as a family member. He'd read all the literature, taken all the counseling, and vowed to do whatever it took to help her stay sober.

And wasn't that *exactly* what she'd just asked him to do? Damn.

"Can you hold out three more weeks until the end of semester?"

"That's a long time to drag out the investigation."

"Best I can do, with finals and all."

"Are you saying you'll come then?"

"Why the hell not? I've never been to Tennessee, and I'll be due a vacation by that point."

"The spirit seems to be confined to the foyer," she said. "I'll simply avoid the foyer."

Sam had to laugh at that. "Strictly the back door for you?"

"Damn right."

"Remember, she might not have anything to tell me, Beth. Only spirits with certain types of needs contact me, just as only certain ones contact you."

Her sigh sounded weary now. "I know, Sam. Trust me, I know. We've both always known . . ."

"And what about the, uh, man?" He cleared his throat. "You, uh, going to be able to hold out on him, too?"

"I . . . I'm not sure I want to."

"That's one hell of a confession, coming from you," Sam said quietly, no trace of mockery in his tone. "Just be careful. Okay?"

"Promise. Now I have to go to a birthday party. See you in three weeks."

"Okay, three weeks. Bye, Beth."

Sam punched the off button and stared for several minutes at the phone cradled in his palm. No sense in denying it. He was worried.

Surely his cousin had considered the probable identity of that spirit in the foyer . . .

One of the farmhands was taking his wife to Knoxville to run errands for several families, and it seemed like Beth's best opportunity to get out of Lorilee's Barbie-doll clothes. At Ty's insistence, Beth gave him a shopping list that included her jeans and T-shirt sizes, a package of simple cotton panties, and a few pair of socks. She could get by with just her Nikes, and she usually went braless anyway. There was no way she would ask Ty Malone to buy her bras.

She'd added basic toiletries, some antacids, and more ibuprofen as well. After meeting Ty's kids, she had a feeling she'd be needing plenty of those.

Besides Lorilee's questionable taste, it made Beth more than a little uncomfortable to wear the late wife's clothes while lusting after her husband. Whether the woman was dead or not . . . However, until the messengers returned from Knoxville Beth really had no choice. She glanced down at the Western-style split skirt the wonderful Pearl had brought her this morning. It was a little loose at the waist, and hit just above her knees. She suspected it was intended to be worn midcalf. Obviously Lorilee hadn't been anywhere near Beth's almost six feet.

The white blouse had two patch pockets, one strategically placed over each breast. At least that was something. Otherwise, since white and braless was not a wise combination—unless she were auditioning for a wet-T-shirt contest—Beth would have been forced to attend a twelve-year-old boy's birthday party as a sex-education visual aid.

The mothers of Brubaker would have run her out of town with tar and feathers for sure. Considering how those genteel Southern belles had turned on poor Lorilee, Beth could scarcely imagine their reaction to a damned Yankee, recovering alcoholic, former-detective, gun-toting, probable slut. The thought made her grin at her revolting reflection.

That Beth Dearborn is nothing but a Jezebel.

She chuckled and finished buttoning the blouse. Her Nikes looked pretty lame with this getup, but they'd have to do. Lorilee's shoes were way too short and wide for Beth's long, narrow feet. At least this outfit wasn't pink, and there wasn't a ruffle in sight.

She glanced at herself in the mirror. Wild hair somewhat tamed after a reviving shower, she didn't look too bad. The goose egg on her forehead had diminished to nothing but a small purple knot now. It could have been much worse, and her headache was completely gone. No more nausea or dizziness either. All in all, she'd recovered very quickly.

Now all she had to do was avoid the damned foyer.

She bit her lower lip and swallowed the lump in her throat as she finished tucking in the blouse. Of course, it wouldn't stay tucked with such a short tail.

"Okay, Beth, so ask yourself the question you've been avoiding," she whispered as she retrieved some lip balm from her backpack. She uncapped the tube and smeared it on, then leaned her hip against the edge of the cherrywood dressing table.

Is the ghost in the foyer the long-absent Lorilee?

Beth sure as hell hoped not. How ironic was that? She might be able to shorten her investigation by weeks simply by engaging the spirit and solving the cause of death.

A sigh squeezed through her convulsing throat at the prospect.

But if Lorilee had died a violent death in her own home, and there was no body . . .

"Don't go there, Dearborn." She shoved away from the dressing table. *Wait for Sam. Wait for Sam. Wait for Sam.*

She dropped the lip balm into her backpack and noticed her Glock. With kids in the house she had to put that someplace where curious fingers wouldn't come across it. The Malone gang had already proven their moxie during their morning visit to her room. No telling what trouble they might find if she wasn't around.

She had a shoulder holster, but that seemed like overkill in Brubaker. Another grin tugged at her lips. She could just imagine Pearl's reaction, and the Glock didn't exactly go with her outfit.

Well, that settled it. "Where I go, you go," she muttered as she slung the backpack strap over her shoulder and headed into the hallway.

She made her way down the stairs toward the parlor, reacquainting herself with the floor plan as she went. Two sets of stairs—one going to the parlor at the front of the house, and one to the kitchen and the rear. No reason for her to ever venture into the foyer again until after Sam arrived.

Three weeks. She could do this.

But what if that spirit really was Lorilee? The fact that she was trying to contact Beth meant she'd died violently.

This is a hundred-and-something-year-old house.

She paused on the landing and stared out the window, drawing several deep breaths. The spirit in the foyer could have been there for a century, waiting for someone with Beth's empathic gift to cross the threshold. No reason to believe it was Lorilee.

Except for the fact that Lorilee was missing and no body had ever been found.

Knock it off, Dearborn.

"Three frigging weeks. That's all," she whispered. Several cars were parked in front of the house, and the sound of kids' laughter drifted up the stairs.

Mark was gradually recovering—so Pearl claimed— from the disappointment that only neighboring children who lived on *this* side of the washed-out bridge would be able to attend his party.

This would be a first—Beth Dearborn at a twelve-year-old's birthday party. Hell, she'd never even had a birthday party of her own. Sam was the only kid who'd ever had anything to do with "weird Beth." She chuckled and rolled her shoulders. Of course, Sam was every bit as strange as his cousin.

Beth reached the bottom step and froze. Balloons, pretzels, confetti, and God knew what else flew around the formerly immaculate parlor. She ran a quick head count and came up with five boys in addition to Mark. Grace sat quietly at a table draped with bright yellow paper.

And Beth thought life as a homicide detective had been dangerous.

"They've got to be kidding," she muttered. But this party was her opportunity to meet some of the women whose names were on the list Ty had given her. Lorilee's friends and her parents would be here, which meant Beth had to suck it up and make nice.

Where were all the parents? This mob definitely needed supervision. She swept the room with a detective's gaze, realizing all the adults had wisely retreated.

Well, hell. Where did that leave her? Stranded here with the inmates? Since the only way she knew out of the parlor was through the foyer . . .

No, there was another way. She squinted through the floating confetti and spotted the archway she'd seen Sarah emerge from last night carrying cocoa. Relieved, she headed in that direction, through an alcove, but stopped short of the kitchen.

Because there wasn't room for her there. Every square inch of floor space was occupied by a human form. Mothers of every shape and size scurried around, filling plates with food as Pearl sliced pizza and Ty poured root beer into plastic cups. He spotted her and grabbed her wrist, dragging her into the melee.

"Make yourself useful." He handed her a tray filled with cups. "Take these out to the kids."

Her eyes widened. "Have you been out there in the last few minutes?"

"That bad?"

"Worse."

"Sarah, take over here?" he asked his oldest child, who was clearly trying to fit in with the older women.

Poor kid. Beth struggled against the urge to rescue the girl from a life of mediocrity. She'd already shown she had potential, and then some.

"Beth and I are going to bring peace to the natives before any more food leaves the kitchen."

"Good luck," Pearl warned. The woman smiled, despite looking more than a little harried. "The grandparents will be here any minute."

"Ah, hell—er, good," Ty muttered as he steered Beth back through the semisacred archway.

"Grandparents that bad?" she asked, certain he hadn't meant for his words to be overheard.

He chuckled. "Yes and no."

She tried to ignore the warmth of his hand on her elbow, and wondered if he realized he hadn't released her even after they reached the parlor.

"Payday on Saturday night in old Dodge City couldn't have been this hazardous," he said.

"At least they aren't armed." She glanced down at his hand on her elbow, then up at his face.

"Thank God for small favors." He met her gaze and she watched a muscle in his jaw twitch. His Adam's apple traveled the length of his throat, and he licked his lips. His eyes darkened from blue-green to cobalt, and he leaned closer.

Surely he wasn't going to kiss her here. Not that she would try to stop him. Would she? His warm breath fanned her cheek as he held her gaze. She couldn't move. Couldn't think. Even the madness around them seemed to fade.

His grip on her arm tightened slightly, and his nostrils flared. She sensed the battle waging inside him—should he or shouldn't he? Damned if he did and damned if he didn't? Oh, she knew the feeling well.

Her body warmed in anticipation. She leaned closer. Wanting. Needing. Enough of this self-control, dammit. Maybe this wasn't the time or the place for a first kiss, but she *wanted* this.

Needed it . . .

Clearly, so did he. The air between them felt charged like last night's lightning. They would be good together. Damn good. Sex with Ty Malone had *multiple orgasm* written all over it.

The mere thought sent a molten flood of moisture and warmth coursing through her. Beth swallowed hard. And waited. Ty suddenly shook himself, pulled back, and dropped her elbow, the moment lost. She blinked, gathering what remained of her wits. *Damn.*

What had come over her? It wasn't like her to become so engrossed in a man that she lost track of what was going on around her.

His gaze dropped to the backpack slung over her shoulder, clearly trying to change the subject to anything except what was uppermost in both their minds. "You wear that thing everywhere?"

She nodded once, trying to capture her equilibrium along with her bearings. "Pretty much."

He gave her a crooked grin, then put two fingers between his lips and produced an ear-splitting whistle. Every hell-raiser in the room froze to stare in total silence.

"Incredible," she whispered.

"Works every time," Ty said with a wink.

The confetti gradually settled to the floor. "If you boys expect any grub—especially *cake*—you'll go outside and run five laps around the house, and then I expect you to be sitting at that table with angelic expressions when your mommas enter the room. Got it?"

They scrambled over each other to the door, while Grace still sat waiting like a good little girl.

Maybe too good, Beth realized, remembering Grace's earlier behavior in her room. Poor kid. Losing a mother at such a young age had to have some kind of serious impact on a girl.

Whether that mother had left of her own free will or not.

There you go, Dearborn—back to work. You're on the job. That's the ticket. Maybe remembering that would keep her mind off Ty's almost-kiss. And keep her from wondering why, why, *why* he hadn't followed through . . .

She shot Ty a glance from the corner of her eye. Damn. He even looked great while setting a frigging table. Did the man ever look bad? Last night, when he'd shown up after the storm, with his hair messy and his clothes soaked and soiled, he'd looked good enough to eat.

And now . . . clean-shaven, dressed for his son's birthday party, he looked good enough to eat. *Mine. Better than cake.*

Oooookay. Enough of that. Back to the task at hand. Forks on the left. Right? When was the last time Beth Dearborn had set a table?

"Cat got your tongue?"

Ty's voice stroked her already-scrambled hormones.

She suppressed a shudder and looked up to meet his gaze. Why couldn't the man ugly himself up just a little?

"Cat? You have a cat?" she hedged.

One corner of his mouth quirked upward, and he shook his head slowly. "Only in the barn." He sighed and dropped the napkins on the table. "The little monsters will only stay outside for a few minutes. All hell will break loose in here again any second. Your headache all gone now?"

"Good as new." She smiled and licked her lips, wishing this guy didn't make her feel so damned giddy. A seasoned pro like her shouldn't feel like a silly schoolgirl. Yet Ty Malone reduced her to little better than a mass of walking, breathing hormones without even touching her.

She simply *wanted* the man. Or maybe it had been too long since she'd been laid. Who the hell knew for sure?

"Should I make myself scarce?" she asked. "Go upstairs and work in Lorilee's study, maybe?"

Ty shrugged. "Some of those women whose names are on the list I gave you will be here today."

"Right." She knew that, but right now escape seemed safer. Still, Beth Dearborn didn't run away, and the sooner she solved this case, the sooner she could leave Brubaker, Ty Malone, and the resident ghost.

She drew a shaky breath. "Guess my work today is down here where the action is, then."

The swinging doors opened, and two mothers came through carrying trays filled with fried chicken. The spicy aroma wafted through the room, triggering a rumble from Beth's belly.

"Miss breakfast?" Ty teased with a wink.

Beth didn't bother telling him she'd been too busy entertaining two of his children this morning to worry about food. "Something like that."

"You're going to need all your strength before this is over."

The look he gave her had double entendre written all over it. Beth took a step back. She was in bad shape. All this guy had to do was look at her, and she was a puddle of want and need and hormones.

"I'm fine." She cleared her throat as the women cast her covert glances before returning to the kitchen. "Betcha I'm the talk of the town about now."

Ty chuckled. "That's one bet I'm not taking. Odds are against me."

"Daddy?" Grace interrupted.

Beth had almost forgotten about the quiet little girl, but there she was, standing beside her father. "May I go help Pearl in the kitchen?"

"Sure, kiddo. Go for it."

They both stared after the girl as she disappeared through the swinging door.

"She's a sweet kid," Beth said.

Ty released a long, slow breath. "They all are. I worry about them."

She nodded, and wandered to the window overlooking the valley. It looked so peaceful now, nothing like last night. Her car sat where she'd left it, but the door was now closed and the lights off, no thanks to her.

She rolled her shoulders and clenched her fists. Her stomach tightened into a knot that had nothing to do with lack of food, and everything to do with the proximity of the man standing so close.

She half turned to face him. He'd almost kissed her. She knew it as well as she knew her own face in the mirror. Why hadn't he? A knowing smile tugged at her lips. Probably for the same reason she didn't grab him by the hand and drag him upstairs to have her way with him right now.

Okay, so he hadn't kissed her because the kids were in the room. Now they weren't. She drew a deep breath.

Maybe Ty Malone needed a little encouragement.

CHAPTER EIGHT

For crap's sake! I almost kissed the woman right here in front of the kids.

Ty busied himself straightening some of the pandemonium before the boys' mothers saw it, knowing his efforts would be inadequate, but still better than nothing. At least Pearl would never know about the pretzels in the aquarium. He'd managed to scoop what the fish hadn't eaten out quick enough. Only time would tell if they'd live to tattle about it.

What the hell had come over him, leaning toward Beth that way? And—dammit all to hell—he grew hot and hard all over just thinking about how close he'd come to . . . to . . . His collar tightened around his throat, and his jeans tugged sensitive anatomy in a particularly uncomfortable, potentially embarrassing way.

He drew a deep breath or three and lined up the eating utensils the way Beth had placed them earlier—or guessed at it anyway. At least the kids hadn't barged back inside yet. Thank God for small favors.

Beth was busy removing pretzels, chips, and confetti from the furniture. Good idea. The grandparents and parents would need places to sit while Mark opened the loot. He gave her a thumbs-up gesture and her cheeks reddened, even as she scowled. What a confounding woman. She blew hot and cold quicker than springtime in Tennessee. One thing he knew for sure: a man would never be bored with a woman like Beth Dearborn in his life.

He stiffened and gnawed the inside of his cheek. Not that he'd been bored with Lorilee, of course. Guilt pressed down on him. Where the hell had that come from? He shifted and cleared his throat.

"Break's over," Beth said over the thunder of sneakers and boots in the foyer.

"Stampede coming." Chaperones were probably a good thing about now, he decided. They would help remind him to keep his hands—and other things—to himself. He glanced at the way the buttons of her white blouse strained against her breasts as she leaned across the table to right an overturned cup.

Maybe . . .

Behave yourself, Malone. He was acting like a horny teenager instead of a responsible adult and father.

The boys gathered around the righted tables, diving into chip bowls again, leaving trails of crumbs across the yellow tablecloths. "Right back where we started," he muttered.

"Pretty much." Was that humor or exasperation in Beth's voice? He looked at her and saw mischief dancing in her hazel eyes. Why that pleased him, he wasn't sure, and he sure as hell didn't want to examine it now.

"What time will Grandpa get here?" Mark asked from his side, rubbing his hands together while wearing a greedy, eager grin.

Ty couldn't help but return his son's infectious smile, thankful to have his son to anchor him back in reality. He rested his hand on Mark's bony twelve-year-old shoulder.

Lorilee's dad still doted on the kids. Spoiled them rotten, when he wasn't busy trying to mold them into his own image—at least as much as his young wife would allow. She only tolerated the kids in moderation. "I expect them anytime now."

"Them? Oh." Mark slouched a little.

"You didn't expect Grandma Ruby to miss your birthday party." Ty ruffled his son's shaggy dark hair. *Boy could use a haircut.* "Did you?"

"I s'pose not."

"'Grandma Ruby'?" Beth echoed.

He didn't realize she'd come over to the table until she spoke. "Lorilee's stepmother. Her daddy remarried a few years after Lorilee and I got hitched."

"Ah." Beth slid her backpack off her shoulder and removed her notepad from yesterday, scribbled a few lines. "Thanks."

Ty chuckled and shook his head. The doorbell rang and the mothers, along with Grace, Pearl, and Sarah, all started into the room, chattering away. "Lord, give us strength," he prayed.

The boys and even Grace all giggled. Young fools—they actually thought he was kidding.

He met Beth's gaze and she mouthed an *amen*, but he saw the corners of her mouth twitching. Heh. He figured her for about five minutes with this crew. Ten, tops.

With a sigh, he headed toward the sound of Pearl's voice in the foyer as she greeted Bill and Ruby Lee

Brubaker. Cecil had found some urgent chore or another to delay his arrival—smart man—leaving Ty the only adult male present, other than his father-in-law.

"Wilson over at the hotel gave me a call yesterday," Bill said as he passed his Stetson to Pearl. "Said there's a lady insurance investigator in town askin' around 'bout Lorilee. You know anything a—"

"Good to see you, Bill," Ty interrupted, pounding his father-in-law on the back in greeting. *Wilson's been a busy old fart.* "You should get over more often. The kids always enjoy your visits." *Even if they generally give me indigestion.*

"That boy of yours needs to learn about running a bigger spread. Send him over for the summer, once school's out."

Ty avoided his father-in-law's all-too-familiar dig about how much smaller his farming operation was than Brubaker's. How many times had the old man tried to coerce and shame him into folding his farm into the larger family spread? But Ty and Lorilee had worked too long and hard to build this place, and he wasn't about to let it be swallowed up by a power-hungry old man.

"Ruby Lee, I swear you look younger every time I see you," Ty said, bending down to kiss the petite redhead's cheek. And she did look overtly younger. Hadn't Pearl mentioned a lift or tuck or something? The discreet pinch his housekeeper delivered to his rib cage was answer enough. "Come on into the parlor. The natives are getting restless."

"Is it true about the investigator, Ty?" Ruby Lee asked, batting her heavily made-up eyes.

"Yes, ma'am. It's true."

"Dunno why you couldn't leave well enough alone," Brubaker muttered. "Leave well enough alone, and let this matter rest in peace."

"That's exactly what I'm trying to do, sir," Ty said, clenching his teeth. It was a wonder he hadn't worn them down to nubs by now. "This is a birthday party. Okay with you two if we change the subject?"

"Sure, sure." Bill appeared somewhat chagrined. He heaved a heavy sigh, patted Ty on the shoulder, then headed into the parlor. The kids greeted him loudly. The old man might be greedy and annoying, but he was a much-loved and loving grandfather, and had been a doting father to Lorilee. Ty always tried to remind himself that her disappearance had hurt Bill as much as it had him.

"Maybe the washed-out bridge will send that investigator packing her way back from where she come," Ruby Lee said. "You think?"

"Oh, I wouldn't count on that." Ty cleared his throat. "Let's get to the party before the hellions tear the house apart."

"What a plan," Pearl muttered.

Ty met his housekeeper's gaze, and the woman rolled her eyes behind Ruby Lee's back. "That husband of yours is a coward, Pearl Montgomery," he whispered as they entered the parlor.

"No, I ain't either, Ty Malone," Cecil said from behind them. "I married this feisty old woman, didn't I?"

"Point taken."

Pearl laughed as her husband leaned down to kiss her cheek. Then she looked up at Ty and asked, "Why didn't you tell Mr. and Mrs. Brubaker about Beth Dearborn bein' here, Ty Malone?"

Good question. He'd been about to, but something had stopped him. "I'm not sure. Guess I didn't have enough time."

"Hmm . . ." Pearl seemed unconvinced.

Frankly, so was he.

"Don't matter now," Cecil said. "Reckon they're about to find out for themselves."

Ty followed the direction of Cecil's gaze. Beth had her trusty notepad in hand and was heading straight toward Bill Brubaker.

"Holy shit," he whispered. The woman could at least wait for an introduction.

Cecil rested his large hand on Ty's shoulder and chuckled. "I got me a feelin' there's nothin' holy about it, son."

The theme song from *Dallas* played in Beth's head as she watched William Brubaker lumber into the room. "Larger than life" was an apt description for the Southern landholder, after whose ancestors the town had been named. Tall and broad through the shoulders, he carried himself like a far-younger man. Years of working outside had worn his skin to a leathery gold that contrasted handsomely with his thick head of silver hair.

So this is Daddy Warbucks.

Beth intended to waste no time getting to know Lorilee's father. With her notepad and pen in hand, she wound her way between mothers whose names she didn't yet know—and who stared at her with more-than-passing curiosity—and headed straight toward her target.

The bouncing redhead who bobbled in behind him couldn't be "Grandma Ruby." Could she? Beth hesitated a second too long, considering that possibility. Just long enough for Ty to intercept her on the five-yard line.

He gave her elbow a squeeze. A hard one. "Now, now," he said for her ears only. "At least wait for a proper introduction before you unsheathe your claws."

If they'd been alone, she would have demonstrated the precise move she'd used to earn her second-degree black belt. Instead, she hissed. Quietly.

"This *is* a birthday party." He leaned closer. "Remember?"

With a sigh, she slipped the notepad into the pocket of her denim skirt, where it would be handy. "I promise to behave, if you *promise* to introduce me to people."

He gave a curt nod. "I said I would, and I will. Thank you for behaving."

"Sure. No problem." Damn, but the man had more charisma—or something—than the law should allow. And she was a big girl. She should be way beyond this.

Get over it, Dearborn. With great effort, she turned her attention back to Lorilee's big daddy.

"Twelve years old, Mark," the older man said boisterously. "That's almost a man."

"Oh, boy," Ty muttered through a sigh.

Even though she'd never been a parent, Beth somehow understood. "Yeah . . ."

"He's center stage now, and there's no stopping him," Cecil said from behind them.

"I'm afraid so," Ty confirmed.

Pearl had disappeared into the kitchen again. Sarah stood beside her grandfather, her pretty face pale, her eyes wide. Beth made a mental note to spend more time with the oldest Malone child. After all, she was the one who'd called Beth here last night, and—according to Ty—had asked to have her mother declared legally dead.

"Let's eat this chicken before it gets cold," Pearl suggested, emerging again from the kitchen. "Then we'll get to the cake and, oh, maybe some presents, if somebody insists."

Timing was everything, and Pearl Montgomery obviously knew exactly how to keep peace in this family. Beth made a mental note to stay on the woman's good side. She could be a great ally in this investigation, but she could just as easily become an impediment, if she so chose. The woman had power and influence, whether or not she realized it.

Beth had a hunch Pearl knew it, but had too much class and genuine affection for her employer to use it casually. No, Pearl was smarter than that. And so was Beth.

"Better grab some food before it's all gone." Ty gestured toward the buffet table and grinned. "Mark picked the menu. Pizza and fried chicken."

Ty passed her an empty plate. "Once folks settle down and start eating, I'll introduce you to a few people." He narrowed his eyes and added, "Remember, this is a birthday party."

"Trust me, I heard you the first time." So much for sexual tension. He'd certainly put her back in her place, and that's exactly where she needed to keep her head. On her job and off her damned hormones.

Beth grabbed a drumstick and a slice of cheese pizza, silently blessing Pearl for managing to add salad to Mark's menu. It seemed unlikely the fresh greens and vinaigrette had been a twelve-year-old's idea.

She felt someone watching her as she poured iced tea into a glass, but forced herself not to look up to identify the culprit. Slowly, she brought the glass to her lips and leveled her gaze over its rim.

Grandma Ruby's stare was icier than the tea. Interesting. The woman was obviously curious about Beth, and why shouldn't she be? Everybody else here was a known entity.

"So, did you wash in with the storm last night?" a silky voice asked from right beside Beth.

She'd been watching the redheaded grandma and hadn't noticed the woman beside her in the buffet line. "Something like that," Beth said with a shrug. "I was on this side of the bridge when it washed out. I'm Beth Dearborn."

The blonde looked over Beth's attire with open curiosity. "Lucy Wilkes. The twins are mine." She inclined her head toward the party table. "You aren't from these parts."

It wasn't a question. Beth knew hostility when she heard it. This Southern flower was no shrinking violet by any stretch. "No, I'm here on business."

"Business?"

So how much did Ty want these people to know about this investigation? Beth rocked back on her heels and blew a wayward curl away from her mouth. Right now she just wanted to sit down somewhere and eat. "If you'll excuse me, I need to—"

"We all heard there was an insurance investigator in town yesterday," Lucy persisted.

Beth's opportunity for a graceful escape disappeared. Where the hell was Mr. Remember-This-Is-A-Birthday-Party now?

"How about that?" Beth took another sip of tea and looked around the room. A few gazes riveted on her and Lucy, but most people were busy with their plates and conversation.

"So?"

"So . . . what?" Beth decided playing dumb was the better part of valor. "Really, I'm half starved, so I'm just going over here to—"

"Are you her?"

One of those . . . Lucy Wilkes had busybody written all over her. Beth narrowed her eyes and pressed her lips into a thin line. She wished her hands weren't full so she could clench her fists for effect. "Guilty as charged. Happy now?"

The woman had the audacity to blink in feigned innocence, as if she hadn't coerced Beth into confessing her identity. At least Lucy finally slunk away and left Beth to her rapidly cooling chicken and pizza.

She found a vacant seat in the corner and settled down to eat, repositioning her backpack. Later, she would lock her weapon in the trunk of her car, so she wouldn't have to worry about the children accidentally getting their hands on it. After all, the likelihood of her needing it here wasn't high.

A voice interrupted her first bite. "So . . . it's you. You're the one."

Beth looked up and saw a short, stout woman nod knowingly before pivoting on her heel to march away to a cluster of other moms who had their heads together.

"Oh, boy." Beth bit into the drumstick. "Bet I'm the flavor of the week," she muttered around a mouthful of herbs and spices that put the Colonel to shame. *Pearl should franchise.*

Beth cast a covetous glance toward the back staircase. What were the chances of smuggling a plate of fried chicken up the stairs to her room, or anywhere in this big old house that was unoccupied by either the living or dead?

Murmurs swept through the room, and the stares directed at her became more numerous and overt. *No escape now, Dearborn.* Besides, she was here to work. The sooner these people knew who she was and why she was here, the sooner she could get on with her life. Right?

Her conversation with Sam this morning had triggered that old mental soundtrack of her mother's nagging voice. *Marry a nice boy and settle down, Beth.* A sad smile tugged at her lips as she set her empty plate on a nearby table.

The woman had died before Beth made detective, and had been harping at her only child for years about making her a grandmother. Acid joined the fried chicken and cold pizza in Beth's stomach. Memory lane was not on her mental GPS today. *Eject tape now.*

Beth finished the iced tea—sweetened, of course—and wondered how long birthday parties lasted. How long would it take for everybody to get their fill of gaping and gossiping, before she could ask some questions? Shouldn't they get to the "Happy Birthday" business soon? She walked around the buffet table and stared out the window at the cars parked in the circle drive. Hers looked even more out of place than she felt.

"How much will it take to make you go away?"

The whispered words were clearly intended to sound menacing, but Beth couldn't suppress the chuckle that bubbled from her throat. This entire day was shaping up like a scene from the latest television-mystery cozy.

The cloud of expensive perfume already told her the walking, talking cliché's gender. Despite that knowledge, she really didn't expect to find herself staring down into the angry green eyes of Grandma Ruby herself.

The woman was about five feet nothing and built like Dolly Parton—easy to see why the old man had been attracted. "Would you like to repeat that?" Beth encouraged. Emboldened, she thrust out her right hand. "I don't believe we've met. I'm—"

"I *know* who you are."

"Oooookay." Beth dropped her hand back to her side. "And you're Mrs. Brubaker. Correct?"

"That doesn't matter." She looked around nervously, as if she actually might believe most of the mothers in the room weren't staring right at them. "I just don't want my Bill to be upset by . . . this."

"This . . . ?" Beth's fingers itched to reach for her notebook and pen, but she folded her arms instead. This would be even better on tape. Pity she wasn't wired. "This . . . what?" she repeated, knowing exactly what *this* Grandma Ruby meant. What Beth didn't know was *why* it was so important to the woman.

"Investigation about Lorilee." Ruby leaned closer. "Bill was crazy about his little girl, and when she ran off like she did . . ."

"*If* she did." Beth definitely had to add the stepmother to the list of nonbelievers.

Ruby stiffened and her cheeks flamed, contrasting horribly with her dyed hair. The woman had obviously been a natural redhead once upon a time, but now covered the gray with far too much zeal. "She was spoiled rotten, that girl. Trust me, she stole her daddy's money and ran off to Europe."

Beth remained silent, waiting to see if Ruby would continue. When she didn't, she nodded and said, "That's why I'm here, Mrs. Brubaker—to find out for sure what happened to Lorilee."

"But I *told* you—"

"There's no proof." Beth studied the woman's face, making mental notes about her level of anxiety. "My job is to prove one way or another if she's dead or not."

"Not. Definitely not." Ruby shook her head rapidly and fished a handkerchief from her pocket. After managing a few impressive tears without mussing her heavy mascara, she added, "She ran off and broke her family's hearts. I just don't want her daddy upset again. That's all."

Beth knew beyond any doubt that wasn't all. She wasn't sure why or how she knew, but she'd learned to trust her instincts—more than just her empathic ones—in this line of work. "I'll do my best not to disrupt your family any more than necessary," she promised. "But I have a job to do, and I intend to do it."

Ruby pressed her lips into a thin line and narrowed her green eyes. "Damn Ty for stirring up this mess again." Without another word, she spun around and returned to her husband's side, her Italian heels clicking across the oak floor.

Beth noticed Ty emerging from the kitchen with the birthday cake on a wheeled cart, candles blazing. The crowd burst into the "Happy Birthday" song. Beth took that opportunity to fish her notepad from her backpack, so she could scribble down a few key points about her encounters with Lucy Wilkes and Ruby Brubaker.

So far it seemed the only person she could list as a friend to Lorilee Brubaker-Malone, outside Pearl and her immediate family, was Rick Heppel.

Interesting. Why had the woman once known as Brubaker's "guardian angel" fallen from grace so far and so fast? There was more going on here than a simple disappearance. But what?

She wrote a question mark on her notepad and felt someone's gaze on her again. Beth looked across the room toward the archway leading to the foyer, where she'd had the close encounter of the empathic kind. A tall, lean cowboy leaned against the wall, his hat pulled low over his eyes, obscuring his features.

The man was not here for the party—at least not as a guest. That was obvious. He must have been an employee, but why was he staring at her?

And why did she suddenly feel unreasonably comforted by the presence of her backpack and Glock?

The crowd burst into applause at the end of the song. She looked away from the cowboy long enough to watch Mark blow out his candles before his grandfather handed him an envelope and a package.

Ty looked up from his son's activities and toward

the foyer archway. Beth noticed the way he stiffened, and his brow furrowed. Tension radiated from the man.

She followed his gaze back to the archway.

But the cowboy was gone.

CHAPTER NINE

What the hell was Gary Harlan doing here? Ty caught Cecil's gaze, and the older man followed the intruder when he ducked out the front door. Mark's birthday party was not the time to follow up on an old grudge. Cecil would make sure Harlan didn't set foot back inside this house today.

Bastard has a lot of—

"Dad, look!" Mark held out an electronic hand-held video something-or-other. "See what Grandpa gave me?"

"*And* Grandma Ruby," Bill gently reminded his grandson.

"Yeah, and Grandma Ruby." Mark squirmed when his stepgrandmother gave him a squeeze.

Ty was as grateful as he knew his son was when she kept it brief and stepped away. Boys crowded behind Mark to examine and comment on the device. "Looks complicated," Ty said.

"Kids these days figure these things out a lot faster than we do," Bill explained.

"I'm off to the powder room. 'Scuse me." Ruby left in a cloud of the expensive perfume she always wore.

Ty tolerated Ruby for the same reason Lorilee

had—she made Bill happy. Otherwise, she was shallow, self-centered, and downright annoying. Shaking his head, he turned his attention back to his son's gift.

Even though both Ty and Lorilee had asked the older man repeatedly not to spoil the kids, he never listened. They always received the latest and greatest gadgets and gizmos. Sarah had a fancy MP3 player from her last birthday, and Grace had an electronic keyboard that did everything except her homework and cook dinner.

It wasn't that he couldn't afford to give the kids some of these things. His spread did well enough now. He and Lorilee had wanted their children to learn the value of work and saving for special items, so they would learn to appreciate them more.

However, since their mother's disappearance Ty had lost the heart to argue about the expensive gifts. Plus, he recognized the old man's need to fill some kind of void in his own life through his lavish generosity. He'd treated his own daughter the same way, and now he was transferring that to Lorilee's children.

With a sigh, Ty nodded. "Thanks, Bill."

"You bet. It's not every day a boy turns twelve."

"Cake and ice cream, anybody?" Pearl called. The crowd shifted from the gift table back to all-important dessert, leaving Ty alone with his father-in-law.

"Ruby said that Amazon in the corner is the insurance investigator." Bill shoved his fists into his trouser pockets. "That a fact, son?"

"Yes, sir." Ty held the older man's gaze. "She wants to talk to you about Lorilee."

Bill huffed out a sigh and raked his beefy fingers

through his hair. "Dammit all to hell, Ty . . ." He looked down at the toes of his custom Tony Lamas, then looked up and asked, "Why? Is it the money, son? I would have been happy to write you a check for the insurance money instead of putting the family through this crap."

Ty had anticipated this. "No, Bill—it's the lies. We want the lies and gossip to end."

"What if the lies and gossip *aren't* lies, Ty?" Bill's voice remained low, but his eyes snapped with barely suppressed anger. "What if you dredge all this up only to find out it's all true? That Lorilee ran away and left us all to wonder whether she's dead or alive?"

"Momma wouldn't do that." Sarah's voice trembled.

Ty hadn't noticed his daughter come in from the kitchen. Damn. "Sarah, honey . . ."

"No, Daddy. I'm not a baby anymore." She faced her grandfather and drew a stuttered breath, released it slowly before continuing. "Grandpa, I asked Daddy to do this. I *begged* him to do this. I want Momma's name cleared. I don't want people thinking she ran off to live it up in Europe, when she's really dead."

Silent tears streamed down the girl's cheeks. "Sarah, honey, please don't cry." Bill reached toward her, but she shied away from his embrace.

Ty knew the rejection had to smart. "Bill, we have a right to put this to rest, once and for all. Let us try. Do it for the kids. Hell, do it for your daughter's memory."

Pain played itself out in the man's eyes. Finally, he

held his palms upright in surrender. "I can't stop you."

"No, in all honesty, sir, that's a plain fact. You can't." Ty held his father-in-law's gaze. "But you can sure help by cooperating with Ms. Dearborn."

"Please, Grandpa?" Sarah reached for his hand.

Her emotional timing was perfect—definitely her mother's daughter. Pride in his oldest child swelled within Ty's chest.

"I'll talk to her." Bill half turned and looked across the room at Beth Dearborn, who was fidgeting with objects on the bookshelf. "I swear, she could probably go bear huntin' with a switch."

Ty had to chuckle at that, though he kept his opinion about the investigator's long legs private. "She's tall enough. That's a fact."

"I think she's a very nice person," Sarah intervened somewhat defensively.

"No one said she isn't." The girl obviously still felt guilty for bringing Beth out here in last night's storm.

Ty placed his palm in the small of his daughter's back. He wouldn't nudge, but he hoped she would take the hint and give her grandfather the hug he obviously needed. Hell, Ty could use one himself about now.

Sure enough, Sarah rose on tiptoes and planted a kiss on Bill Brubaker's wrinkled cheek, then wrapped her arms around the man's neck and rested her head against his barrel chest. The old man's expression softened as he held his oldest grandchild.

"Thanks, Grandpa. I'm sure Ms. Dearborn can help us find the truth."

"We'll see, honey." His sigh ruffled Sarah's blonde hair. "I'll go talk to her now, but don't get your hopes too high. You hear?"

"I just want the truth, Grandpa."

Bill met Ty's gaze over Sarah's head, his expression solemn, but his unspoken warning was unmistakable. Any trouble stirred up from this investigation would land squarely back in Ty's lap.

"Why don't you give Pearl a hand with the birthday cake, and I'll introduce your grandpa to Ms. Dearborn."

"Okay."

Once Sarah was out of earshot, Bill jabbed his index finger at Ty, then dropped it to his side. "Dammit, Ty."

"You gave your word, Bill."

Muttering under his breath, he took a few steps and stopped. "My God. Is she . . . is she wearing Lorilee's clothes?"

Ty shook his head in disbelief. "You actually recognize that getup?"

"Just answer me."

"Yeah, she is."

"Why, for God's sake?"

"Because of the bridge. Remember?" Annoyed with himself for allowing irritation to edge his words, Ty dragged in a deep breath. "Sorry, Bill. Tempers are short. She came out here to talk to Sarah and ended up stuck on this side of the bridge. Pearl put her things in the wash, so . . ."

"All right, fine. Fine." Bill squared his shoulders. "Let's get this over with."

"Bill?" Ty had to ask one thing first.

"What?"

"What was Gary doing in my house at my son's birthday party?"

Redness crept from Bill's collar and up both sides of his neck to his ears. "I told him to wait outside."

"You didn't answer my question."

"Ty . . ."

"He's trouble, Bill."

"So you say. Look, I don't want to get into that now, Ty." He looked up at the ceiling and mouthed something under his breath. "I broke my driving glasses, and he was the only hand in the bunkhouse, so Ruby asked him to drive us over here."

"Ruby couldn't manage to drive the car herself?" Ty put his fists on his hips. "You know how things are between us since Mom died."

"I know. Sorry. Won't happen again, Ty." Bill jabbed a thumb toward Beth Dearborn. "Can we *please* get on with this before I change my mind?"

The mountain is coming to Mohammed.

Beth cracked her knuckles and tried to pretend she didn't know what was happening. Even though she hadn't been able to overhear the conversation taking place across the room, instinct and several covert glances had alerted her that she was the topic.

And now Ty was bringing Daddy Warbucks to meet her, as promised. It wasn't like her to feel nervous, but she wiped her suddenly damp palms on Lorilee's denim skirt before meeting the woman's father. Maybe that was it—she was about to meet the allegedly dead woman's father while wearing her clothes.

That was a first, even for Beth. Having dead people in her head was one thing, but having their clothes on her body was another. Of course, from all accounts, William Brubaker was among the nonbelievers, regarding Lorilee's fate.

"Ms. Dearborn," Ty said stiffly, clearly uncomfortable with the entire situation. "This is Bill Brubaker—Lorilee's father. Bill, Beth Dearborn is with Avery—"

"Yeah, yeah. I know who the hell she is. We can stop pretending I don't." Brubaker waved his hand dismissively. "You go eat cake with the kids and leave us be."

Beth made the mistake of letting Ty capture her gaze with his incredible turquoise eyes. She inclined her head very slightly, hoping to reassure him that she would "behave," as promised. Of course, she'd also promised him and Sarah both that she would do her best to find the truth, and a little misbehavior might be necessary from time to time . . .

"Get on with you now, son," Brubaker said, his tone relatively mild now, all things considered. "We'll be fine. Ms. Dearborn and I are both grown-ups, and neither one of us is armed and dangerous."

Speak for yourself. Beth grinned, and managed not to blush, though she thought Ty might have given her backpack a more-than-cursory glance before nodding and walking away.

That man sure filled out the backside of his jeans well. That was one of the first things she'd noticed about him out on the highway when he'd stopped to change her tire.

"Okay, so what do you want to know about my Lorilee's disappearance?" Brubaker asked.

He took her elbow and steered her toward a pair of chairs in the corner. She found the gesture annoying and macho, though she recognized he was a victim of his generation and upbringing. For that reason, and to get the answers she needed, she let it go. This time . . .

"Here, let me take your bag." He reached for her backpack when she started to lower herself into a chair with it still on her shoulders.

"No, no—it's fine where it is."

He gave her a look as if he found her totally insane, and said, "All right." The chair looked ridiculously small beneath his large frame. He rested one booted ankle across the opposite knee, and draped his hands there as well. "Fire when ready."

If he only knew . . . Beth suppressed a chuckle and removed her notepad and pen from her pocket. "Do you mind . . . ?"

He shrugged. "Suit yourself, but I really think this is a huge waste of time."

"So I've heard."

He narrowed his eyes. "What's that supposed to mean?"

Easy, Dearborn. "Just that most people around town believe your daughter left and is alive somewhere in Europe." She met and held his gaze. "Is that what you think, too, sir?"

He remained silent for several seconds, lowered his chin to his chest, then looked at her again. "I . . . Yes. I don't want to, but what choice do I have, with that letter and all?"

"Right. The letter you never had analyzed."

He stiffened, and she thought for a moment he would stomp away in a huff. However, he simply sat staring, an expression of amazement in his eyes.

"You've got grit, Ms. Dearborn," he finally said. "I'll grant you that."

"Thank you, sir." She smiled. "I'll take that as a compliment, coming from someone like you."

"Fair enough." Sadness filled his brown eyes, and the wrinkles across his forehead deepened. "Lorilee's my only child. I spoiled her rotten after her momma died."

"That's understandable, sir." Beth waited, hoping he would continue without too much urging. She didn't want to inadvertently steer him in the wrong direction, just in case he was about to reveal something useful.

"She was a good girl. I thought she was anyway." He stared beyond Beth at something she suspected only he could see. "She sure loved these kids. That's why it didn't make sense at first."

Beth waited and watched as he stroked his chin thoughtfully, still staring across the room. "What didn't make sense?" she asked quietly.

He jerked his head around and pinned her with his gaze. "The *why* of it. Why did she just walk away from those little kids? Grace was barely out of diapers, for Christ's sake!" He swallowed audibly. "And Ty. And . . . and me. Neither of us ever mistreated her. Always the opposite. She never wanted for anything—at least not that I knew of."

He fell silent again. Beth didn't make any notes, because she feared it would distract him, and she didn't want him to stop, now that he'd started. "You're right, sir," she said finally, hoping he would continue. "It doesn't make sense."

"You know, Lorilee is an artist. A painter." He smiled then. "She has some real talent, but of course I'm biased." The sadness crept back into his features. "Some folks think she went to Paris to paint . . ."

Time to get some answers. So far, he'd been pretty consistent about referring to his daughter as if she was still alive. "What do you think, sir?"

"I . . ." He heaved a sigh and shook his head. "Until that letter came, I was right there with Ty, demanding the sheriff find out who'd hurt my . . . baby." His voice caught on the last word. "But that letter . . ."

"Where is that letter now, sir?"

He looked at her, confused. "I haven't seen it since that first day." He shoved a stray lock of hair back from his eyes. "The sheriff must still have it."

"So it was addressed to you." Beth made some quick notes. "Is that correct, sir?"

"Right."

"And you gave it to the sheriff?" she urged when he fell silent again. The letter could be the most damning evidence regarding Lorilee's fate.

"Yes, including the envelope it came in, because of the postmark." He removed a handkerchief and mopped perspiration from his brow. "It was mailed from the UK somewhere."

"Was the letter handwritten or typed, Mr. Brubaker?" Beth already knew the answer from the newspaper articles, but she wanted his reaction.

"Typed." He looked around the room. "I wonder where my wife got off to. I'm about ready to call it a day. These youngsters can wear an old man down." He rose, and Beth stood as well.

"Did you recognize your daughter's signature on that letter, Mr. Brubaker?"

"I didn't pay close attention to it, but she signed her name, all right."

"Did you have it analyzed?"

"Analyzed?" Brubaker glowered down at her now.

"Why in Sam Hill would I do that, Ms. Dearborn? My only child ran away, money was stolen from my operation that *she* had access to, and she's never been seen again." He squeezed his eyes closed, his pain palpable. "I'd say that pretty much tells the story." He opened his eyes and pinned her with his gaze. "Wouldn't you?"

"How do you know she took the money, Mr. Brubaker?" Beth asked cautiously. "Did you trace it somehow?"

His teeth clenched so hard she actually heard them, then he released his breath slowly. "I trusted my daughter. My flesh and blood. My *child*." He swallowed audibly. "I was a fool. She had full access to my accounts. She always did."

Without another word, he stomped away. Beth followed his path across the room to where his bouncing baby wife stood waiting in the foyer. She patted his cheek and offered all sorts of ridiculous comforting gestures while still managing to shoot arrows in Beth's direction with the merest glance.

"Get anywhere with that?" Ty asked.

"Huh." Beth scribbled a couple more notes down, then look straight at Ruby Brubaker. "How much do you know about the wife?"

"Ruby?" Ty turned in that direction as the couple disappeared into the foyer and left the house. "She showed up here as a medical assistant to the town doctor shortly after Lorilee and I got married. Bill had a dislocated shoulder. Next thing we knew, he'd eloped."

"Wow." Beth would definitely be running some background on Ruby Brubaker. "And what about that lanky cowboy I saw earlier? He didn't come all the way inside—just hung out by the door and glowered at me."

"Bastard."

"Uh-oh." Beth made another note. "And the bastard's name would be . . . ?"

"Gary Harlan." Ty spit the name out like battery acid.

"No love lost there, I take it." Beth waited, recognizing by now that Ty did everything in his own time, including talk.

"Works for Bill."

"Hmm. For how long?" Beth held her pen poised over the notepad, anticipating more. She didn't know what, but instinct and training told her more than any dying empathic gift that there was a hell of a lot more to Gary Harlan—at least where Ty Malone was concerned.

With a sigh, Ty cocked his head and looked down at Beth. "Since he was born." He shoved his hands into his pockets. "I'd better help clean up some of this mess and make nice with the guests who are heading out now."

"Hey, wait just a minute, buster." Beth tugged on his shirt sleeve when he tried to walk away. "Are you saying Harlan's parents worked for Brubaker? So he's lived there his whole life?"

"Something like that." Bitterness edged Ty's words. "You'll hear about this through the grapevine anyway."

"So why don't you save me the trouble?" Beth pulled her belle smile and batted her lashes. "Hmm?"

He arched an eyebrow and shook his head, letting her know the innocent ploy didn't work on him. "I was born there, too."

"I . . . see." *The plot thickens.*

Ty looked away, then faced her with what could only be described as a lifetime of pain etched across his handsome face. "Gary Harlan and I had the same mother."

Whoa. Beth hadn't seen that one coming. "Your last names are different."

"Different fathers. I don't rightly know how many times she married." The smile on his face was more grimace than smirk. "Rumor has it Brubaker himself got to her more than once."

"Oh . . . no." Beth released a long, slow breath. "Are you telling me he's Gary Harlan's—"

"Daddy?" Ty tilted his head. "That's the theory. The old man refused paternity testing, and Mom died back in ninety-seven."

Beth waited for him to continue. When he didn't, she asked, "So you two grew up as brothers?"

Ty snorted. "Not hardly. My dad got custody of me, thank God." He nodded matter-of-factly. "He was a good man, a hard worker, and he recognized the trouble of staying around these parts."

"Why did you come back?"

A muscle twitched in his jaw, and he actually reached out to touch her arm. There was no malice or anger in the contact—only sadness and a plea that matched the haunted expression in his eyes. "That's a long story for another time," he said. "Remember, today's a birthday party."

Beth's throat clogged and convulsed. Her eyes burned. Damn. Tears were not her way. She couldn't trust her voice, so she reached out to touch his hand where it still rested on her opposite arm.

Their gazes met and held. Something foreign and powerful passed between them. She wasn't prepared for this kind of connection.

"Thank you." He gave her hand a squeeze, then walked away to fulfill his duties as birthday-party host.

Leaving Beth to stare and wonder.

And worry . . .

CHAPTER TEN

Despite the full day of activity, sleep eluded her. Abandoning all hope of sleep, Beth climbed out of bed and padded barefoot across the cool wood floor to the open window. Balmy spring air and moonlight spilled through lace curtains, and goose bumps dotted her bare skin. The mild weather was like a peace offering compared to the violent storm from last night.

What a difference a day makes.

Despite the clement temperature, a shiver skated down her spine. Probably lingering effects of the storm. Besides, it served her right for standing around naked, though that was certainly preferable to trying to sleep while being to being strangled by pink ruffles and lace.

But who was sleeping? She shook her head in frustration and ran the fingers of both hands through her wild mass of tangled curls. That blessed and coveted state of REM had been a total stranger tonight. She'd lain in bed listening to the regular chimes from the grandfather clock downstairs and the other nocturnal sounds of a century-plus-old house. In truth, Beth found the noises the Malone house made charming. The place had real character—something lacking in most modern construction.

No, she knew damned good and well why she couldn't sleep. Stubborn, independent, all-business Beth Dearborn was plain, old-fashioned horny. And that had *everything* to do with the sexy owner of this charming, creaky old farmhouse.

"Damn you, Ty Malone," she muttered, leaning on the windowsill with a half smile playing at her lips.

She couldn't remember the last time a man had insinuated himself into her thoughts, her emotions, or her hormones so quickly or completely. Beth pressed her forehead against the cool windowpane, giving that matter further thought.

Maybe the reason she couldn't remember the last time was because there'd never been one—not to say she wasn't experienced with men. Though her sexual encounters were selective and typically far between, she certainly didn't consider herself inexperienced.

But in the past, she'd always maintained a certain emotional distance in her relationships that had allowed her to remain in control. Like last night's storm, the thought of surrendering that control completely in the throes of passion was terrifying.

She couldn't do that. She *wouldn't* do that.

Drawing a long, slow breath, she straightened and stared down at the swath of moonlight strewn across the circle drive in front of the house. Her car still sat where she'd abandoned it the night before. She'd been so agitated by that electrical storm, she could barely remember driving from Heppel's place to the Malone farm.

What was that? A dark shape shifted on the far

passenger side. A shadow? Some wild animal? If so, it was a damned tall one. It emerged from behind her car and then disappeared.

Now she wished she were fully clothed, so she could dash down the steps and out the front door—correction, the back door. Of course, by the time she got there, whoever or whatever it was might be gone. If it existed at all.

So, instead, she maintained her naked vigil from the second-story window, confident, at least, that she could see but not be seen behind the lace curtains. That was small comfort, considering . . .

A narrow beam of weak light suddenly appeared from beneath her car. "What the devil . . . ?" Was someone vandalizing her car? But who would do it? And, more important, *why*?

The piece of junk sure as hell wasn't worth stealing. Either it was a kid committing random vandalism—and somehow Beth seriously doubted that was as common here as on Chicago's South Side—or something far more sinister was taking place right before her eyes. For what they were worth in the moonlight.

The shadow could have been an optical illusion, but the flashlight beam—or whatever it was—definitely existed. Well, it had. It disappeared as suddenly as it had appeared.

She narrowed her eyes, clutching the windowsill more tightly, leaning closer to the glass. Who was out there, and what were they doing to her car?

Didn't the Malones have farm dogs running around that would bark at something like this? No, Beth remembered seeing a kennel by the barn, where the dogs were kept. They weren't roaming free, as Heppel's old hound did.

There was the shadow again, standing beside her car. *Creep.* She waited. After a moment, the tall figure walked toward the far side of the house. Through her partially open window, she actually heard the faint crunch of boots on gravel.

What else would she hear? She waited, anticipating the start of an engine as the vandal fled the scene of his crime. But she heard nothing once the steps faded into the night.

Whoever had crawled beneath her car was on foot.

Which probably meant he didn't have far to go.

Or he was already home . . .

Acid churned in her belly. Just because she wanted to sleep with the man didn't make him a saint. For all she knew he was personally responsible for Lorilee's disappearance.

"No . . ." She rubbed her eyes. Ty was good with the kids. He seemed so genuine. It just didn't wash.

"Listen to yourself." She'd dealt with true masters of deceit over the years. Until she knew for sure what had happened to Lorilee, anything was possible. Anything . . .

"Well, so much for sleeping." Beth waited a few more seconds in case the vandal decided to return, then grabbed her freshly laundered T-shirt off the chair, where she'd left it with her jeans and undies for morning, and tugged it over her head. She pulled on the jeans, then slipped into her tennies without bothering to tie them. Before bed, she had managed to slip out to lock her Glock in the trunk of her car, thinking she was relatively "safe" out here. Now she wasn't so sure that had been wise. Still, she didn't want to risk one of the Malone children getting their hands on it.

Was someone trying to harm *her*, or just inconvenience the annoying investigator by further screwing up an already screwed-up car?

She fully intended to find all the answers. Beth couldn't discount the fact that—other than the less-than-stellar sperm donors at Gooch's Garage—Ty Malone was the only living being besides Beth Dearborn who knew that it would only take one more flat tire to render her decrepit vehicle completely useless.

"Well . . . shit."

After grabbing her key ring with the small penlight and shoving it into her pocket, she slipped out the door and down the stairs. On autopilot, she started across the parlor toward the foyer, but stopped just short of that dangerous area of the house. This time she actually detected the familiar sense of dread that commonly preceded her empathic encounters.

My God. Her cursed, so-called gift really was attempting an all-out comeback. "Sam, hurry, dammit . . ."

Beth stood frozen for a few seconds, squeezed her eyes shut, then backed up and swung around to sneak out through the kitchen and mudroom. Except for the incessant ticking of that frigging clock, the house was quiet and still.

She stepped out the back door and winced when the screen squeaked far more loudly than she remembered it doing in broad daylight. Where was the vandal now? Was he long gone or still lurking about nearby?

The barn, chicken yard, kennel, and any other structures housing potential animal aromas were—as Pearl had explained—wisely situated some distance from the main house. The only buildings close by were the garage, the bunkhouse—Ty had told her they were really stretching to call it that, with only three full-time hands occupying it—and the small house where Pearl and Cecil Montgomery lived.

Of course, there were many acres of forest along the creek where someone could hide. Beth would never find the culprit in the middle of the night, and she'd have to wait until morning to get a good look at her car.

She crept slowly along the side of the house toward the front, where her car was parked, continuously scanning her moonlit surroundings. This was probably a total waste of—

"Ooompf!" She ran smack into something tall, warm, and all male. The impact caught her by surprise, and she lost her balance in a very un-Beth-like manner.

Instinct and years of martial-arts training took over. Before he could draw another breath, the man was flat on his face with her knee in his spine.

"What the—"

"Malone?"

"Yeah, I think so." He wheezed out a chuckle. "Where'd you learn to do that?"

"Police academy."

"Back in Chicago?"

"Right." What the hell was he doing out here now?

She didn't want it to be him. Had he done something to her car?

"Do you suppose you could take your knee out of the middle of my back now?"

She cleared her throat and got to her feet, offering him a hand. "Sorry. Knee-jerk reaction."

"Yeah. No kidding?" He rubbed the back of his neck. "What are you doing out here in the middle of the night?" he asked as if reading her thoughts.

Beth knew better than to feed him answers, and Ty Malone's proximity to her car in the wee hours of the morning did *not* bode well, no matter how good he felt. "Getting some air. I couldn't sleep."

"That's what windows are for." His tone didn't sound accusatory, though his words bordered on it. Then, unexpectedly, he reached out to gently grip her upper arms. "But I'm sorry you can't sleep."

She stared at him, bathed in silver, still touching her. "What are *you* doing out here?" She kept her tone as casual as possible.

"Checking my mare." He inclined his head toward the barn. "She's due to drop a foal any day now."

"Ah." She really *wanted* to believe him. His thumbs traced warm circles against her bare arms, sending shockwaves of longing straight to her core. Her breath caught. "Um . . . how is she?"

"Beautiful."

"The mare?"

"You."

Was it her imagination, or had he stepped closer? His breath was warm against her cheek. Definitely closer. "What are you doing, Ty?" she asked, barely able to breathe, let alone speak.

His grip tightened, then eased as he slid his open

palms to her back. "Something I've wanted to do since I stopped to change your tire."

Beth's heart slammed mercilessly into her ribs, and she met him halfway. "I'm probably going to regret this, but the feeling is mutual," she whispered. Without hesitation, she draped her hands behind his neck.

Just a taste, she promised herself as he leaned toward her. *Just a taste . . .*

Ty had lost what was left of his mind.

The minute she had thrown him to the ground and planted her knee in the small of his back, he was lost. Nothing mattered except getting closer.

A lot closer . . .

Cecil claimed Pearl called it sleep-deprivation psychosis when he came in after being up all night in the barn with a mare. Ty didn't have a brain left to worry about right now. It was all physical. Blood, heart, bones, flesh, skin . . .

Yes, skin. He wanted more skin. His against hers. Bare and slick and hot. Everything heated, melted, ached, hardened. He tugged her more firmly against him, pleased when she didn't protest. When her arms slipped around his neck, he took that as consent to move in for a good, old-fashioned lip-lock. If she had any other ideas, she'd sure as hell better say so now.

Their breaths mingled as he lowered his lips to hers. She smelled of mint toothpaste and woman. He drew a sampling breath through his nostrils, then another through his mouth, before he brushed his lips to hers.

"Mmm."

He teased her lips with his tongue, and she

opened. She wasn't shy, this one. She tilted her head and took his mouth with a hunger that left him breathless.

The flame in his loins burned hotter than Pearl's blue-ribbon barbecue sauce. He pulled her still closer, devouring her mouth, tasting, exploring. Their tongues mated, imitating a much more intimate act.

He stroked her back, brought his hands to the slender curve of her waist, then the plump round-ness of her butt. Cupping her, he backed her against the side of the house and urged her against him, showing her what she was doing to him, and what he wanted to do to her . . .

In response, she buried her hands in his hair, deepened their kiss, pulled his tongue deeply into her mouth. He encouraged her when she wrapped one of her achingly long legs around him to pull him closer to her feminine heat.

Damn jeans. He couldn't remember ever being so aroused from a mere kiss. He braced her against the wall, so he could free one hand to explore her long, athletic body. He ached to bury himself inside her and match his strength to hers stroke for stroke.

Dragging his mouth from hers, he kissed his way down the long curve of her throat and tugged up her T-shirt to bare her breasts to the cool night air. She eased her other leg around his waist.

Ty urged her higher, marveling when she didn't resist. Her breasts were right in front of him, her T-shirt shoved above, baring her flesh to his pleasure. He stared at dark nipples against milky flesh, bathed in the promise of moonlight.

Then he used his tongue to taste, to slowly, metic-ulously stroke and savor. She moaned. It had been so long since he'd tasted such sweetness. Based on her response, maybe he hadn't forgotten how to pleasure a woman. If he didn't expire from his own hunger first . . .

"Oh, God." The soft thud had to be the back of her head hitting the house.

He chuckled against her warmth, then drew a deep breath, all traces of humor gone. Gently, he nipped her with his teeth, then closed over her and drew her nipple deeply into his mouth.

Her pleasure was palpable. She clutched him to her and her legs tightened around him. She pressed her heat against him, and he had to use his hands to hold her in place again to keep from dropping her. He lowered her body to a spot that made him groan. Pure and simple, down and dirty, right here, right now—he wanted to bury his cock deep inside her.

She reached down to cup the sides of his face with both hands, dragging his mouth from her breast and back to hers. Spontaneous combustion was a distinct possibility.

"I want you," she murmured against his lips. "Right here. Right now."

"Ditto." He eased her downward until her feet touched the ground, but kept brushing his thumb against her nipple. "But not on the ground." He kissed her gently. "You deserve better than that."

A small gasp tore from her; then, without warning, she squirmed away. With both hands on his shoulders, she gave him a shove that sent him sprawling.

"What the hell?" Ty staggered backward, more from surprise than the impact, though Beth Dearborn was no weakling. "I take it that means no."

"Got it in one." Beth righted her T-shirt and took another step away from him. "Were you out front messing with my car tonight?"

"Huh?" Ty's brain was still in a hormone fog. He shook his head to clear it. "What in blazes are you talking about, woman? You know damn good and well what I've been 'messing with' tonight."

"Typical male." She folded her arms in front of her. "You can just forget that happened. Just a moment of weakness on my part."

"Yeah. Sure." Ty rubbed his pectorals, where she'd shoved him. "So you say, but I don't think so."

She was silent a few moments—a few too many, to Ty's way of thinking.

"Think whatever you want," she said finally. "Doesn't matter. Just answer my question."

"What question?" He released a long, slow breath, desire waning in light of total frustration.

"Did you vandalize my car?"

"Vandalize your—" Ty shook his head and held his hands out in front of him. "Woman, you are nuts."

She muttered something under her breath that sounded totally obscene. "I *saw* someone crawling around under my car just before I came outside."

"Really?" Should he believe her? "You positive?"

"Yes. I think so."

"Which is it?"

"Dammit." She rubbed her arms with both hands. "Positive. I think."

"Let's have a look." Chuckling, Ty headed toward the front of the house, but paused and looked back over his shoulder. "Though I'd rather get back to what we were doing."

She look at him through the moonlight. "Bad idea. Really bad idea. I—I behaved unprofessionally. My apologies."

"Apology not necessary or accepted." He continued to stare at her for a beat, then turned to continue toward the front of the house. What an intriguing, gutsy, *crazy* woman.

And he thought he was the one with the hang-ups, living like a frigging monk all these years. Renewed guilt pressed down on him. Well, shit. That was all he needed. Lorilee had been gone a very long time. He had no reason to feel guilty. Besides . . . he doubted needless guilt was going to help him keep his hands to himself, with Beth Dearborn living under his roof. Not after the pseudo-tonsillectomy she'd just given him . . .

He grew hot and hard all over again just thinking about it.

So don't think about it, Malone.

Right. He raked his fingers through his hair and almost tripped over a downspout on the corner of the house. She grabbed his arm.

They both stood like frozen silver statues in the vanishing moonlight. He swallowed audibly, his throat thick, and other parts of his anatomy rapidly following suit.

"Look, we're both grown-ups, last time I looked," he said, resisting the urge to cup her pretty face in his hands. That massive amount of hair dwarfed her face, giving it almost a pixie quality—a strange thought to have about such a tall woman.

"And I'm here on assignment." Her voice was surprisingly steady. She released her breath slowly, dropping her hand to her side. "I've always prided myself on professional behavior. *That* was not professional behavior—at least not for *this* profession."

He chuckled quietly. "Point taken, but it doesn't change what happened." Now he did reach out to cup her cheek, brushing his thumb just beside her lips. "Or what we both feel. And want . . ."

She captured his hand in both of hers, pressed her lips to his palm. A jolt went through him at the contact. He'd gone from celibate to ready and willing in no time.

He reached for her and tried to pull her into his embrace, but she shied away and dropped his hand. "Ty, please . . . don't."

After a few deep breaths to steady his hormones and slow his pulse, he gave a curt nod. "We'll try it your way," he said. "For now."

"Thank you." She pointed toward the circle drive. "I'm going to have a look at my car now."

"We both are." He took a step, then stopped and put a hand on her shoulder. "Beth, I have to tell you, after what just happened between us—"

"I have a job to do."

"Let me finish," he said, but let his hand fall to his side. "I just want to give you fair warning that I am not a man to be trusted."

She looked up at him sharply. "What do you mean by that?"

He held her gaze in the deepening dark. "Just what I said."

CHAPTER ELEVEN

Beth couldn't breathe.

Somewhere between coming outside to check on her car in the middle of the night and this moment, she had almost had sex on the ground with a client. One more kiss, one more touch of his mouth to her breast, one more nanosecond, and she would have torn off her clothes and shouted, "Take me! Take me now!"

She drew in that elusive breath.

Beth Dearborn didn't *do* things like that. Uncontrolled acts of passion were un-Beth, unwise, and unsafe—at least for her. Oh, sure, she liked multiple orgasms as much as the next woman, but only if she was the one calling the shots.

Maybe she should stick with the kind of "man" that required batteries, and had on and off switches. She sure as hell wished she could turn off the urges coursing through her right now.

Permanently off.

Oh, but that would mean no more multiple orgasms. On second thought . . .

Damn, but she wished Sam were here right now. Sam was the one person in the world she could talk to about anything, including Ty Malone and her sexual frustration.

And—*face it, Dearborn*—tough, smart-ass Sam was the only person in the world who could help Beth stay sober, no matter what. *He'll be here in two weeks, twelve days, and ten hours.*

She drew another shaky breath, following Ty at a safe distance. Fortunately, it was dark enough that she couldn't make out the shape of his ass, but she remembered it well enough to fill in the missing details.

Who could have imagined that a farmer from Tennessee could kiss like Ty Malone? Renewed heat washed through her from head to regions better left unacknowledged. Her nipples, still hard and moist from his mouth, brushed against the soft fabric of her T-shirt. At this moment, the son of a bitch wasn't even touching her, but he was still tormenting the hell out of her. "Creep."

He stopped and looked over his shoulder. "Did you say something?"

"Nope," she lied. "Car's right over there."

"Yeah, I know." She saw his teeth flash in the waning moonlight when he looked back over his shoulder. "I got your backpack out of it for you yesterday morning. Remember?"

Had that been yesterday? Already? "Wow, how time flies," she deadpanned.

"Ha. Ha." He covered the last few steps to her car and leaned on the hood. "So . . . where do you think you saw someone?"

Beth wasn't about to give him any more information than he might already have. "One side or the other. Definitely not the front or back." She stooped on the driver's side and used her penlight in an attempt to illuminate the mechanical workings beneath the vehicle. "I can change a tire and put oil in it, but this is all Greek to me."

Ty pulled a slightly larger but no brighter light from his pocket and stooped beside her.

He has a flashlight. But was that little thing powerful enough to create the beam she'd seen from her upstairs window? "Why don't you go shine your light from the other side while I shine mine from over here?" she suggested. "Maybe they'll meet in the middle."

He aimed his light in her face, but it didn't blind her enough to make her miss the expression on his face. No, the look he gave her suggested he found her insane. "Whatever you want, Dearborn."

He rose from his crouch and she fell back on her haunches. "Shit," she muttered under breath.

"I heard that," he said as he walked around the front of her car.

Was she that transparent? Had she completely lost her touch, or was he that cool? Or that innocent . . . ? She hoped for the latter—seriously hoped.

After a moment, a weak, narrow beam came from the far side of her car. It seemed unlikely that this pitiful instrument had created the light she'd noticed from her window earlier. "Do you see anything?" she asked, hoping he wouldn't see through her foolishness.

"I see the underside of a total piece of crap."

"Eat my—Er, never mind." She reconsidered her words, as she'd have liked nothing better than to have his mouth on her again, and vice versa. Besides, her car really was a piece of crap. He would know, having changed her tire just a couple of days ago. "You know what I mean, Malone."

"So we're back to *Dearborn* and *Malone*."

She let that one go. He'd called her Dearborn just a bit ago, and she hadn't commented. After all, she was the one who told people to address her by her last name more often than not. Still . . . having heard him use her first name like a caress earlier in the evening, its avoidance now seemed almost like an insult.

"Something's wet and sticky under here," he said. She heard a scraping sound she attributed to a man's sliding under a car on gravel—made sense, considering—and leaned to her side, hoping her pitiful penlight would offer some additional help.

"Not rainwater from last night's storm?"

"I said sticky." He grunted, and she heard him scooting on gravel again. "I'll be damned."

"What?" She flopped completely onto her side, aiming her light as far under the car as possible. "What the hell is it, Ty? What did you find?"

Or do . . . ?

Though she really didn't want to believe he'd done anything to her car. Furthermore, if he had, he must have hidden a larger flashlight somewhere before he'd run into her, because he didn't have it on him presently. For now, she had to pretend he was innocent.

"What is it?" she asked again.

"Definitely not rain." He grunted, and it sounded like he was scooting back out from under her car.

She pushed to her feet just as he did the same on the passenger side. "Then what is it?"

"Can't be sure, but I'd say brake fluid." His voice was solemn. "I think it's leaking."

"So that's what they were doing." Beth gnashed her teeth and switched off her penlight. "Guess we'll have to wait until daylight to be sure."

"Yep." The crunch of gravel told her he was coming toward her, even though he had also turned off or put down his light.

She noticed something else for the first time. The footsteps she'd heard earlier had been heavier and definitely from hard-soled shoes—like boots. It sounded to her like Ty was wearing sneakers.

"Um, Ty?"

"So now I'm Ty again?"

"For now."

He touched her forearm, and she couldn't suppress the shiver that raced through her. "Mind if I ask you a personal question?"

A low chuckle drifted to her on the cool night air. "I reckon that's allowed, considering we've shared spit and all."

"Gosh, what a sexy thought." She rolled her eyes, but couldn't prevent a grin from spreading across her face. "Seriously . . . what kind of shoes are you wearing?" She flipped on her penlight and aimed the weak beam toward his feet, and made out what she thought was something red. That was about it.

"My shoes?" He looked down. "An ancient pair of Keds, because Pearl can toss 'em in the wash after I've been in the barn." He brought his gaze back to hers. "More practical than my boots. I wear 'em fishing, too, unless it's too cold."

Even though she couldn't see his eyes, she could

feel his gaze on her. The man had some weird kind of power over her, and she didn't like that—not one bit. No one was allowed to have power over Beth Dearborn. No, sir. Not allowed.

The dead had done that most of her life, and look where that had gotten her. No, she had to remain in control at all times. Losing control meant losing everything . . .

"Keds?" Despite her confused resentment toward him, her relief about his choice of footwear made her grin again. "That's great. I'm glad."

"You are?"

"Yeah, really glad." It was all she could do not to throw her arms around him and give him a great big kiss.

He aimed his penlight right in her face again. "Beth Dearborn, you are one really strange woman."

Now she did laugh—a low, sultry sound Sam had always called her "naughty laugh."

She put one hand on her hip and said in her best belle imitation, "Honey, you don't know the half of it."

He leaned so close to her face she felt the warmth of his breath. "That's what I'm *afraid* of."

Ty stripped off his clothes and fell into his lonely bed with Beth Dearborn on his mind, wreaking havoc with his libido. The woman oozed sex appeal, and it was clear she wanted him as much as he wanted her.

He flopped onto his back and stared blindly at the ceiling. The woman had issues. Cecil would call it "baggage." Even recognizing that didn't do a damned thing to cool Ty's urgent need.

He was in bad shape.

He rolled onto his side and punched his pillow. A full day of work was only a few hours away, and he hadn't slept at all. His mare still hadn't dropped her foal, which meant another sleepless night, if she didn't deliver soon. He'd give Doc Barnes a ring today, just in case.

All right, get some sleep, Malone. Enough lusting after the crazy lady.

Though *crazy* wasn't the right word to describe Beth Dearborn. *Haunted? Tortured? Troubled?*

It had been years since he'd visited what his dad had called "Lily Palm and her Five Sisters," but he didn't want that now. Masturbation couldn't come close to satisfying the raw, burning need eating away at him. Only the woman who'd ignited this flame could extinguish it.

And that was just what he *didn't* need.

Exhaustion crept over him, and he wished he could order his body to sleep on command. Of course, he knew from personal experience that wasn't possible. Lord knew he'd spent enough sleepless nights after Lorilee's disappearance trying.

Lorilee. Odd that she was the cause of Beth Dearborn's being here, yet the niggling guilt he felt about the prospect of being with another woman—even after all these years—was also because of her. Talk about a catch-22 . . .

Lorilee . . .

He thought back to that long-ago day when he'd made his way back to Brubaker after his dad's funeral, and the first time he'd laid eyes on his future wife. She was the prettiest girl he'd ever seen—petite and blonde and spoiled rotten.

Ty had returned in search of the mother he hadn't

seen since age three. He had no memory of her, and his father had told him she was dead. Only after his dad was gone did Ty discover the truth while sorting through the man's legal documents—a divorce decree, custody order, and so forth. So he and Ty's mom had divorced, and his dad had taken Ty far away from Brubaker, Tennessee.

At nineteen, Ty wasn't ready to lose his dad and head out on his own. He had only one semester under his belt at Oregon State before a rain-slick highway and a horrible accident ended his dad's life. After that, Ty didn't have the heart to return to school. Instead, he'd sold the small house where his carpenter father had raised him, and set out in search of the mother he couldn't remember.

Ty didn't know what to expect when he reached Brubaker. He used a fake last name when he first showed up at William Brubaker's employment office. The big man said they were hauling hay and needed strong backs. He put Ty right to work on Cecil Montgomery's crew.

That very first day, Ty knew he wanted to work the land. He loved being outside under the sky, getting dirty, and working with nature. A week went by before he gathered enough courage to ask Cecil about his mother. She didn't work there anymore. She'd retired and moved into town a few years earlier, but her son was there.

Ty folded his hands behind his head, still staring at the dark ceiling. Nancy Malone had been a lush. There was really no other word for it. When he showed up at the front door of her small ranch house in town that same evening, she was beyond tipsy. Even so, the first word out of her mouth was his father's name. That figured—after all, he looked just like his dad.

She'd thrown open the door and called him Tyrone. A sad smile curved his lips. No one had called him that since grade school, when one kid had laughed about his rhyming name. Ty had beat hell out of him, and that had been the end of it.

He'd told her yes, just as a gangly man in his early twenties walked in the door. Ty had seen him around the Brubaker spread a time or two.

"So you're my long-lost kid brother," Gary had said, but his tone made it clear he was far from pleased to see Ty. "How about that?"

That first night, right there in Momma's living room, Gary had announced his intention to marry the boss's daughter. Ty immediately noticed how much that disturbed their mother, but Gary seemed oblivious.

At her request, Ty had moved into the spare room, announced his true identity, and taken his rightful place as her son. The next day, Gary moved into the bunkhouse at the Brubaker spread.

Gossip being what it was in a small town, Ty heard the rumors about Gary's paternity. It didn't take a rocket scientist to understand why their mother didn't want him dating Lorilee Brubaker.

His possible half sister.

Ty tried to befriend his half brother, but was immediately rejected. His presence was unwelcome—that was made abundantly clear. He'd come to Tennessee in search of family after losing his dad, but what he'd found was a cesspool of scandal.

And Lorilee Brubaker. Sweet, pretty, innocent, seventeen-year-old Lorilee . . . He'd fallen as hard and fast for her Southern-belle ways as he had for farming and ranching. He'd vowed to wait for her to grow up enough to marry, but they'd been too much in love to wait, of course.

Ty was an irritant to Gary from all sides. First, their mother loved Ty, too, and Gary couldn't abide sharing. He'd been an only child all his life, and suddenly he had to share his momma with a half brother he'd never known.

Second, Cecil Montgomery declared Ty a "natural-born farmer," and made him a foreman almost immediately. His rise in status and open acceptance in town made Gary resent him even more.

And Lorilee.

No one ever came right out and told Gary that Lorilee was off-limits. That she might be his half sister. He seemed totally ignorant of the gossip Ty had already overheard during his short time in Brubaker.

So when Ty and Lorilee were seen together around town, Gary started making threats. The tires on Ty's old truck were slashed first. Then his room at his mom's house was ransacked. The few precious photos he had of his father were strewn around the room, and one had been deliberately destroyed.

When Lorilee came to Ty and told him their young love had created a child, Ty went to William Brubaker and asked for his daughter's hand in marriage. And he told the old man that his half brother had been undermining his every step, and that that would have to stop. He didn't like using his position as Lorilee's husband against Gary, but he couldn't let Gary hurt her. It was clear by then that Gary would do anything to help Gary, regardless of whom he hurt along the way.

Ty sat up in bed, his chin resting in his hands. He'd never forget the day he and Lorilee had married. Bill had arranged a private ceremony at the house, after Lorilee had confessed her pregnancy. Gary made sure the other hands knew all about it and raised a ruckus. Firecrackers went off on the lawn, and Ty's truck was decorated with tin cans.

So much for discretion.

Somehow, his creep of a half brother had learned about Lorilee's unplanned pregnancy and written her due date across the back of Ty's tailgate. It didn't matter that Gary could be a half brother to both him and Lorilee. Ty spent part of his wedding night beating Gary Harlan to a bloody pulp.

Oddly, that was when Ty seemed to have won the grudging respect of his new father-in-law.

Ty swung his legs over the side of the bed and planted his bare feet on the floor. "Well, hasn't this been fun?"

He stood and padded barefoot to the window, shading his eyes against the rising sun. Enough pretending. Between his libido and his memories, he wasn't going to get a wink of sleep.

With another sigh, he headed for the shower.

A cold one.

CHAPTER TWELVE

Beth passed out the moment her head hit the pillow. She'd have been safer downing an entire pot of coffee and staving off sleep entirely, because this level of exhaustion was a surefire prelude to one hell of a nightmare.

In other words, empathically speaking, she was at her most vulnerable while sleeping. She'd become a control freak in her mission to distance herself from her so-called gift. Not only had it driven her to drink, but she'd almost lost her mind.

That last case, the loss of control, had pushed her to the brink. She'd not only feared for her sanity, but for her own life.

Battling her way through alcohol withdrawal had been bad enough. The sheer terror of encountering another needy spirit before she was ready still had the power to make her physically ill.

Some people snored when they slept. Others belched and farted like Heppel's hound. But not Beth Dearborn. No, she had to dream in wild, vivid, too-often-violent Technicolor.

Sometimes her slumber was peaceful and undisturbed. Other nights—especially those when she was extremely exhausted—she had visitors.

Dead ones. Repeat offenders. Despite the years of separation between now and that last horrible murder in Chicago, the memories of being repeatedly stabbed, shot, strangled, drowned, hanged, suffocated, mutilated, and burned to death insisted on periodic visitation rights. Sure, she could do her best to stay away from the active spirits of those who'd died violently, but she couldn't purge herself of the morbid, haunting memories of those she had already encountered.

Of course, before she'd walked—rather, run—away from her gift and her career, there'd been many times in her life when she had quite deliberately opened herself to these empathic invasions in order to solve a murder. And no matter how horrifying, once an encounter was underway, she was at its mercy until the victim moved on to the other side and released her. She had no control, and that was too risky.

Layers of shadow and light filled her mind as she drifted. A blurry face drifted by—a woman. Someone she'd never met.

"I know you're here," the woman said. *"You can help me. Please help me."*

No, she couldn't go back to the foyer. Was the spirit getting stronger? Could it reach her here now? As Beth struggled to keep herself from drifting into a deeper sleep, her last coherent thought was a fervent prayer that God not allow the ghost in the foyer to overtake her while she was helpless.

Her dream transported her to another place and time. At least there were no faces in this new dreamworld—only two nameless bodies with mouths, teeth, lips, tongues, flesh. Ty's? Beth's? They met, parried, touched, sought, and tasted . . .

So it was *that* kind of dream.

She hadn't meant to touch him. That was her last coherent thought before his hands streaked up and filled themselves with her breasts. His throaty moan spilled into her mouth like forbidden wine.

Then he was tugging away her shirt and shoving back from the table all at once. "To hell with it," he muttered against her greedy mouth, and then he lifted her.

Her arms and legs wrapped around him like silken rope, her shirt dangling from one wrist where the buttons held. Beneath, she wore a plain cotton camisole—something Beth didn't even own—but in her dreamworld it felt as erotic as silk lace.

He handled her as if she were small and light, instead of the long-legged woman she was. As her erratic pulse pounded in her ears, she thought he could have carried a mountain.

They weren't outside in the dark now, but somewhere in the house—the kitchen?—in broad daylight. Sunlight streamed through a tall window next to the mudroom door. Even the risk of being caught didn't dim their fierce hunger.

Her busy mouth never paused, racing from cheek to jaw to ear and back, while little whimpers purred in her throat. He started out of the kitchen, stumbled over a loose throw rug, and knocked her back against the doorjamb. She only laughed, breathlessly now, and tightened the vise of her legs around his waist.

How could he possibly walk and carry her this way? It didn't matter. All that mattered was having Ty Malone. All of him . . .

Their lips fused again in a rough, desperate kiss until he tore his mouth free to fasten it to her breast, suckling greedily through tissue-thin cotton.

The pleasure of it, dark and damning, lanced like a spear through her system. This was more, she realized, as the blood coursing through her veins began to hum. More than she'd expected. More than she might even have wanted. But there was no turning back.

He whirled away from the wall.

"Hurry," was all she could say as he strode toward the stairs. "Hurry."

His footsteps rang in her ears. Hurry. Hurry. Beth clung like a burr as he all but leaped up the stairs.

He turned left at the top of the stairs, then right into a bedroom where sunlight spilled like liquid gold through open curtains. She welcomed him as he fell with her onto the neatly made comforter.

There was no thought or need for gentleness, for soft endearments or slow caresses. They ravished each other, recklessly shoving aside pieces of clothing, pulling, tugging, kicking off shoes, all the while feeding each other ravenous kisses.

Her body no longer belonged to her. She was losing control. Completely. She rolled and reared while her breath seared out in burning gasps. Seams ripped, needs exploded.

His hands were rough from hard work. Another time they might have smoothed over her body like butter. But now they grasped and showed no mercy, bringing her indefinable joy that soared through her system as that dreaded storm had torn at the sky two nights past. Now, with no barriers between them, he drew her sensitive nipples into his mouth.

She gasped, not in pain at the none-too-gentle scrape of his teeth and tongue, but in pure carnal bliss as a merciless orgasm tore through her.

She hadn't anticipated it would come so fast and so pro-

found, nor had she ever relinquished control enough to experience the utter helplessness that followed. Before she could do more than wonder or worry about her loss of control, renewed need surged through her.

She'd never imagined, never, that sex could completely devour her and leave her trembling. But she trembled beneath his hands, under the wild demands of his mouth. For another crazed moment she was totally vulnerable, defenseless, her body liquid and her brain stunned into capitulation by the power of her own climax. Then he was gone.

Darkness pressed down on her, the air thick with dread. Where was she now? She knew this place. Chicago. Lakeshore Drive. That last time . . .

Not again. Not again.

"Wake up, Beth. Wake up," *the shreds of sanity commanded.*

Blood. Crashing rivers of it erupted from the corners of her mind.

The shimmering steel blade ripped and retreated again and again. Crimson waves of pain pierced her. Dripping life's blood . . .

Death tugged at her, greedy and demanding, dragging her into the victim's world, toward the cold, the dark.

Not yet . . . She had to see the face. The killer's face.

Beth bolted upright in bed, sweaty sheets tangled around her, a silent scream tearing through every cell. She held her head in trembling hands, waiting for her heartbeat to slow. The ragged sounds of her breathing filled the room.

"Just a damn dream." She drew a deep, shaky breath and shoved her wild hair back from her face. Well, part dream and part nightmare.

But the dream—no matter how delicious—had

shattered her control and made her vulnerable to the nightmare. She squeezed her eyes shut, allowing herself to remember, just for a moment, what it had felt like to have Ty's mouth and hands on her.

"Oh, God."

But she had to maintain control. No matter what. Maybe once Sam engaged the spirit in the foyer, Beth could let down her guard just a little, but not completely. Maybe . . .

And she remembered the voice just as she drifted off to sleep, and the face—a woman's face. *Help me,* she'd said. *I know you're here.*

Was the ghost in the foyer gaining strength? More importantly, was it Lorilee? Beth had seen photographs, and she knew from family comments that Sarah closely resembled her mother. The face in her semidream state could have been Lorilee. Whoever she was, her spirit was trying to contact the empath in residence, and that was one very reluctant Beth Dearborn.

"Hurry the hell up, Sam."

Beth spent some time washing away the dregs of her dream-nightmare in the shower, organizing her thoughts and notes, going through the Rolodex Ty had given her, and planning her strategy for the day. She also figured that would give the master of the house plenty of time to get out to his field—or whatever farmers did during the day—so she wouldn't have to face him.

After all, her car wasn't going anywhere, and that was the most important thing she had to do this morning—examine the damage. It could wait until Ty was away from the house.

"Coward," she muttered to herself.

So she wasn't exactly a coward, but when it came to touchy-feely stuff, she was less than forthcoming. And her dream of Ty had definitely backed her into a touchy-feely corner in the wee hours of this morning. She wasn't ready to face the man or her feelings just yet. Later, she'd face the man, because she had no choice if she wanted to finish this investigation. Much later—okay, probably never—she *might* face her feelings.

First things first. She called a federal judge who owed her a favor and explained the situation regarding the letter, allegedly from Lorilee. The appropriate steps would be put in motion today, ordering the sheriff's office in Brubaker to turn the evidence over to Avery Mutual, which would have the signature analyzed by a handwriting expert.

Beth checked that item off her list and opened her laptop. Ty had a wireless network, but it was secure, of course. She should have asked him for the password. Or maybe Beth could hack into it. It was worth a try. She tried combinations of the kids' names with various symbols, birth dates, the usual common password suspects. No luck there.

She flipped through Lorilee's file. Her wedding date leapt off the page. "Hmm." Beth typed it in month first, date first, then she tried the year first and spelled out the month. "Bingo!" She was online.

She was able to network her computer with the farm's operation within a matter of minutes. "Thank you, Apple, Mac, and Steve Jobs." She didn't expect to find anything particularly useful or incriminating, but just being connected to the outside world again was good.

After sending a quick e-mail to Sam to remind him of his promise to come to Brubaker, along with directions to the farm and an update regarding all the primary players in her investigation, she sent another to an associate at Avery Mutual, alerting him about Lorilee's letter. She didn't want any screw-ups or delays with the handwriting analysis. That had waited long enough already. Ty had provided another sample of his wife's handwriting, so that was a go.

Then she spent a little time looking through various farming operations. Most of it was simple accounting software, a few databases—boring stuff. Then she saw the webcams.

"How cool is that? High-tech *Green Acres*." She clicked on the icon that said "Barncam." Ty walked right past the camera, almost as if he knew she was watching. Of course, that was impossible. Still, she should probably feel a little guilty, spying on him this way. But in her line of work, she'd learned to squelch that useless emotion a long time ago.

He opened a stall, and she wondered if she could get any audio. Granted, the internal speaker on her laptop wasn't all that great, but she turned the volume up full blast and waited.

"Hey there, girl," Ty said in a gentle voice. "Are you going to have that baby today?"

She saw the top of his head and the mare's as he stroked the animal's long neck and continued to speak in soft, soothing tones. The beast nuzzled his sleeve lovingly and nickered.

"I'll take that as a yes." Ty rested his forehead against the mare's neck. "Not sure I can stay awake all night again, Cissy."

A lump lodged in Beth's throat as she watched Ty and the horse. He continued to speak softly to his mare while he stroked her neck. The trust between the man and his horse was undeniable. Was that what they meant by "horse sense"? Did Cissy know something about human nature Beth couldn't begin to understand?

Or maybe all those years in Homicide had left her jaded. "Go figure." She slammed the mental vault on those memories. Last night's nightmare had been more than enough.

With a sigh, Beth rested her chin on her fist and tapped her touch pad with her other hand to keep the screen from going dark. She focused on the clean, square line of Ty's jaw, the way the muscles worked in his neck as he stroked the mare.

He'd touched Beth differently. Feverishly. There'd been no gentleness in either the reality or the dream. Beth's nipples hardened and her body warmed from the memory. That had been a first-class wet dream, but it had also served as a reminder that she needed to hold herself back enough to protect herself. She couldn't let down all her shields again.

"I envy you, Cissy," she whispered. Beth wanted nothing more than to feel the unconditional love and trust she was witnessing right now. Her relationship with her cousin was the closest she would ever come to that kind of trust, because he shared his own personal version of the Dearborn curse.

But oh, how she would have loved to give herself over to the kind of passion she'd experienced in that dream, and feel the kind of trust she saw in Cissy's soft brown eyes right now.

But she couldn't. Beth Dearborn had a job to do and an empathic gift to keep at bay until Sam showed up to strike some kind of bargain with the spirit in the foyer.

Unless it turned out to be Lorilee.

Then what? "Then I find out who killed her. And why," she murmured.

Beth clicked her way out of the webcam, purged her cache and cleared her history, then put her laptop to sleep. "Sheesh. I'm jealous of a damn horse."

She gathered her gear and headed down to the kitchen, hoping to find Pearl before she went out front to crawl under her car again. She wanted to spend some casual time with the woman, see if she might glean a few tips about how best to approach Bill and Ruby Brubaker. She needed to talk to Gary Harlan, too, and another visit to Rick Heppel's was probably on the agenda.

It wasn't as if Beth didn't have enough to keep herself busy. Maybe that would help keep her mind off Ty Malone's kisses.

In the kitchen, she discovered some hot coffee still in the pot, but no other sign of human life. Everybody had gone about their daily business. She found a mug and helped herself to the bottom of the pot. After two big swigs, the caffeine started to work its magic. She felt almost alive.

She drained the cup and left it on the counter, then headed out through the mudroom and into the overly bright morning. The sun was working overtime today. She shaded her eyes and then headed around toward the driveway.

At the front corner of the house, she stopped to

stare at a tow truck backing up to her car. "What the hell . . . ?"

Running the last several yards to where Ty stood, she grabbed his sleeve. "What's going on here?" she demanded.

He blinked. "Friend of mine has a garage in Marysville." Ty aimed his thumb that direction. "Don't have to cross the bridge to get there."

"Hey, that's *my* car. I'll decide if it gets towed or not."

The man driving the truck hopped out to attach the winch. "I'll need the key to this heap."

"That heap belongs to me." She pushed past Ty and approached the bearded man. "Did you happen to look under the car to check the brake line?"

"No, ma'am. Ty said it was leakin' fluid. That's all I know."

Beth had to know if the line had been cut or not. Was Ty trying to get rid of the evidence, since he knew she'd seen someone messing around her car last night? Or was he honestly just trying to be helpful?

Shit.

"Do me a favor and have a look at my brake line first. Will you?" She sighed when Ty rolled his eyes. He sure didn't act guilty of anything.

"Sure, lady. Whatever you say."

"Thanks, Mitch," Ty said, inclining his head as if giving the man permission to obey the crazy lady's silly request.

Mitch dropped to the ground and inched under Beth's car, let out a low whistle a second later. He slid back out and scrambled to his feet while wiping his hands on a grease rag.

"Lady, a brake line don't wear out that neat and straight." He shook his head.

"Meaning what, Mitch?" Ty asked.

Mitch shoved his greasy rag into his pocket. "Looks like they were both cut, Ty."

CHAPTER THIRTEEN

Ty watched Beth retrieve her backpack from her trunk, then remove a pair of sunglasses from the driver's side visor. She hadn't spoken since Mitch's revelation about the cut brake line. Last night, she'd asked Ty if he'd been "messing around" with her car.

And now she was clearly fuming about it, but keeping it to herself. He hated that. Why couldn't she just let it fly instead of stewing?

One of the ways he'd been able to tell when Lorilee had been drinking was by the way she controlled her temper. As a rule, she'd tended to get angry and get it over with, unless she'd been in the rum bottle. Then, she'd sulked.

Which type was Beth Dearborn? Right now, he figured her for the suspicious type. Of course, considering her line of work, that probably came in handy.

He really didn't know much about her at all, except that she came from Chicago, used to be a cop, and worked for an insurance company. Oh, and she was single. He released a long sigh as she slammed the car door and swung the leather backpack over her shoulder.

"Give us a call when you have some idea how long

it'll take, Mitch." Ty pulled out his wallet and handed the man a twenty. "A little extra for crawling under the car."

"And humoring the crazy lady?" Beth asked, her tone unreadable, her hazel eyes glinting with suspicion.

"Heh." Mitch rolled his eyes in Ty's direction and muttered his thanks, then headed for the cab of his truck. "I'll give you a call after we get it on the lift and find out what parts cost from the nearest Honda museum."

"Very funny. A real comedian." Beth kicked at the loose gravel as they both stood and watched the truck drive away with her little car secured on its flatbed. "Well, isn't this just dandy? My luggage is in Brubaker, my car's going to Marysville, and I'm stuck here."

"There are other vehicles here you can borrow," Ty reminded her. "Besides, you said most of your research starts here in Lorilee's files."

She drew a deep breath and looked over her shoulder at the house. "So I did." Then she shaded her eyes and leveled her gaze on him. "So, Ty, who cut my brake line? And why?"

"That's a damn good question." He hooked a thumb through his belt loop. "What do you think?"

"First rule? Opportunity. You had that by being out here last night, and here you were trying to get rid of the evidence this morning."

He threw his head back and laughed out loud. The woman was either crazy or the most brazen one he'd ever met. After a moment, he realized he was laughing alone. "Okay, so I had the opportunity, but I don't have a motive." He leaned close to her face. "I *asked* you to come here. Remember? I *want* you to investigate Lorilee's disappearance."

"And whoever cut my brake line doesn't." She didn't even blink.

"You're good." He shook his head slowly. "Yeah, I'd say that sums it up. Somebody doesn't want—"

"Me here." She shifted the pack to her other shoulder. "Which means somebody has something to hide."

"Interesting." He rubbed his chin, the raspy sound of his thumb against his whiskers sounding in his head. He hadn't shaved this morning, because he'd been in a hurry to check on Cissy. "I wonder what."

"You don't know?"

Something snapped in Ty. He grabbed her upper arms and gave her a little shake. "I did not cut your damn brake line. I'm one of the good guys. We're on the same side. Remember? I think those were your words." He dropped his hands to his sides. "Will you stop suspecting everybody and learn to trust once in a while?"

Her eyes widened and she blinked repeatedly. Her expression went from shock to shuttered in record time. He'd obviously struck a nerve. Trust. Beth Dearborn had trust issues. She was like a skittish wild mustang, full of courage and spirit but frightened at the same time.

"Well, you're right," she said finally. "I'm sorry I suspected you."

He wasn't sure she really meant that, but he'd accept it for now. "Good. So we're going to work together to find out what happened to Lorilee. Right?"

"That's the plan," she said, then took a deep breath that drew his gaze down to her breasts.

"If you keep walking around here without a bra, I can't be held responsible for my actions, ma'am."

Her face flared crimson so fast he thought, at first, he might have been mistaken. "My God—you're blushing." He tried not to laugh, but couldn't prevent the low chuckle. "I'll be damned. I made Beth Dearborn blush."

"You did not. It's . . . just the sun." She folded her arms and stuck her chin out. "I don't blush."

"Sure." He winked. "It's okay. I won't tell anyone."

"You're actually enjoying this." She shoved her hand through that wild mass of hair, but the wind had it flying in her face again in no time.

"What are you hiding from, Beth?" he asked, his tone serious now. "Sometimes I think you use all that hair to hide from the world, to hide your eyes."

He tilted his head at an angle when she stood frozen with her hand holding her hair away from her face. Their gazes locked, and he suddenly knew he was right. She was definitely hiding, but from what?

"Well, I'd better get to work," she said, breaking the spell. "I'm going to start in Lorilee's studio, if that's all right."

"You have run of the place." He reached out to slip his finger through one of her curls. "But be careful. I don't like knowing someone cut your brakes. What if you hadn't known and had driven out of here?"

She looked at his hand instead of at his face, but at least she didn't shy away now. Maybe she would learn to trust him. "Whoever got to my brakes wasn't just sabotaging my car, Ty." She lifted her chin and met his gaze now. "They were trying to kill me, or at least hurt me enough to slow me way down."

He swallowed hard. His stomach tied into a knot of dread. "Shit."

"I'm a big girl, and I know how to take care of myself."

"I found that out last night when you threw me to the ground and planted your knee in my spine."

She smiled. Really smiled. Her entire face was transformed, and her eyes sparkled. The woman sure was beautiful when she smiled like that. He found himself wishing she'd do it more often, and that he could be the cause.

She pointed at him with her index finger. "Don't you be forgetting that lesson, cowboy."

With that, she spun around and walked back to the house, swinging her hips with her signature long stride. "I am *not* a cowboy," he muttered.

"Did I say you was?" Cecil asked from right beside him.

"How long have you been standing there?" Ty narrowed his eyes and turned to face his old friend.

"Not nearly long enough, I reckon." Laughter sparkled in Cecil's dark eyes. "But that don't matter now, son. Your mare is ready. Doc Barnes is on her way."

"Hot damn." Both men ran toward the barn.

Beth slipped in through the back door, hoping to find the kitchen empty. Of course, earlier, when she'd been hoping to find Pearl there, she hadn't been. Now the woman was busy peeling carrots at the sink.

The short, plump woman looked over her shoulder to identify the intruder. "Mornin', Ms. Dearborn."

"Beth. Remember?" She wanted to befriend this woman who'd known Lorilee her entire life, and Ty much of his. Plus, instinct told her Pearl Montgomery was a woman worth getting to know. She was one of the good people in this world, and her husband probably was, too. "Pretty outside today."

"That it is." Pearl studied Beth a few moments. "Did you find yourself any breakfast? I'd be happy to—"

"No, don't go to any trouble. I overslept, so I'll just have lunch when it's time." Beth smiled. "I wanted to thank you for helping me the other night after I fell and hit my head."

"You're welcome." Pearl paused in her peeling and stared out the window. "Don't know what got into Sarah, calling you that way. She knows better."

"It really wasn't her fault, and—as you pointed out—it's better that I'm stranded here than on the other side of the bridge."

"True enough." She started scraping carrots again. "Making stew for dinner. Beef and barley."

Beth wasn't much of a cook, and her mother had generally opened or heated dinner, or they'd ordered pizza. "I don't think I've ever had it."

"If you like it, I'll give you the recipe." Pearl wiped her hands on her apron and dropped the peeled carrots onto a cutting board, where she diced them into chunks. "Was old Mrs. Brubaker's recipe."

"Lorilee's mother?"

"Her granny." Pearl smiled, one gold tooth flashing amid many white ones. "That old woman lived to be a hundred and one, and ran the kitchen until the day she died."

"Sounds like an interesting person."

Pearl gave a wheezing chuckle. "That's one word for it."

She went to the stove and stirred a massive kettle of sizzling meat. "You want to brown the beef before you start adding vegetables." She dumped a bowl of diced onions and another of minced garlic into the pot. Then she rinsed and cleaned two green bell peppers and tossed them in as well.

"You want to hand me that pot of thyme from the window there, Beth?"

Beth rose and stared at the row of small herb pots lined up along the kitchen windowsill. "Um . . . which one is thyme?"

Laughing again, Pearl picked up a pot and held it up to Beth. "Take a whiff."

"Nice."

"That's thyme." Pearl pinched some off with her fingers and sprinkled it into the sizzling pot. She picked up a different herb. "This un's rosemary." She let Beth smell it as well before she repeated the entire process.

The kitchen filled with wonderful aromas as Pearl kept adding and stirring items into the pot. Beth's stomach rumbled hungrily, making the older woman chuckle again.

"Lorilee was always skippin' breakfast, too." She smiled sadly. "There's sandwich fixin's in the fridge. Help yourself."

"Thanks. I guess I'll do that." Beth pulled bread and cheese out of the refrigerator. "Can I make you one, Pearl?"

"No, I ate breakfast with the kids and Cecil, so I'm good for a bit yet." Pearl pointed at the food.

"You go ahead. Plates are over there." She aimed a thumb across the room. "And there's iced tea in that pitcher."

Sweet tea. Blech. "I'm more of a water person, actually."

"Suit yourself."

Beth smiled to herself as she constructed the sandwich and poured herself a glass of water, then took a seat at the table. "So the kids have school today?"

"Yes, and Mark is still fit to be tied that the schoolhouse isn't on the other side of that durned bridge." She laughed again. "The girls, now, they both like school pretty much."

"That's good." Beth had hated school, mostly because she'd had no friends. She was too weird growing up, trying to come to terms with her gift and learn to control it. Since her gift had come from her father's side of the family, and he'd died when she was an infant, the only people she'd ever had to share her secrets with were Sam and his father, who was also gone now. Their mothers had always tried to stay out of it. Though they knew about the family gift from their husbands, they didn't understand it well enough to help their children. So she and Sam had been more like siblings than cousins.

Beth took a bite of the sandwich and reached for a flier on the table. Some kind of cancer fund-raiser. Sam's mom had died from breast cancer. What a horrible waste.

"Some hairdressers have donated their time and are coming to the school for this," Pearl explained, when she saw what Beth was reading. "I think they need at least nine inches of hair to make a wig for chemo patients, or something like that."

Beth took another bite of her sandwich and chewed thoughtfully. She probably had enough hair to make three wigs and still have some left over for herself. A smile spread across her face. Ty thought she was hiding behind "all that hair." Well, maybe she had been, but no more. Someone else needed it more than she did.

Besides, for some crazy reason, she needed to prove to herself she wasn't hiding from anyone or anything. At least no one living.

"So when is this fund-raiser, Pearl?" she asked. "I feel the need for a change."

"That's the spirit. It's this afternoon." Pearl put the lid on the stew. "We'll both go. I'll get a trim, and you can donate hair for wigs. Won't they be surprised when they see you?"

"I'll bet they won't be the only ones." Beth finished her sandwich. "Don't tell anyone. We'll surprise everybody."

Pearl laughed again. "We sure will. They won't have a big turnout today, because folks from Brubaker won't be able to get to the school, so they'll need all us country folks to make it worthwhile."

Imagine that—Beth Dearborn as "country folk." She smiled again and finished the water. "Maybe on the way, you can tell me more about Lorilee and her parents."

Pearl looked over her shoulder and nodded. "Sure, I don't see why not. If you think it might help."

"You never know what might help. Thanks. I'll just get my things."

"And I'll dump all this into the slow cooker, get my car, and meet you in the drive."

On her way up the back staircase, Beth promised

herself she'd visit Lorilee's attic studio as soon as they returned. This would give her another chance to observe the locals. Maybe she'd run into Bill and Ruby Brubaker again, or the very strange Gary Harlan.

Maybe she'd get some inkling of who might want to see her dead.

In her room, she dropped the antiquated Rolodex into her backpack alongside her Glock and put her cell phone in the outside pocket. She paused in front of the dressing mirror to stare at her wild mane of hair.

"Hiding, huh?" She held it away from her face with both hands. "Probably."

With a sigh, she swung her backpack onto her shoulder and headed for the door. "Definitely time for a change."

Ty was as nervous as an expectant father. He'd raised Cissy herself from a foal. She was the daughter of Lorilee's beloved Tennessee walking horse, which had come to the farm with her after their marriage. Ty had hesitated to have Cissy bred, but Sarah and Bill had both insisted they keep the line going.

So here they were, waiting and pacing while Amanda Barnes examined the mare. Cecil patted Ty on the back. "She's from good, strong stock," he said, reading Ty's tension. "She'll do fine."

"I should call Bill."

Cecil appeared thoughtful. "I'd wait until after the fact, were it me." He arched a woolly brow. "But it's your call."

"I like it your way." Ty grinned. "You're pretty smart for an old fart."

"That's what Pearl says."

"Sure it is."

Cecil guffawed and slapped Ty's back again. "You're the darnedest." He grew solemn after a moment. "Y'know, that investigator and my Pearl took off somewhere together this afternoon."

"No kidding?" Now that surprised Ty. "I thought she was hell-bent on going through all of Lorilee's records in her studio today."

"Apparently my Pearl made her a better offer."

Ty thought back to this morning, and Mitch's discovery about the brake lines. "I hope they're careful."

"Pearl's a good driver, Ty. You know that." Cecil narrowed his eyes. "What's eatin' you, boy?"

"Somebody cut Beth's brake lines last night."

"What?" Cecil's alarm showed in his face. "Why in tarnation would someone do such a fool thing?"

"To stop her from finding the truth." Ty kept his voice low. "Why else?"

Cecil's expression remained solemn. "If anybody tries to hurt my Pearl, I'll kick their ass into the stratosphere."

Ty placed a comforting hand on Cecil's shoulder. "And I'll help. The bastard won't stand a chance."

"It's a filly!" Amanda shouted from the stall. "She's breach, but she's coming fast now."

"I'll be damned." Ty and Cecil both rushed to the stall and stared over the door as Amanda Barnes worked her magic on Cissy. The veterinarian massaged the mare's bulging, contracting abdomen as she urged the gangly-legged filly from the warmth of her mother's womb.

In what seemed like only seconds later, the filly was out and her mother was licking her clean while

Amanda dealt with the afterbirth. "They both did great. No worries here," she called from the stall floor.

Cissy decided that enough was enough of all this human intervention and lurched to her feet. Then she licked and nuzzled her foal until the new-born imitated her mother. Within minutes, the filly was suckling as her mother continued to lick her clean.

"Good work, Cissy," Ty said, giving her a thumbs-up.

"Do you still have that treat I gave you earlier?" Amanda asked.

"Oh, sure." He pulled it out of his pocket. "Looks like a sugar cube."

"That's what she'll think. Vitamin." Amanda finished gathering her equipment and stepped out of the stall. "Go on in and see if she'll let you say hi."

Ty entered the stall slowly. Even though Cissy was his horse in every way, he never knew how a mare would react to human contact with her foal. Cissy bobbed her head as if saying, "Come on in and see what I did."

He kept his eyes on Cissy and offered her the cube open-palmed, stroking her neck. "Aren't you the best?" She took the cube and made a soft nickering sound.

"Extra sweet feed for the next two weeks," Amanda said to Cecil. "As much as she wants for now, then taper back once she and—Hey, what's this young lady's name?"

The filly's long legs made Ty think of Beth Dearborn, but he figured that would be inappropriate. "I haven't decided." He looked back over his shoulder. "The kids'll want to be in on it."

"Sure, that makes sense." Amanda Barnes leaned on the stall door with Cecil. "I don't think she's going to mind if you touch her foal, Ty."

No, neither did he. Ty kept one hand on Cissy's neck and reached down very gently to touch the still-damp back of the nursing filly. "You did good work, girl. Real good. Looks like she'll be a dapple gray, like her momma."

"That's my guess, too." Amanda pushed away from the stall when her beeper sounded. "Have another stop to make on my way home."

"Thanks for coming. Glad you're on this side of that damn bridge."

She laughed. "Me, too. Considering my work, it makes sense."

Ty left the stall and followed Amanda out of the barn while Cecil measured the sweet feed for Cissy.

"I'm sorry we missed Mark's party," she said. "Cory has a terrible cold, and I didn't want to spread it around."

"Appreciate that."

"Lorilee would be proud of how you've managed the kids, Ty." Amanda reached out and put her hand on his arm. "You torture yourself too much. Let the investigator do her job. You're doing the right thing."

"Thanks, Amanda. I hope you're right."

"I was Lorilee's best friend. Remember?"

"And maid of honor at our wedding." Ty sighed and stared off toward the road. The sight of Pearl's car heading toward the house barely registered. The kids would be home in an hour or so, and they'd want to see the foal.

Amanda continued to talk, but Ty barely heard her. He was too busy watching Pearl park her car.

She'd obviously noticed the veterinarian's truck and assumed it was because of Cissy, because she parked close to the barn.

He watched the short, plump woman and the long-legged one walking toward him. He'd recognize that stride anywhere, and couldn't help but remember those legs wrapped around his waist last night.

As they drew closer, he noticed something else. Her hair. She'd cut her hair. A lot! He chuckled. That figured. All it took was for someone to accuse her of hiding behind it, and off it came.

"What's so funny?" Amanda asked, looking in the direction of his gaze. "Oh, it's Pearl. Is that the investigator?"

"Yes. Yes, it is."

"Well, I'd better run. I need to stop at the Holmes place on the way home."

"Thanks for coming, Amanda."

"Are you kidding? I wouldn't have missed it." She gave Ty a hug. "Cissy is family, and so are you."

She waved to Pearl, then headed for her truck at a brisk pace, obviously trying to make up for the time she'd spent chatting with Ty. As Pearl and Beth drew closer, Ty stood transfixed.

Beth's hair was a cap of soft, dark curls now, with some loose strands grazing her cheeks and eyes, and a little fringe around her collar. The closer she came, the prettier she looked. Those eyes . . .

"Did Cissy have her foal?" Pearl asked when they reached him.

He nodded. "A healthy gray filly. Go see for yourself. Cecil's in there."

Pearl left him alone with Beth. "What happened to all that hair?"

"Donated it to charity." She drew a deep breath. "I didn't need it anymore."

He studied her eyes for several seconds. "Not hiding anymore?"

She gave him a tight smile. "We'll see. Won't we?" After a minute, she inclined her head toward the barn. "I've never seen a newborn horse. May I?"

"Sure." He turned toward the barn. "And, by the way, I like it."

"What?"

"Your hair."

She nodded, matching his stride toward the barn. "So do I." She paused at the open door and he stopped beside her. "Um, one question."

"Shoot. You're the investigator."

She arched an eyebrow and tilted her head at an angle, suspicion oozing from every pore. "Who's the redhead?"

CHAPTER FOURTEEN

At this moment, Beth wished she still had that mass of hair. She could have used a handy place to hide. Ty's stare told her she'd asked a really stupid question, and she was *not* stupid. Nor was she the typical jealous-female type. Far from it.

Damn. She drew a deep breath and summoned her detective persona.

Be professional, Dearborn.

"Anyway, none of my business. Never mind." She took a step toward the barn, but he put a hand on her shoulder.

"Amanda Barnes is an old friend and our veterinarian." His tone was calm and unaccusing. "You'll find her in that Rolodex of Lorilee's. They were best friends from childhood. She's on the list of names I gave you the other day of people you should talk to."

Beth remembered the name. She nodded. "Thanks. I'll do that." She inclined her head toward the barn. "Let's have a look at the baby horse so I can get back to work and your lives can get back to normal."

"Baby horse?" He grinned.

"Uh, foal?"

"Right. I really do like the hair." He reached out to play with the short waves around her face. "Really sets off your eyes. You have beautiful eyes. Very expressive." He leaned closer. "They give you away, you know."

She stiffened. "I have no idea what you mean." He couldn't possibly know her secret. At least, she sure hoped not. "Anyway, the horse . . ."

"Have it your way." He dropped his hands to his sides. "She's a beautiful filly, all legs." He allowed his gaze to drift down the length of her and back to her face. "Like someone else I know."

Beth cleared her throat. "Filly, my ass." She hesitated at the barn door. "You know, I think I'll head back to the house and see the filly later. I need to make up for the time I lost this afternoon."

"Sure." Ty gave her a tight smile that said he didn't buy her excuse.

Well, that made two of them. Truth was, Beth had to put some distance between herself and Ty Malone—even temporarily. Right now she wanted to throw her arms around him and thank him for saying he liked her haircut and for talking about her eyes. No man had ever done that, and it made her feel . . . silly and all squishy inside.

Get a grip, Dearborn.

She'd made it to thirty-one without hearing that kind of mush, and she didn't need it now. She'd finally become resigned to spending her life alone and miserable, just one step ahead of a bottle of bourbon, and she couldn't afford to become dependant on a man. She managed to avoid his knowing look—the you're-hiding-again-even-without-the-hair look—and headed toward the house at a brisk pace.

Her backpack swung heavily against her side, and she shifted it to the left just as a loud cracking sound erupted, and something slammed into her. The impact sent her sprawling. Pain and instinct sent her scrambling behind a tree.

Her heart raced. She turned hot, then cold. Her belly clenched. No mistake. She'd been here, done this.

Someone was shooting at her.

She tugged her bag around to examine. Sure enough, a bullet hole was in the soft leather. She reached inside and removed what was left of her Glock. The bullet was lodged in its holster, but the gun itself had blocked the bullet and bruised bloody hell out of her ribs. Better that than a gaping hole in her side. The gun had saved her life yet again, and now it was destroyed.

The caliber of the bullet was from a powerful, long-distance rifle. She kept the useless weapon handy from instinct, then retrieved her cell phone and found the entry for Ty's number.

"Was that a gunshot?" he answered.

"Yes, keep everybody in the barn and call the sheriff."

"We aren't stupid. Otherwise we would have run out after you," he said on a sigh. "You okay?"

"I'm fine, but call."

"He'll have to send somebody from Marysville."

"That damn bridge." Beth chewed her lower lip. "Whoever it was is probably long gone by now, and they fired from long distance."

"How can you tell that?"

"Ammo."

"Are you hit?" Ty's voice rose. "Cecil, call the sheriff. Somebody's taking potshots at Beth."

"My backpack stopped it."

Silence filled the line for a few seconds. "What's in there? Lead?"

Beth grinned in spite of the possible danger, though instinct told her the shooter had taken one shot and fled. "Something like."

"Try Rick Heppel," Ty said to Cecil. "Ask him if he can fly the sheriff out here before the kids get home."

"Good thinking," Beth said. "Can Grandpa get the kids and keep them from coming home until we know it's safe?"

"Good thinking. Pearl's doing that now," Ty returned. "We make a good team. Where, exactly, are you?"

"Behind the big tree with the tire swing, near the back door." Beth continued to scan the horizon in the general direction from where the shot had come. "I think the shooter is gone."

"Why's that?"

"Because he probably thinks he got me, since I went down and didn't get back up."

"And you think he was after you why?"

"Same reason he sabotaged my brakes."

"God dammit all to hell." He sighed into the phone. "At least this time *I* have an alibi."

"That's true. You do." She waited a minute. "Is Heppel bringing the sheriff?"

She heard Ty talking to Pearl and Cecil, but

couldn't quite make out the words. "Yes, he's doing it. I hear his chopper taking off now."

Sure enough, the chopper rose just beyond the tree line. Interesting. Beth hadn't realized how close his place was as the crow flies, so to speak. On foot, a person could go back and forth—as long as they didn't mind crossing the creek—within a few minutes between the two farms.

A chilling thought raced down her spine. Heppel could have walked over here and cut her brake lines last night.

And with the right weapon and skill, he could sit on the roof of his hangar and pick her off from there without much difficulty. He was a trained army vet.

"Hey, Ty?" she said into the phone.

"Yeah?"

"Did you tell Heppel why we need the sheriff?"

"No, I didn't. Just that it's an emergency."

"Did he have any kind of reaction?"

"He asked if we need a doctor, too."

"Damn. Just stay put until they get here. And Brubaker's definitely getting the kids?"

"Yes. And taking them home with him after school."

"Good."

Beth heard the sound of footsteps and had her mangled Glock leveled at the intruder in one smooth motion. In a crouch, she kept the weapon aimed straight at him.

"Ty, you fool!"

"You have a gun," he said, staring, cell phone still held to his ear. "A big one."

She released the hammer and turned on the safety,

then slid the weapon carefully into her backpack. "I told you to stay in the barn."

"You also said you thought the shooter was gone." He pocketed the cell phone. "So I'm a guy. Shoot me. Er, nix that—bad choice of words. I needed to make sure you're really okay."

"I'm okay. See?" She sighed. "Will you at least get down? I could've shot you." *Well, not really.*

"With that big gun."

Beth laughed. "Yes, with my big gun." She didn't tell him it was a broken big gun.

Ty dropped to the ground and crawled on his belly until he was beside Beth. "Let me see the bullet."

Beth held out her palm. "See?"

"Definitely from a rifle." He picked it up and examined it. "Now I guess I have a pretty good idea what it hit in your backpack."

"Good thing it did."

"I'd say so." He returned it to her, his expression solemn. "You could be splattered all over the backyard, Beth."

"Don't I know it." She shoved the slug back into her pocket. "They were afraid of not getting another chance. And as far as we know, the shooter thinks he got me."

"Yeah." A look of dread settled across his handsome face. "Can we change the subject?"

The worry in his eyes filled Beth with warmth. No one but her mother and Sam had ever worried about her before. Oh, maybe her commander a couple of times, but mostly because of the trouble she always caused.

She leaned close and kissed his cheek. "Thanks for caring."

Now it was his turn to blush.

He cleared his throat. "You think we can make a run for the back door now?"

"Yeah, I think so." Beth touched his sleeve. "But I'd rather Cecil and Pearl didn't try to come from the barn until after the sheriff arrives."

"Me, too." Ty called Cecil and told him they were going in and that he and Pearl should stay put.

Together, Ty and Beth darted through the back door, the mudroom, and into the empty kitchen. Ty sniffed the air appreciatively. "Beef and barley stew."

"How did you know that?"

"The nose knows." He grinned and tapped her nose. "You scared the hell out of me when we heard that shot."

She didn't want to meet his gaze, but something compelled her. For some reason she couldn't look away. "We need to teach Pearl to lock doors."

He grinned again. "None of us lock doors around here, Beth. It's a farm. Lots of coming and going."

"Exactly." She shrugged. "Whoever took a shot at me will probably try again. They want me gone, Ty." She grasped his upper arms. "I'm not leaving now. I'm determined to find out what happened to Lorilee. Nobody's taking potshots at me and getting away with it."

"There's my girl."

My girl? Taken aback, Beth blinked several times. "Well, I have a job to do, and I intend to do it." She finally broke eye contact. "Leaving the house wideopen all the time is problematic."

"Locking the door and unlocking it all the time on a farm is, too." He reached out and caught her chin in his hand, tilted her face upward, and brought his lips down on hers.

The kiss was short but potent. Beth swayed and he reached for her, but she summoned her stubborn dignity and pulled back. "What was that about?"

"I don't think it requires an explanation." He cleared his throat. "We established last night that we want each other."

"So we did." She faced him again, determined to change the subject. "I think the webcams you have set up can be put to use for security."

"What?" He shook his head. "You lost me. What does that have to do with kissing?"

She smiled. "Not a damn thing." A whirring sound reached her ears and she pointed upward. "Hark! It's a bird. It's a plane."

"Cute."

"Where will he land that thing?"

"The only place open enough besides my fields— and he knows better—is out in front of the driveway."

She pushed through the swinging doors into the parlor, then stopped in her tracks. He ran right into the back of her. "What is it?"

"I'll go back this way and meet you out front."

"Um . . . what the hell's wrong with the front door?"

She met and held his gaze for several seconds as the chopper landed. "It's a long story, Ty, and we don't have time right now."

"That's a cop-out if I ever heard one."

"Well, I used to be a cop. Get over it." She darted into the kitchen and headed for the back door. "Let's get going."

Shaking his head, Ty followed her, instead of going through the front door. "I want to hear this long story, Beth Dearborn," he said, following her around the corner of the house. "Tonight. After dinner."

She stopped, and he ran into her again. "Will you stop doing that?" he asked.

She winced from the horrible bruise spreading across the side of her torso, but the pain helped remind her she was alive. "You wouldn't believe me if I told you," she said, her tone deadly serious. "I'd have to show you, and I can't do that. You don't want me to do that. Trust me."

He rubbed her shoulder. "Okay. For now."

"For now."

Sam had to save her from herself, because she was more convinced than ever that the ghost in the foyer had a story worth telling. Either it was Lorilee or, she'd be willing to bet, it knew about her.

Someone definitely didn't want her here, and sure as hell didn't want her dredging up the truth. Well, tough, because that was exactly what she was determined to do.

"We're still going to have a talk after dinner," Ty said. "Get used to the idea."

"Fine, dammit. We'll talk, but I can't tell you what you want to know, Ty."

"Maybe you don't know what it is I want to know."

His tone indicated he wasn't talking about her secrets now. She swallowed the lump in her throat and started walking toward the front of the house again. "Let's go talk to the sheriff."

* * *

Pearl invited everybody to dinner and managed to throw together something suitably vegan for Rick, who had also visited the school fundraiser today and was only half as hairy as the last time Ty had seen him. Was that why Beth kept glancing at him, or was there another reason?

Ty certainly couldn't discount the fact that the man lived in the same general area from where the shot had been fired. Beth hadn't said anything about being suspicious of Heppel, but Ty sensed it.

His weird neighbor may have had opportunity to sabotage Beth's brakes and take a shot at her, but *why* would he have done such a thing? If it was true, there was only one possible explanation, and it didn't set well with Ty at all.

Lorilee. Was Rick Heppel the man responsible? After all these years, would it turn out to be their next-door neighbor? A man his wife had befriended and trusted?

Ty watched everybody eat, relieved, for once, that the kids weren't home. The place felt empty without them, but it was best this way. He'd drive over and pick them up in the morning, since it was Saturday. Meanwhile, they could spend the night being spoiled by their grandfather and endured by their Grandma Ruby.

As he watched his guests share the meal, he couldn't convince himself of Heppel's guilt. The big man always seemed so gentle. Lorilee had thought so, and Pearl did as well. Try as he might, Ty just couldn't imagine him as a cold-blooded killer.

"So you have the bullet, then?" Sheriff Bailey asked after Beth finished telling him the story of how her backpack had stopped the bullet.

She reached into her pocket and retrieved the piece of metal, only slightly blunted from its impact with her backpack and its contents. Ty ran a hand through his hair. Thank God she packed a piece. He almost laughed aloud with relief, but held himself in check.

Dan Bailey was a good ten years older than Ty, but he carried his age well. He'd been re-elected six times, and—other than Lorilee's disappearance—had solved every case that had come along. Of course, like most of Brubaker, he believed her case had been solved, that she'd abandoned her family and fled to Europe.

"You were right. Definitely a long-range rifle," Dan commented when Beth handed him the bullet to examine. "I suppose it could have been a poacher with lousy aim."

"Bullshit." Ty's tone was sharper than he'd intended, but they might as well get everything out on the table. "Someone deliberately cut the brake lines on her car last night."

Dan's brows arched in surprise. "Really?" He looked at Beth. "Where's your car now?"

"Einstein here had it towed to Marysville." Beth grinned when Ty scowled at her.

"Mitch's Garage," he provided without being asked. "He checked the lines himself."

Dan nodded and actually made a few notes on a memo pad he pulled from his pocket. "I'll call him when I get back to the office." He took a few more bites of stew. "Pearl, you are the finest cook in the county."

"Don't let these fine men be forgetting it, either," the woman said with a giggle.

"Not in this lifetime," Cecil said, and gave her cheek a peck.

"That's a promise," Ty agreed.

"Thank you for preparing something special for me, Mrs. Montgomery," Heppel said. "It's delicious."

"You're welcome. And I've told you before to call me Pearl."

"Looks like someone doesn't want you here, Ms. Dearborn," Dan said as he pushed his bowl away. "You're here to investigate Lorilee's disappearance for the insurance company, as I understand it. Correct?"

"Actually, sir, to prove or disprove her death," Beth corrected, "since there's been a claim filed for her life insurance."

"What's your background, Ms. Dearborn, before insurance investigating?" Dan asked. "If you don't mind sharing."

"I don't mind at all." She kept her gaze leveled on the sheriff. "I was on the Chicago Police Department. Homicide."

Dan let out a low whistle. "Impressive credentials."

Cecil added, "Don't that beat all?"

"Homicide?" Ty hadn't known that part.

"Yes, Homicide." Beth toyed with the food remaining in her bowl. "Really delicious stew, Pearl."

"All right, so it's a life-insurance claim," Dan continued, as if they'd never strayed off topic. He rubbed his chin thoughtfully. "And Ty, being the beneficiary, would want you here. So that rules him out."

"Damn straight," Ty said.

"I think we can rule out Pearl and Cecil, too." Dan smiled. "And you said they were both in the barn at the time anyway."

"That's right." Cecil reached for a roll. "Got us a new filly."

"Always good news." Dan turned the bullet over and over between his thumb and forefinger. "What about you, Rick? Do you have a rifle this might fit?"

Everybody turned to stare at the old hippie. He seemed very calm for someone who'd more or less just been accused of attempted murder.

Rick placed his fork on his plate and folded his hands in front of him. "I don't own *any* guns."

"None at all?"

"I'm a pacifist."

"Since Nam?" Dan poked.

Heppel lurched to his feet, nearly tipping over his chair. "We aren't talking about that. Not now. Not ever." Though his words were harsh, his tone was almost fiercely calm.

Pearl rose and patted Rick's arm. "No, son. We aren't. Sit, sit. It's fine. Sit."

The look Pearl gave everyone at the table put an immediate end to Rick's interrogation. The big man did as she asked, but he sat stoically and didn't resume eating.

Ty noticed the way Pearl handled Rick was different from the way Lorilee had treated him. Lorilee had treated Rick as an equal. She hadn't let him pull that crap with her—at least it hadn't seemed that way to Ty. However, the pair had spent a lot more time alone together than Ty would have liked. Of course,

Rick was old enough to have been Lorilee's father. Still . . .

Pearl, on the other hand, treated him almost maternally, though they were probably near the same age. In fact, Heppel might have had a few years on her.

He sensed the cogs turning in Beth's brain. She sat right beside him, at the place usually occupied by Sarah. So far, she'd remained fairly quiet, but he figured that would change. He also noticed she hadn't touched the wine Pearl had served with dinner. After being shot at, you'd think she could've used a belt or three.

Just thinking about it made him reach for his. He'd have preferred three fingers of the Irish whiskey his father had always kept for "medicinal purposes." Dad hadn't consumed alcohol often, and when he did it was always Jameson's. He called it his one indulgence, and it was. John Malone had been a hardworking man of modest means, and had lived his life and raised his son that way.

Ty refilled his wine, which was rare for him. He wasn't much of a drinker as a rule. Not after living with Lorilee. As the years went by and her secret drinking increased, he'd realized the importance of the children having one sober parent around. He suppressed the sigh threatening to escape and turned his attention back to Dan and the conversation.

"I'll take this bullet in to Forensics," he said. "But without a weapon, you know it won't do much good."

"Unless there's a previous record." Beth reached for her water glass and took a sip.

"Is the wine not to your liking, Beth?" Pearl asked. "I have a white chilled, if you pre—"

"No, it's not that, Pearl," she interrupted. "I don't drink." She shrugged and set down her water glass. "Rick doesn't eat meat and I don't drink alcohol. No biggie."

"I should've asked first." Pearl stood and removed Beth's wineglass, passing it over to Cecil. "You aren't going anywhere tonight, old man."

With a laugh, he took the glass. "Only with you, old woman. Only with you."

Ty had never met a cop, or former one, who didn't drink. As she'd said, "no biggie," so he dismissed it and concentrated on what was important.

He leveled his gaze on Dan. "Look, I know you and most of the town gossips wrote off Lorilee's disappearance after that bogus letter came."

He held up his hand when Dan started to speak. "Hear me out, please."

Dan set aside his fork and leaned back in his chair. "I'm listening, Ty."

And he was. The man's expression definitely seemed receptive enough. So Ty drew a deep breath and looked around the table before continuing.

"The kids and I have put up with a lot of crap these past seven years. Gossip and rumors and stories about fake sightings."

"I know. I've had to investigate them."

Ty nodded. "And they've all turned out to be false for the same reason, Dan. The same reason I've known all along."

"Because Lorilee was murdered," Rick Heppel said quietly, his arms folded, his chin on his chest.

"She was murdered and her body hidden somewhere so we wouldn't find her."

Every person at the table turned toward Rick. Only the grandfather clock in the adjoining room made any sound at all, when it chimed seven times.

"And how do you know that, Rick?" Beth asked in a matter-of-fact tone. "Unless you were there?"

CHAPTER FIFTEEN

Beth kept her gaze glued to Heppel. He matched her stare for stare, the silence stretching. Finally, he leaned back in his chair and said, "You're the cop. Figure it out."

"Now, Rick . . ." Dan pushed to his feet. "That's uncalled for, and you know it." He resumed his seat after a moment. "You made a damn strong accusation. If you have something to back it up, share."

"Yeah, share," Ty said, his tone etched with acid as he emphasized each word with his finger. "I've spent seven years trying to find out what happened to my wife. If you know, we'd really appreciate it."

He didn't reach for his wine this time, but water. And drained it. Beth could have used a refill herself, though the wine was sounding better and better. But no . . . not after last night's nightmare. She had to be extra careful.

Extra alert.

Especially with the word *murder* now out of the closet. "I asked you this question at your place, Rick," she continued, her tone still as mellow as she could make it. "What makes you so certain Lorilee is dead? And more important, why are you so convinced she was murdered?"

He nodded. "Fair enough. I'll share." Rick steepled his fingers under his chin, staring across the room at something only he could see. "Ty, Pearl, Cecil, and I all know she wouldn't have left her babies. Agreed?"

They all murmured in agreement.

"That don't prove she's dead, or that she was murdered," Dan argued.

"Then where is she?" Rick half turned and seemed like a different person—more educated, more outspoken, more confident. "After all these years, if she didn't leave under her own power—and the people who knew her best know she didn't—then where the devil is she, man?" He slammed his fist down on the table, much as he had that night Beth had eaten dinner at his place. "Where, dammit?"

"Thank you," Ty said, and reached across the table with his right hand extended.

"For what?" Rick eyed Ty's hand with open suspicion.

"For saying it outright and honestly."

Rick shook Ty's hand, and Beth made a mental note to scratch Heppel off her list of suspects. She trusted gut instinct, and even though her empathic and psychic abilities did not extend into this realm, she just knew.

"What happened today, and the fact that someone is working so hard to keep me from uncovering the long-buried truth, lends credence to Rick's theory," Beth said, choosing her words carefully. "What do you think, Sheriff?"

Sheriff Bailey leaned toward her and said, "Your office got a court order for the letter. Happy?"

Beth smiled and took another sip of water. "Not yet, but it's a start."

"It's about damn time," Ty said.

"The letter," Rick repeated. "*The* letter? The one that started all the lies about Lorilee?"

"One and the same." Ty leaned back in his chair. "I never even laid eyes on that letter. Bill wouldn't let me see it. He was so upset by it, he just wanted to sweep it all under the rug and move on. Said he felt betrayed by his own flesh and blood."

"Trust me, I remember." The sheriff sighed again. "He's gonna have my hide over this."

"No, he won't," Beth said, still smiling. "I already told him about it." She did her Southern-belle eyelash thing again.

Pearl actually laughed. "Don't you beat all."

Cecil said, "Amen. It's time Lorilee's memory was cleared, and this mess put to rest once and for all."

"Well . . ." The sheriff looked around the table, his expression one of resignation. "Looks like I'm outnumbered here."

"That's a fact," Ty said.

"I have an apple crisp in the kitchen if anyone's of a mind for dessert," Pearl said, rising with dirty dishes balanced in both hands.

Cecil groaned and imitated her actions. "I'm so stuffed, I couldn't eat another bite."

Echoes of agreement swept around the table, and everybody followed the woman—despite her protests—to the kitchen with their own dishes in tow. Beth couldn't help feeling a pang of envy for the deep love and respect every person present—including Rick Heppel—obviously felt for Pearl Montgomery.

Though she was a housekeeper, she was a queen in this house, and treated like part of the family. From what Beth had seen, she deserved every ounce of that respect.

Beth hadn't met a lot of people in her life she truly admired, but Pearl and Cecil Montgomery were at the top of her list. Ty was lucky to have them here for his children, and for himself. And to his credit, he clearly knew it.

Rick Heppel announced it was time for his "bird to fly" while he was still awake enough to pilot it. While Cecil helped Pearl clean up the kitchen, Beth and Ty walked out to the chopper with Rick and the sheriff.

"Stay in touch, and let me know if anything else suspicious happens," the sheriff said as he climbed into the small helicopter. "Damn, I hate these things."

Rick Heppel laughed. "I heard that."

"Hey, Rick," Ty called. "I'm not sure I've ever heard you laugh before."

Rick grinned through his beard in the lighted cockpit. "You hadn't earned it before, cowboy."

"I am not a cow—"

Ty's words were drowned out by the starting engine and whirling blades. Beth and Ty ducked and hurried back toward the house as the chopper rose into the air and headed toward Brubaker.

When they reached the front steps, Beth stopped and tugged on his hand. "Remember? I don't do front doors," she said.

"Oh, that." He took a step closer and pulled her into his arms, allowing his hands to snake downward and cup her butt, tugging her firmly against his erection. "What *do* you do, Beth?"

"I know you're there. Help me!"

She knows we're here. We have to move away. "We're too close."

"I want to get a lot closer," Ty whispered, nuzzling the lobe of her ear.

"Not here." She pulled away and tugged on his hand. "Wait until Pearl and Cecil go home. Besides, you said we're going to talk. Remember?"

"Me and my big mouth." He followed her quick strides with plodding steps. "I need to check on Cissy anyway."

"I'm goin' to do that now," Cecil said as he headed out the back door. "That's what your fancy webcam is for, anyhow. Then me 'n Pearl are callin' it a day."

"Thanks, my friend," Ty called. "It's been a long day."

"So we'll go help Pearl finish in the kitchen," Beth said, heading around to the back door as fast as she could. The spirit in the foyer was definitely gaining strength.

She met Pearl at the mudroom door. "All done. I just started the dishwasher. All you two have left is turnin' off the lights. Oh, and lock the doors tonight, Ty."

Ty sighed and Beth laughed. "That's what I keep telling him." She aimed her thumb over her shoulder. "But he says you don't do that on a farm."

Pearl held up the jailer's ring of keys she had hanging around her neck. "Then why do you make the kids do it when you or I aren't here, Ty?" She laughed at his sigh. " 'Night, you two."

" 'Night, Pearl," Ty called. Once she closed the door behind her, he slid the bolt. "It's locked."

"Go check the front door, too."

"Come with me?"

"No, Ty. I'm tired. I'm going up—"

"We're having a talk. Remember?"

"Yes. I remember." She turned off the kitchen light as he headed for the front of the house, then went to the back staircase.

"Meet me in my room at the top of the stairs," he called back to her through the empty house.

Top of the stairs, left, then right. Wasn't that the room from her dream?

She almost tripped on the bottom step, but gripped the banister and pulled herself up one step at a time. Maybe they'd just talk.

But she knew better. This thing between them had been coming to a head since the moment he'd stopped to change her flat tire. She had to make the choice in order to be in control, and that was exactly what she was doing now. It was time. Past time.

Sure, they both had enough baggage to keep every bellhop in Chicago busy for a year. But even her self-enforced pragmatism couldn't deny how her feelings were evolving.

Take it slow, Dearborn. Control . . .

With a secret smile, she remembered the other stop she'd made besides Gooch's Garage that afternoon, and reached into the front pocket of her jeans to make sure the three-pack of condoms was still there.

It was time.

Resigned and more excited than she cared to examine, she just hoped only two of them occupied his bed tonight.

* * *

There she stood beside his bed. Light from the hall-way spilled through the open doorway into the dark room, bathing her in a golden glow. He couldn't wait to run his hands through her soft, short curls.

She obviously knew that talking wasn't upper-most on his mind, since she was waiting for him in the dark. Beside his bed.

"All locked," he said, walking over to stand right in front of her. "Happy now?"

"Almost." The tone of her voice told him she wanted him as much as he wanted her, if that was possible.

"I'm out of practice, you know."

"Then you're due a workout."

"Holy . . ." He released a long, slow breath and nibbled the lobe of her ear. "Be gentle with me," he teased.

"Not a chance, cowboy."

"It's a good day to die."

Ty gently pressed her down to sit on the edge of his neatly made bed and stood with his hands on her shoulders. Her unique, haunting scent wafted up from her closely cropped curls to fill his senses. No fancy perfume here. She smelled clean, fresh, and sexy as hell.

He barely knew this woman, yet she'd invaded his life, his home, and his mind with a gusto that left him breathless. He wanted her in ways he hadn't believed he was still capable of wanting a woman. She'd made a part of him that had died return to the living. She was a gift of fate, or perhaps it was simply time.

She reached toward him, brought her hands up to cup his face. They felt cool and soothing against his burning skin. With the tips of her fingers, she drew an invisible line from the lobe of his ear to his mouth, then gently stroked the contour of his lips. Lips that wanted to sample every toned curve, every valley, every soft inch of her.

Beth didn't have an ounce of extra flesh, but she wasn't scrawny by any means. She leaned toward the athletic side—probably all those martial arts. He smiled down at her.

"Something funny?" she asked, her voice huskier than usual.

"I was just remembering when you threw me and buried your knee in my spine."

One corner of her full mouth curved upward. "Did I hurt you?" Her eyes smoldered. "Want me to kiss it and make it better?"

"Oh, yeah." He caught his breath in anticipation. "Definitely."

"Well, I might have a few bruised ribs you can tend the same way . . ."

Though he didn't like to think of her being shot at or in pain, he swallowed hard when she stepped flush against him. Without hesitation, she captured his mouth with hers. His arms snaked around her waist and pulled her hard against him.

Her lips were soft and sweet, like Pearl's best dessert, only better. Much better, and far more enticing. She parted her lips, drawing him inward to taste and explore.

And he did. God help him, but he was lost. Maybe a part of him was using her to heal himself. Maybe he had no right.

Then why did this seem so right? Why now? Why this woman?

Sweet. That one word described and explained so much. After years of torment, of grieving, of living hell, he'd found this sweetness. Not her personality, but her response. Her generosity. Her spirit.

A still sane part of his brain knew Beth Dearborn would hate being thought of as sweet. Later—much later—he would tell her, and she might throw him to the floor again. At another time and place, the thought might have made him laugh. But not now.

He fused himself—mind, body, soul—to the sweetness. The now.

Their mouths became feverish, studying, claiming, consuming until Ty thought he'd die from craving more of her. She oozed more natural sexuality than any female he'd ever known, seen, or even imagined.

And then some.

She explored him with eager hands, her long fingers caressing the spot on his slightly bruised back where her knee had been planted night before last. Then she pulled his shirt from the waistband of his jeans. Her sighs of longing echoed his and filled his mouth, arousing the inferno that already burned him to his very soul.

Beth's movements became more frantic, almost jerky. Ty sensed her need matching his, and he knew she would not deny them tonight.

His shirt had snaps instead of buttons, and she took full advantage, ripping it open in what he considered a Beth-like manner. Her usual caution had no role here. She groaned into his mouth when her hands met his bare torso, and she broke their kiss to explore new territory, tracing small circles around his nipples with her tongue.

He was hot and hard and horny as hell.

"Beth?"

"Hmm?"

With a groan, he grabbed a handful of her T-shirt and tugged it upward, forcing her to break contact long enough to pull it over her head. "No bra," he whispered.

He barely caught a glimpse of her newly bared flesh before she resumed her teasing. He'd never known a man's nipples could be so . . . so . . .

Then she nipped him with her teeth and he growled. She lifted her head to stare at him and he swallowed. Hard.

How long would she torment him? How long would she make them both wait for what they both so obviously needed?

As if she'd heard his silent question, she unfastened his belt buckle, then released the five buttons of his fly.

"What's in there?" she asked, pressing the palm of her hand against his throbbing erection. "Mmm."

"Easy, Beth," he warned. "It's . . . been a while."

"Me, too." Her tone was filled with empathy. She pressed her bare breasts against his chest. "I want you, Ty."

"I'd say the same, but it'd be the understatement of the year."

His gaze dipped lower to her breasts, nicely rounded against his ribs. The only light in the room came from the hallway. "I should've turned on the lamp."

"We'll do that next time."

Next time. There would be a next time. He almost came then, but held himself in check. "I feel like a high-school kid going all the way for the first time," he confessed. "Don't know how long I can—"

She pressed a finger to his lips. "Stop."

Maybe he couldn't see her as clearly as he'd like, but he sure as hell *felt* the woman. Her nipples were firm nubs against his chest. She wasn't small and delicate. Not Beth. She was tall and sturdy and fearless, though she oozed feminine sexuality with every breath.

And for now—at least tonight—she was his.

His hands slid over smooth skin as he opened her jeans and savored the gentle slope of hip to waist. Then he brought his hands around and filled them with her delectable breasts. She responded by thrusting her hips even more firmly against him, and punctuated that with a strangled gasp.

He could definitely relate.

"I want all of you," he murmured.

"Ditto." She eased her hands into his jeans, flush against his hips, shoving them downward. "So what's stopping you?"

"I don't have . . ." He was a grown man. He should have kept condoms around, but there hadn't been a call for them in years. "Protection."

"I do."

He chuckled. "I should've known." And he kissed her hard and fast and deep.

She trembled as he savored every inch of her exposed flesh against his hands. But he wanted more.

He eased her down to the bed, dropped to one knee beside her without breaking their kiss. He cupped her breast again, brushed her nipple with his thumb until her moan filled him. She was everything he'd dreamed she would be. More.

Dragging his mouth from hers, he kissed his way

down her long, slender neck and found the rampant beat of her pulse. Gathering what patience he had left, he rested his lips there until she pressed her breast eagerly against his hand.

Her small, firm breasts had beckoned to him since that first day out on the highway. The fact that she walked around braless all the time added to her appeal. He seriously doubted she did that to entice men. No, Beth Dearborn probably did it for either comfort, practicality, or downright orneriness.

And he didn't care. All he knew was the need to taste her. He kissed his way lower, then returned the torture she'd inflicted earlier by using his tongue to trace the shape of her swollen nipples.

"Oh," she whispered, and gripped the back of his head with her hand. "That feels . . . amazing." She offered more of herself to him.

Starving for what she offered, he closed his mouth over her and feasted. She panted and raked the back of his neck with her short nails. Her soft purrs and moans urged him on, reminding him what they both wanted.

The feel of his erection brushing against his jeans reminded him that they weren't nearly as naked as they could be. "I think it's time we both shed some denim," he said.

"Past time."

He started to slide hers down her thighs, but she grabbed his wrist.

"Wait." She reached into her front pocket and withdrew something. "We'll need these."

"More than one. Good girl."

He pushed his jeans down and stood to completely rid himself of his boxers and socks. In the partial light from the doorway, he saw her reach toward him, holding her arms up to urge him back to bed.

Unable and unwilling to resist her invitation, he slid his long body against her softer one. They fit well together. Almost as if they'd been made for each—

Don't go there, Malone. Not now. Not yet.

She turned to face him, her mouth hot and hungry. Now all he had to do was remember how to ride a wild mustang.

Beth savored Ty's unique taste, hot and commanding. His kiss was thorough, wet, wicked, and she welcomed it, even while she yearned for more. Much more.

She wondered what surprising breakthrough she might discover next in this man's bed. His gentleness, wildness, sense of humor? Oddly, she felt no fear now, only wonder and want. No invading voices or memories—no horrifying images or nightmares. Only Ty.

Still, the niggling voice in the back of her mind told her to hold back, just a little. Keep control. Don't let go completely. Don't let down her guard. Don't let them get her when she wasn't looking.

Yet . . . as his lips left hers to drift down her throat again, the voices were drowned out by the roar of desire through her blood. Her breasts swelled against his firm chest, and she ached to feel his hot mouth tugging against her again.

Naked and yearning, she relished each touch of his lips, each stroke of his tongue against her flesh. She felt vaguely distanced from her body, almost an observer, yet acutely conscious of every spiraling need that thundered through her.

Like the storm, her mind tried to reason. *You're letting go, Beth. Losing control.*

But she couldn't stop this. She'd finally met a man strong enough to push her beyond her coveted self-control. No, not just him. It was their mutual, combined desire and need overshadowing all else. And she had no choice but to allow it to burn free.

That realization brought her a moment of terror, and she stiffened.

"You all right?" he asked, nibbling the lobe of her ear. "Should I stop?"

She laughed, a low throaty sound. "If you do, I'll have to throw you down again and have my way with you."

He didn't laugh. He hovered over her. "You'd better open that condom now."

"Oh, my." Beth caught her breath and opened one of the packets. She hadn't even had the chance to explore his body as much as she wanted yet. "You want to play rough, cowboy?"

"Right now I don't even care if you call me cowboy." He kissed her again to punctuate his statement.

The emptiness inside her clenched deep and hard where Ty would soon fill her. She tingled all over as she eased her hands between their bodies. He rose slightly to accommodate her.

He was hot. So hot. A scorching fire swept through her as she closed her hand around his impressive erection. "My, my," she whispered. "You *have* been holding out on me."

"You're killing me here."

"Not yet, I'm not." She savored the petal-softness

at his tip, the vital, pulsing power of his length. This was Ty, and she wanted him more than anything.

All of him.

Her hands trembled slightly as she rolled the condom over the tip of his penis and slowly down the length.

"Definitely killing me."

His words and his gasp made her laugh quietly again. The act of protecting them both didn't dampen their desire. On the contrary, it merely fueled their need.

Beth wrapped her arms around his muscular back and dragged her long legs up the backs of his. "What are you waiting for now?" she invited.

Her body cried out for his warmth as he abandoned her to the cool evening air and kissed his way down her belly. Instinctively, she tightened her grip on him, but he winced and slipped from her grasp, lowering himself between her thighs.

Beth hadn't anticipated this—not the first time. Anticipation erupted as gooseflesh as he kissed the curve of her hip and slipped his hands beneath her bottom to hold her. The part of her that wanted to maintain control tried to object, but couldn't. She couldn't break away.

She wouldn't.

He held her pleasure firmly in his hands, angling her hips to his will. There was a quiver of pleasure deep in her core, and it spread ruthlessly as he kissed her inner thighs and eased them farther apart.

Even though she knew his intent, she still gasped when his mouth covered her slickness. The man's tongue was wicked and wild and wonderful.

So much for being out of practice.

Scalding weightlessness filled her body as he brought her higher and higher toward total loss of control. She could only pray she returned unscathed.

All she knew was this gift of pleasure—beautiful, delicious, wanton pleasure. She'd denied herself this level of abandonment all her life, unless asleep or drunk or possessed by a dead spirit. This Beth savored pleasure and joy only for herself and for the now.

Just this once. Just this once . . .

He'd awakened in her something she'd never known existed. This strange, foreign, alien thing within her. This ability to want and need and *give* in turn. This slumbering yet potent emotion of which she'd been blissfully unaware until now.

Until Ty.

The fever ravaged her as she heard a strange animalistic sound and vaguely registered it as her own primal growl of pleasure. Her need was primitive, almost savage.

She buried her fingers in his hair and held him to her as she climbed toward a place she had tried, in the past, to avoid. Now she had to find it or die. Everything she had depended on this moment, his mouth, her body, and the incredible joy.

He pushed, he sought, he claimed. His hands on her hips held her captive as he ravaged her with the sweep of his tongue, the scrape of his teeth. Her head tossed from side to side and her hips thrust upward, demanding more than she could bear.

The first climax hit her like a punch as she shattered in his grasp. A tsunami of convulsive joy swept through her, carrying her away on a sensual voyage.

She had relinquished control, and nothing bad had happened. Beth wanted to shout her discovery to the world, but her lover was busy bringing her back to reality, and reminding her there was still more to come.

She felt herself actually blush at the double entendre. *What has* come *over you, Dearborn?*

Then, as he kissed her thighs again and eased himself slowly upward, she remembered what—and who—had come over her. He teased her belly button with his tongue and cupped her breasts with his farmer's hands. Every inch of her was so sensitized, she wanted to shout from the merest touch of his lips, his fingers.

But she knew there was more. And now he would give it to her—all of it. All of himself.

A foreign stinging sensation began building behind her eyelids, and she blinked. Beth Dearborn did *not* cry after good sex. What was that about?

She couldn't take the time to analyze her emotions now, because Ty and her hormones were in total command.

He touched her face, his fingers long, rough, and enticing. She tried to see his eyes but couldn't, so she conjured their turquoise depths from memory. It was enough, for now.

His mouth covered hers again, and she tasted herself, strange but not unpleasant. She moaned when he finally covered her with his body, all the while stroking her tongue with his own.

She might not have been with a man for a while,

but she wasn't some innocent virgin. She knew what came next. She wrapped her legs around his waist, reached between them, grasped his throbbing penis in her hand, and guided him home.

"Now, Ty. Now."

His deep thrust made her breath come out in a hiss of pure fulfillment. All those years of running and martial arts had left her toned and strong, and she used her lower body strength to hold him deep and hard and fast.

"This is gonna be over before it started, if you keep that up," he warned, nose to nose.

"Let's try it anyway." Beth wrapped herself around him like shrink-wrap. "Ride me, cowboy."

He tried to laugh, but it came out as more of a gasp. "Don't say I didn't warn you."

His voice was ragged, but his movements were slow and strong. Beth answered him stroke for stroke, hungry for every blessed inch, answering and wanting more.

Wet and hot, her body hugged and held him. A sigh left her lips each time he withdrew and returned to fill her again. And again.

She felt so whole, so . . . wanted.

As he found his rhythm inside her, his thrusts probed deeper, became more forceful. Even with her legs around his waist, Beth couldn't seem to get close enough, couldn't let this end without taking all he had to give.

He answered her unstated plea, demonstrating that she could not only take all of him, but that she could want him even more. The muscles of his shoulders and back were rigid cords beneath her hands.

Each stroke drove her closer to the brink. She fell

into a dark pit of pleasure and sensation, where thoughts and fears lost their power. Where painful memories surrendered to the more potent and pleasant forces of the present.

Her body contracted beneath and around him, drawing him inward and answering him thrust for thrust. Each time he buried himself inside her, she found a more delicious level of madness.

Her mind filled with a rainbow of colors. The colors gave way, blurring and dissolving completely when she came again. She surrendered to the physical urgency as the explosion crescendoed. She expected to make her way gently back to reality, but it happened again and again.

"Oh. My." She bucked against him, on fire. He took her higher and higher into this unknown place, this world of pure carnal bliss. Fractured yet complete, filled with only this man, as he brought her to orgasm again, seeming determined to keep her there.

Then Beth realized why this was different. She felt Ty—literally. Not only him inside of her, but his pulse, his heat, and his sensations. She sensed the length of him and tingled along with him.

Oh . . . oh, God. Did all men feel so hot inside when they had sex? This had never been part of her gift. Why was it different with Ty?

Maybe because she wanted it to be different? Better? More important? No, because it *was* better, different, and more important. She savored feeling what he felt. So she took that next step—that extra risk. She let her guard down even further. Deliberately.

Instead of fear and death and violence flooding her mind, sensation and tenderness enveloped her. No one and nothing except she and Ty existed now.

Joy filled her. Not only did she let him into her body in the most intimate way a woman can take a man, but she shared an even more sacred part of herself. Would he know it, somehow? Until now, she'd only had empathic experiences with the dead. Why this was happening, she didn't know, but she *liked* it.

She *loved* it. Loved him? *Later. Later.*

Slowing her rapid breathing, she gathered her thoughts, mentally unlocked the vault at the back of her mind she'd kept carefully blocked for so long. Ty merged more fully with her, and she welcomed him, savored every nerve ending.

Tears streamed down her face. He thrust into her, and they were one in every way. She was he and he was she, though perhaps only she was aware of it. It was as if she had splintered into two halves that perfectly fit together again as one.

In fact, she'd never felt so complete, so whole.

All the other implications could be dealt with later.

Slowly, she brought her hands to Ty's face and wished she could see his eyes as she felt his emotions join with hers, just as their physical sensations melded.

There were definitely only two people in this bed, and—in many ways—they were one.

He pushed deep, sure, and powerfully into her. She felt like heated silk to him, and he like molten steel. What a combination. Mother Nature definitely knew what she was doing.

She met and matched his every thrust, ready to revisit the joy he'd shown her, and now, to share his. Tiny fingers of heat bloomed inside her until one climax blended into the next. The convulsions merged into one long, exquisitely painful sensation.

Then he buried himself inside her and tensed. The heat built along his length. Pulsing pressure reached an unbearable point. He threw his head back and shouted, as did she.

Beth convulsed around him, taking his completion and her own as one. She shared his orgasm, which made her come yet again. He marked her with his completion, and they rocked together slowly. She held him with her body, her arms, her legs, stroking his back and shoulders as he strained against her, and she actually felt him empty himself.

So that's what it's like. A secret, knowing smile tugged at Beth's lips. *But only women get multiples.*

He peppered her face with tiny kisses and eased his weight off her, then rolled onto his side and gathered her against him. Beth rolled to her hip with her back against him, enjoying the tender kisses he rained across her shoulder.

Her throat filled and tightened, and she realized the combination of his emotions and hers had her struggling against more tears. The need to say the words in her heart drove at her, but she bit her lip to silence them.

Were they hers . . . or his?

CHAPTER SIXTEEN

Near dawn, Beth had a vague thought that she should tiptoe back to her own bed, but she couldn't quite bring herself to leave Ty's side. Besides, the kids weren't here to worry about.

She'd never known sex could be anything like this. And she'd sure as hell never known her gift could come in so handy. A smile curved her lips in the dark room. At some point, Ty must've turned off the light in the hall—probably while ditching the second condom.

She smiled again. If possible, the second time had been even more amazing than the first. And the man had warned her he wasn't sure how long he could last. She almost laughed.

He was an incredible lover. Patient, attentive, well-endowed, and long lasting. In fact, he'd worn her out. She was exhausted.

This new, unexpected perk to her empathy was a little quirk she wasn't prepared to share with her cousin, even though they'd always shared in the past. Sam used to say he envied the drama and magnitude of Beth's gift, while she wished hers could be as simple and undemanding as his. He often compared himself to a psychic errand boy, as the spirits of those who'd passed with something left undone or lost would seek him out to finish what they'd left, so they could move on to their eternal rest.

Beth felt something amazing drift over her as she lay spooned against Ty Malone, an emotion she'd never really known before. Contentment. She felt warm and wanted and safe in his bed. In his arms . . .

Her eyes drifted closed, and sleep overtook her sated body and relaxed mind.

"I know you're here."

The blonde woman's face appeared in Beth's dream, again blurred and semitransparent.

"I know you can help. Please help me."

No, go. Leave me. I can't help you. Helping you will hurt me, Beth tried to tell her.

"I need to go. I'm trapped. Please help me."

Beth didn't want to know the woman's name. Something stopped her from asking. Her subconscious didn't want to know.

"You have to help me. They hurt me. They killed me."

I know. Otherwise, you wouldn't be able to reach me. Please leave me alone. Wait for my cousin. He'll help you. I can't. I can't.

"You won't. You can, but you won't."

Guilt pressed down on Beth's dreamworld. She tried to push it away, but it shoved back with more force.

I can't help you. It will kill me.

"I'm already dead. They murdered me."

Don't ask who "they" are. Don't ask who she is, or was. Don't ask, Beth. Don't ask. Don't care. Don't help. Don't go back to that terrible place.

Nothing matters except staying sober. One day at a time, Dearborn. One day at a time.

"I was drunk," the woman said.

Could the spirit read Beth's thoughts? Did this empathy work both ways? She'd never been sought out in quite this manner before. Of course, in the past she'd usually walked right into the middle of these messes and asked for it.

Now she was running away from it with everything she had. Even in her dreams and nightmares.

I don't want to know about you, Beth told the dream woman. Please go away. Leave me alone. Wait for my cousin. He'll help you.

"I was going to get help, but they came for me too soon."

Stop! Please stop.

Beth saw the blurry woman walking—no, staggering— to the kitchen here in this house. She opened the pantry door and took a bottle from inside an empty oatmeal canister, and poured the rum into a blue glass. She drank it straight—no mix, no ice. Then she went to the sink, rinsed her glass, reached into her pocket, and squirted breath spray into her mouth.

"I needed help," she continued.

Please, don't. I want to wake up now.

"I had already called one of those clinics and made arrangements to check myself in the very next day. I can give you the name of it and you can check."

Beth stopped arguing with the woman and tried to block out her words. But she couldn't. The woman's spirit had gained strength, probably feeding off Beth's proximity. Hope was a powerful thing, and she'd obviously sensed Beth's ability, even in its diminished state.

Was Sam right? Did Beth have a responsibility to help this spirit? And what if she was Lorilee?

"Don't you know who I am?"

Don't tell me. I don't want to know.

"I saw them together the day before," she continued. "Sometimes I stopped at a little bar out on the highway. No one ever recognized me there. Until then."

Stop. Leave me be.

"I will leave here forever if you'll help me." The dream spirit actually sighed. "Make those who hurt me pay for what they did."

I already felt what happened to you.

"Yes, I know. Will you help me now?"

I can't. My cousin can help you. A little more than two weeks and he'll be here. You've already waited this long. Wait. Please wait.

"I'm not sure I can now."

What do you mean?

"Because of you."

Beth bolted up with a silent scream on her lips. She clutched at her throat, her heart lurched and thundered against her bruised ribs. Sweat trickled down her face, her neck, between her naked breasts.

Just a dream. Another nightmare.

But she knew better. She knew. The spirit in this house would not leave her be. To make matters worse, the woman had been a drunk. That was almost laughable, considering.

Beth glanced over her shoulder at Ty. Though she couldn't see his face in the dark, she knew from the steady sound of his breathing that he still slept soundly. At least she didn't have to explain her nightmare to him.

And—oh, God—she needed a drink. Which was precisely why she couldn't have one. She gnawed her lower lip and clenched her fists, trying not to remember the wine in the fridge Pearl had mentioned, or the liquor cabinet in the parlor downstairs.

No, she wouldn't go there. Not now—not ever.

Sam would be here in a little over two weeks. She could hold out that long.

And there was Ty. She didn't want to risk driving him away by getting falling-down drunk. And if she took one sip, she'd drink the entire bottle. Zero control, once she tasted the demon liquor.

So stop thinking about it, Dearborn.

She needed to understand why this one man had been able to share his lovemaking with her on an empathic level, when that had never happened with anyone else. There was some significance to that. She knew it as certainly as she knew her own name.

Very carefully, she slipped back beneath the covers, not wanting to disturb Ty. She wanted—needed— to feel his warmth against her. When his arm went around her waist, she sighed.

A lone tear escaped from the corner of her eye. Even so, she smiled just a little.

"You need a what?" Ty asked, shaking his head to make sure he'd heard Beth correctly.

"A gun." She smiled at him, the sheet tucked just under her arms, her bare shoulders smooth and flawless against the pale sheets. "The sniper's bullet destroyed my Glock."

"A Glock, huh?" He chuckled and nuzzled her shoulder. "Well, I know for a fact we don't have one of those around here, but there are some hunting rifles and an old shotgun."

"No handguns?"

He sat up and looked down at her. "I guess you have a license to carry a concealed weapon." Her answering look made him chuckle again. "There's an old forty-five, and some ammunition as well. You'll need to clean it."

"I just happen to know how to do that." She threw back the covers and swung her long legs over the edge of the bed. "I want to shower and dress before Pearl or your children show up and catch me in your room."

He sat up and caught her hand. "Beth, I . . ."

She bent down and kissed him full on the mouth. "Don't ruin it. There will be time for words later."

He nodded in resignation, unsure of exactly what he'd been about to say anyway. "That's a nasty bruise. Are you sure nothing's broken or cracked?"

Her smile lit up her entire face. "Think about it, Ty," she said and patted his cheek. "Think about it." Then she gathered her clothes off his bedroom floor and left, giving him a magnificent view of her slender backside.

"Mmm, mmm." Of course, she wouldn't have been able to perform the calisthenics in his bed—especially this morning's—with cracked or broken ribs. He grinned and stretched. "Coffee. Definitely coffee."

He pulled on a robe and slippers, then headed for the kitchen, figuring he'd give Beth first dibs on the hot water. Sure enough, as he passed her room he heard the shower come on. The urge to join her there struck him like a punch, and he actually stopped, turned, considered it, but realized Pearl would be scandalized if she came in to start breakfast and caught them in the shower together.

"Okay." He sighed. "Coffee." So he continued his trek down the stairs to the kitchen, ground the beans, measured the water, and started the coffee. While it brewed, he checked the Barncam from the kitchen monitor. Cissy and her filly looked just fine. Better than fine.

He visited a website to check the weather forecast, and that looked good, too. Then he did something he hadn't even considered doing until this very second.

He went to Google and typed in *Chicago* and *Detective Elizabeth Dearborn*. The number of hits was phenomenal—mostly newspaper archives and police reports, court records from cases in which she'd been involved. She'd mentioned once that she had been with Avery Mutual for three years, so he limited his search to prior years.

Why am I doing this?

Because he cared about her more than he should. Because she was keeping secrets, and he could never forget that Lorilee had kept secrets. He would always wonder if those secrets had led to her death. Her drinking? Some of her outings?

Was that the reason? Getting involved—he was *already* involved—with another woman of secrets scared the living hell out of him. Yeah, he supposed that was it. Partly. But there was also plain, old-fashioned curiosity. Why would someone give up a glamorous big-city Homicide position to work for an insurance company? Huge demotion. There had to be a reason . . .

DISTINGUISHED DETECTIVE RESIGNS FROM FORCE

Ty stopped at this headline, dated just a little over three years ago. He scanned the article quickly. It didn't tell him much, except that Detective Elizabeth Dearborn had solved every single murder case she'd been assigned with amazing efficiency, and that her sudden resignation had shocked the community. Though her methods had been considered somewhat unorthodox by some, she always brought evidence to the prosecutor that he could use in court. The article didn't explain the use of the term *unorthodox*, but now Ty's curiosity was really aroused.

When they grew to know and trust each other better, he would ask her himself. Meanwhile, enough snooping. He closed the browser and checked the Barncam again.

Nice.

"I smell coffee," Beth said from the doorway.

Ty looked up, startled. "I didn't even hear you come down the stairs."

"Barefoot." She looked down and wiggled her toes for emphasis. Her dark curls clung damply to the sides of her beautiful face.

"You're gorgeous."

"You aren't so bad yourself," she said, retrieving two mugs from the hooks under the cupboard. She poured them each a mug of steaming brew. "Black?"

"Yup." Ty accepted the mug and blew across the surface of the hot liquid before taking a tentative sip. "Mmm. Coffee."

"My favorite food group," Beth said with a laugh.

"I've heard that about cops." Ty grinned.

"But cops make hideous coffee, so don't ask me to do it." She returned his grin. "They teach us at the academy to make the worst possible pot of coffee imaginable."

He studied her expression as she sipped her coffee. "Do you miss it?" he finally asked, because he wanted to know.

She looked up, startled, then looked quickly away as if to shield her eyes from view. "Yes. Yes, I do." She walked around the kitchen and stopped at the computer monitor. "Ah, I see mother and baby are awake and seem to be fine."

"Yes." Ty joined her there to look down at the mare and foal. Cecil's image appeared on the monitor next. "Ah, if he's up and about, that means I'd better get my ass in gear or I'll never hear the end of it."

She reached behind him and patted the ass in question. "I think your ass does just fine."

He cupped her cheek with his free hand and kissed her mouth. "And yours is magnificent."

"My, my."

The moment Ty left the kitchen, Beth launched the browser on the monitor and checked the history. "Damn." She didn't feel angry as much as she simply felt betrayed.

Why was Ty checking up on her? Why now? Why the morning after, so to speak?

"Dammit, Ty," she muttered just as she heard the keys in the back door. That would be Pearl, of course. She cleared the history herself, then closed the browser window just as the door creaked open.

"Up bright and early, I see," Pearl greeted. "I thought you might sleep in after all the excitement around here last night."

Beth leaned against the counter, holding her mug in both hands. "Another day, another dollar."

"You sound like my Cecil." She chuckled. "He's already down at the barn checking on the new filly."

"We saw him on the webcam." Beth took a sip of coffee.

"Oh, Ty's awake, too." She poured herself a cup of

coffee. "I'll rustle up some breakfast as soon as I start my engines."

Beth smiled at the older woman—someone she admired more every day. "He headed up to shower after he made the coffee," she explained. "I told him to never trust a former cop to make coffee."

"Just like on TV?" Pearl laughed and went to the refrigerator to pull out eggs and bacon.

Beth, when she ate breakfast, was more the yo-gurt-and-granola type. She remembered last night's beef stew and asked, "You don't worry much about cholesterol out here, do you?"

Pearl looked up at her with a knowing smile. "Sure we do, but we eat real food—not the fake stuff you get in the city. You won't find any instant this or con-venient that in my kitchen, Beth. It's all real."

She nodded. "And delicious, I might add."

"Thank you kindly." Pearl retrieved a cast-iron skillet, which must've weighed a ton, from a hook over the massive range. "Are you going to eat a real breakfast this morning, or wait until your belly but-ton is makin' love to your backbone again, like you did yesterday?"

Beth snorted coffee through her nose and grabbed a napkin from the holder on the table. "Don't do that when my mouth's full."

Pearl laughed. "I guess you haven't heard that say-ing before."

"No, I can't say it's common in Chicago." Beth tried to ignore the heat churning in her loins, into her belly, and possibly spreading across her collarbones and up her neck to bloom in her cheeks. Pearl's refer-ence to making love had triggered Beth's memories of her hours spent in Ty's bed. Surely the woman didn't know or suspect, though she did know they'd spent the night alone together here.

And now Ty was checking up on her. Beth drew a deep breath and hoped her displeasure at this discovery wasn't obvious to anyone—especially to Ty.

"I'm just going to call and see what time Bill's bringing the children home, so I'll know how much food to fix," Pearl said, and dialed his number on the kitchen wall phone. She chatted for a few minutes, then asked over her shoulder, "Are you sure it's safe now?"

Beth shrugged. "We have no way of being a hundred percent certain, since we don't know who was shooting at me," she said. "But we do know they were shooting at only *me*."

Pearl repeated that—more or less—to whichever of the Brubakers she had on the phone. After another moment, she held the receiver toward Beth. "Wants to talk to you now."

"Oh, for crying out . . ." With a sigh, Beth set her coffee mug on the table, dabbed at her nose again with the napkin, and took the receiver from Pearl. "Beth Dearborn here."

"Good morning, Ms. Dearborn," a silken drawl said. "We didn't get a chance to speak again at Mark's party. I just wanted to let you know the sheriff upset my husband yesterday, and it's all your fault. You just had to dredge up that nasty old letter again. Didn't you?"

Beth wanted to hoot with laughter at "nasty old letter," but she resisted the impulse. She deserved a medal or something. "I assume I'm speaking to Mrs. Ruby Brubaker. Is that correct?"

"Yes, of course."

"I'll be happy when we have the long-overdue handwriting analysis back from the experts," Beth stated very carefully. "Is there anything else you'd like to know?"

"In the future, I'd appreciate it so *very* much if you'd refrain from upsetting my happy little home, Ms. Dearborn." The woman's voice was sweetened with battery acid.

Pearl pointed a finger to her head and rotated it in the universally recognized signal for craziness. Beth wanted to snort again, but resisted—that made two medals. Yes, she was counting.

"I have a job to do here, Mrs. Brubaker," Beth said very carefully. "And I intend to do it. Your husband and I have already discussed this, and he seemed fine with me dredging all—"

"Dredging what?" Grandma Ruby asked sharply.

"I believe I explained to Mr. Brubaker the necessity of having the letter analyzed. Now if you'll excuse me?" Beth handed the receiver back to Pearl before the woman could say another word. She could hear her raising her voice even after she crossed the room to retrieve her coffee cup.

After Pearl hung up the phone, she said, "Sorry. That woman just grates on the nerves."

"She does, and I don't even know her."

Pearl set the bowl of eggs on the counter. "Mr. Brubaker will have the kids here in about half an hour, so I'll start breakfast now."

"Great. If you don't need me for anything, I'm going to make a few phone calls."

"I've been cooking breakfast by myself a long time, child. Run along."

Beth headed up the stairs to her room, hoping she

wouldn't run into Ty just now. She needed to gather her thoughts after learning he'd googled her.

In all honesty, could she blame him? He barely knew her, and they'd already slept together. Plus, anyone would be curious about why a person would give up a job like the one she'd had for her current position.

So now he probably knew she was the most decorated homicide detective in the department's history. Would he wonder why? Did it matter?

She paused at the door to her room. Yes, it mattered. He mattered. And that's why she was so frigging upset about the whole mess.

Right now she wanted to call Sam. She just wanted to hear her cousin's voice. That was all. Nothing more, nothing less.

It really galled her that Ty didn't trust her, though—she sighed—she had to admit she'd do the same if the situation were reversed. He hardly knew her, after all. Even so, she still felt betrayed and more than a little wounded. Telling herself the man was justified didn't help much.

She walked into her room and saw sunlight spilling through the curtains onto the colorful quilt. Like a spotlight, the sun's rays shone directly on a handful of bright yellow flowers in the center of the bed. Daffodils, maybe. Even a city dweller like Beth Dearborn knew they were early spring flowers.

She stepped farther into her room and saw something else. Closer to her pillow, beyond the spot of sunshine, was a wooden box. On the outside it read "Colt 45." She opened the box. It was in exquisite condition. Someone had obviously taken excellent care of the old firearm. It looked like a John Browning clone. An unopened package of ammunition sat beside it.

She noticed the plate on the underside of the gun case's lid and wiped away the smudges and tarnish to read the words inscribed there.

Presented to Sergeant John T. Malone,
United States Army, for bravery.
August 2nd, 1972.

Beth whistled low. Was John T. Malone Ty's father? Had he served in Nam? And this was his gun?

She sat down hard on the bed with the box clutched in her lap, then reached for the bouquet of handpicked flowers and held them to her cheek, hoping tears wouldn't wilt them.

Maybe he did trust her.

CHAPTER SEVENTEEN

Guilt over his snooping that morning made Ty feel uneasy, and he wondered if he should confess to Beth. Plus, he was curious about why she had left the police force. He supposed he could ask her that without confessing, but it seemed dishonest.

Sometime today he would find the time to talk to her and hoped she would understand. That seemed unlikely, since even he really didn't understand his motive. It had been pure whim.

No, that was a lie. He knew exactly why he'd snooped. Beth Dearborn was a woman with secrets, and that scared the holy crap out of him, because Lorilee had also been a woman with secrets. He didn't want to lose another woman that way . . .

Until he learned the truth about Lorilee, he would always wonder. Would he ever stop wondering? Doubting? Would Beth ever trust him enough to reveal her secrets?

As he completed his early morning chores with Cecil, his thoughts kept drifting back to the night of lovemaking with Beth. The woman was full of surprises, and he had never felt as close to anyone. Something very unique had passed between them—

something he'd never experienced before and had no way to define or describe, even to himself.

All he knew was he wanted it to happen again.

And again.

He needed to think a lot about exactly what that meant, and what she meant to him. How could she possibly fit into his life? Would she want to? A big-city homicide detective living on a farm in Tennessee seemed unlikely as hell.

But she'd left that life for some reason. So, maybe she wanted something else. Something more. Maybe she wanted Ty Malone.

Did he want her on a permanent basis?

He stopped mucking out Cissy's stall and leaned on the pitchfork's handle. She seemed a little distant with the kids, except for Sarah, though she and Pearl sure hit it off well.

His empty belly churned. Coffee and stomach acid made poor partners when stress was thrown into the mix.

What the hell was he thinking? Premature thoughts for sure. Legally, at least, Ty Malone was still a married man.

First things first.

He needed to help Beth complete this investigation to prove his wife was dead, so Lorilee could rest in peace and her reputation could be restored in the community for the sake of their children. That was Sarah's wish, and the reason he'd filed the life-insurance claim and petitioned the court.

And what had brought Beth here. He smiled to himself.

"Hmm. The kinda look you got on your face this

mornin' makes me curious." Cecil's voice interrupted Ty's thoughts. The older man filled Cissy's trough with fresh water and gave Ty a questioning glance. "I ain't stupid, Ty. Me 'n Pearl both noticed the heat passin' between you two."

Ty knew better than to dodge Cecil. The man knew him better than anyone, and had been like a second father to him since his return to Tennessee. He tipped back his hat and met the man's gaze. "Did you, now?"

"Sure. Kinda hard to miss, son." Cecil grinned and winked knowingly. "And Ms.—I mean, Beth—is a fine-lookin' woman."

"That's a fact." Ty smiled. "And competent."

Cecil laughed out loud. "Competent?"

"At investigating." Ty tried to keep his expression bland, but he knew Cecil was on to him. "What are you getting at, old man? Just say it."

"Oh, she's definitely good at her job. Ain't nobody denyin' that." Cecil leaned his elbow against the stall door while the filly nursed and Cissy ate the sweet feed he'd given her. "But I don't think that's what's got you makin' owl eyes after her every move, son."

Ty had to grin at Cecil's word choice. "Point taken," he said. "I'll bet breakfast is about ready."

"I reckon." Cecil's expression grew solemn, and as Ty exited the stall, he placed a fatherly hand on his shoulder. "Just be careful, Ty."

Ty nodded, not trusting his voice. Cecil would know immediately if he lied. And he wasn't ready to tell the old man it was too late for him to "be careful."

He was already in too deep.

* * *

Professor Sam Dearborn looked at the rental-car company's map again. "What the devil have you gotten me into this time, Beth?"

A major tornado had damaged the campus enough to warrant an early end to spring semester classes. As far as Sam was concerned, it was fate, because he was meant to make this trip sooner. The damage was confined to academic buildings, and the students were ecstatic about the short break to prepare for final exams.

And Sam had decided to take this opportunity to check up on Cousin Beth.

She worried him. And they were the only family either of them had left. He'd made a vow to help her stay clean and sober, and she insisted the only way to do that was to avoid empathic encounters.

So here he was in Bumfuck, Tennessee. Correction—he couldn't even find Bumfuck on the damned map!

He looked down at the gas gauge—still more than half-full. What was it Dad used to say? If you have gas in the car, you aren't lost. He smiled in remembrance and looked at the map again as another pickup truck sped past him on the two-lane highway.

Of course, if he'd been able to fly into Knoxville and drive in through Brubaker, he wouldn't be having this problem. But the damaged bridge had required him to approach from the opposite direction. The rental car clerk had seemed competent enough when she'd traced his route with a green marker, so he concentrated on those marks and looked at the road sign ahead.

He was heading the right direction. It looked as if

his turnoff to the Malone place should be right over the next hill. "Just momentary panic." He cleared his throat and glanced at his cell phone again. Ah, finally he had a weak signal. Since he was pulled over onto the shoulder, he decided to warn his cousin of his pending arrival.

"Dearborn," she answered.

"Didn't look at caller ID?" he asked. She usually used his name immediately upon answering.

"Sam!" Her voice sounded odd. Strained. Or maybe she had a cold. "I was about to call you."

"Well, get ready for a surprise. If I'm reading this map right, I should be at the Malone farmhouse within half an hour or so."

Silence.

"Beth?"

"I'm here."

"I thought you wanted me to come."

"I do."

"What's wrong?"

"Nothing. Everything."

"Beth? Speak English."

"Things are getting strange here."

Sam laughed. "Honey, our entire lives have been strange. *We're* strange."

"True." She sighed. "Someone cut the brake lines on my car, first."

"You're all right?" His heart slammed into his chest. "No accident?"

"No, I'm fine." She sighed into the phone. "And then a sniper took a shot at me last night."

"Somebody definitely doesn't want you around, my dear."

"No shit."

"So maybe you should leave."

"I . . . I . . . can't."

"Can't?"

More silence.

"Beth?"

"I don't want to leave."

Sam let his head fall back against the headrest. "It's the man. This Ty person. Isn't it?"

"Yes." Another sigh. "I think it's serious, Sam. I'm scared."

Makes two of us. Sam didn't want anything or anyone to push his cousin off the wagon, but if she had a shot at true happiness, he was all for it. All he knew for certain was that he had to meet this man.

"What are you more worried about now, Beth?" he asked. "The spirit in the house, or this relationship?"

"Both." She cleared her throat. "Sam, I'm more and more convinced that the spirit in the foyer is Ty's wife."

"Why do you believe that?"

"I've been dreaming about her."

"Explain."

"She's trying to contact me when I'm asleep."

"You aren't as capable of shutting her out then."

"Exactly."

"She knows you're there and knows you can communicate with her." Sam tapped his long fingers on the steering wheel. "Let's finish this in person. I want to meet Ty Malone. And the spirit, if she'll engage me."

"I want that, too," Beth said. "More than you can imagine."

Oh, Sam could imagine. He'd been the one to carry Beth into the treatment facility, to sit beside her through the tremors that ravaged her body as she withdrew from alcohol. He'd sat with her through counseling sessions, through AA meetings . . .

He could definitely imagine.

"I'm here now, Beth. I'm here." He chuckled and glanced at the map again. "Well, almost."

"Drive carefully. And thanks, Cuz."

Sam disconnected and eased off the shoulder and back onto the highway—what passed for one in this part of Tennessee, anyway. He hit an open stretch and increased his speed, hoping to find the turnoff soon and make up for lost time.

He glanced in his rearview mirror as he crested the next small hill and saw flashing lights. Seven miles over? He should've known when the rental agency gave him a car with New York plates that this would happen.

Resigned to being even later than planned, he pressed on the brake and pulled back onto the shoulder. The state trooper pulled up behind him, climbed out of his car, tugged on his belt, and started toward Sam's rental.

He sank lower in his seat, thinking about the old Charlie Daniels song, "Uneasy Rider." Good God, he was even driving a Chevrolet. Sam glanced in his mirror again. He definitely should've lost the ponytail and earring before this trip.

"Mornin'," the trooper greeted as Sam lowered the Chevy's automatic window. "Where you headed in such an all-fired hurry, boy?"

Boy? Sam forced a tight smile. "I'm looking for the Malone Farm. Am I lost?" He didn't acknowledge that he'd been over the speed limit. He'd either get ticketed or he wouldn't.

"Ty Malone's place?"

"Yes, sir."

"Next left turn. You're almost there." The trooper leaned against the car, sunlight reflecting off his mirrored sunglasses. He grinned like a Cheshire cat. "I'm not gonna write you a ticket today, because just seein' that hair and bling of yours is enough entertainment to make my day. You got balls, boy. New York plates and a damn ponytail. Don't that beat all?" He laughed and shook his head. "Just ease back on that pedal some. Lots of slow farm equipment pulling on and off this stretch of road. Hear?"

Still chuckling, the alleged officer of the law made his way back to his vehicle and drove away.

"Entertainment, is it?" Sam figured he should be insulted, but at least the asshole had said he had balls. "Damn right."

At least now he knew he was on the right road. "I'm coming, Beth. Hang in there."

The children chattered enough about the new filly to keep breakfast from being as strained as it might have been, considering. Beth's mind was occupied, awaiting Sam's arrival, but she was also busy listening to Bill and Ruby Brubaker's conversation.

Why was Grandma Ruby so adamant that Beth not investigate Lorilee's disappearance? Why had she convinced Bill not to have the letter analyzed when it first arrived? It didn't make sense. Family wanted answers about the people they loved when they disappeared. If Beth had learned anything during her years of investigative work, that was it. Whether it was missing persons or homicides, families wanted *answers*.

And Ruby had convinced Lorilee's father to stop looking for those answers. There had to be a reason, and Beth had a hunch—nothing else to go on—that Ruby's reason might prove important. At any rate, Beth's detective antennae were buzzing.

The moment the meal was finished, all three children dragged both grandparents out to the barn to visit the new filly. Ty had appointed them the job of naming the new addition. Cecil went along to ensure Cissy didn't object to all the attention. Ty promised to join them shortly.

Beth's bullshit detector went on alert. He was lagging behind for a reason, and she was willing to bet it had something to do with her. Pearl went to work cleaning the breakfast dishes and refused Beth's offer of help, so she headed into the parlor, wondering if Sam had managed to get lost despite his assurances that he was so close.

She stood gazing out the front window and felt Ty's presence behind her. They hadn't spoken privately since early this morning, right after she'd caught him investigating her online. Of course, he didn't know she knew.

"What are you staring at?" he asked, and placed his hands on her shoulders.

She squeezed her eyes shut and rested her cheek against one of his hands. "Nothing at all. Just thinking." She turned to face him. "Thank you for trusting me with the Colt, Ty."

"I know you'll take good care of it." He rested his hands at her waist, his thumbs gently caressing her lower ribs. "How's your bruise?"

"Sore, but it will heal. Could've been worse."

"Yeah." He blanched. "Tell me about it."

She saw genuine dread in his eyes, and heard it in his voice. "Thank you for caring." She kissed him very quickly. "Was that Colt your father's?"

He nodded. "Dad was in Nam. When he was discharged with a Purple Heart and a Meritorious Service Medal, his commander presented him with it as personal thanks."

"It's very special. I'll be extra careful with it." She grasped his arms, just above his elbows. "There are things you don't know about me, Ty—things about my past."

"Quick change of subject," he said quietly. "Is it bad?"

"It's . . . hard for most people to believe." She smiled and drew a deep breath. "My cousin is arriving this morning. In fact, he should've been here by now."

"Cousin?"

"Yes, his name is Sam." She stepped away from Ty and back to the window. "He's a college professor. Philosophy." She shot a wry grin over her shoulder.

"Philosophy?" Ty arched an eyebrow. "Okay. So why is he coming to Tennessee, Beth? What aren't you telling me?"

"Ty . . . I know you googled me this morning," she said without really thinking. His shoulders fell, and the guilty expression on his face almost made her laugh. "Ty?"

"That's why I sent everybody out to the barn. The guilt is killing me." He pressed his lips into a thin line and exhaled slowly. "I don't know what made me do it. The computer was there, and I was checking weather—farmers do that. The next thing I knew, I'd typed your name into the search engine."

She tilted her head to one side. He seemed sincere, but she sensed there was more. "And . . . ?"

"I guess I wondered why you gave up the glamorous life as a hero to work as an insurance-company dick." He flashed her a sheepish grin.

"That's understandable, and part of what I need to explain." She sighed. "And what Sam will help me explain once he arrives."

He narrowed his eyes, his grasp on her waist tightening. "Beth, does this have anything to do with what happened the first time you walked in this house?"

"Yes." She swallowed hard, trying not to remember.

"And what you told me last night about having to 'show' me?"

"Yes again." She shook her head very slowly. "None of this will be easy for you to understand or accept, but it may give both of us a lot of answers."

"I trust you," he said, and pulled her into his into the warmth of his embrace. He kissed the top of her head, the lobe of her ear. "Mmm."

"I wish we could disappear upstairs together for a while," she whispered.

"Are you reading my mind?" Ty chuckled low.

Guilty pleasure at sharing his feelings oozed through her. "Mmm, something like that." How would he feel about knowing just how much he'd shared with her last night?

He held her at arm's length and gazed into her eyes. "A Chevy screaming rental with New York plates is creeping up the drive."

"Sam!" Beth started toward the front door, then

remembered why she couldn't. "Damn." She did an about-face and raced toward the kitchen and the mudroom door, but not before she received the whispered plea from the foyer loud and clear.

"*Help me.*"

CHAPTER EIGHTEEN

Beth bolted out the back door. Ty gave Pearl an apologetic glance and followed as fast as he could. The woman could *run*.

Of course, with legs like hers, he should've known. She launched herself into the arms of the tall man who'd barely climbed out of the rental car. Definitely a family resemblance, but if Ty hadn't known in advance, he might've been jealous of the warm reception she gave the guy.

She stopped hugging him, but kept hold of his hand when Ty reached them. "Ty, this is my cousin, Sam Dearborn, from Chicago." She looked at her cousin. "Sam, this is Ty Malone."

Cousin Sam was a tall one. He towered over Beth, who had to be at least six feet. The ponytail and diamond stud seemed out of place on such a big man.

He extended his right hand. "Welcome, Professor Dearborn."

"Oh, please—call me Sam," he said in a deep voice that matched his size as he shook Ty's hand. "I gather Beth has been learning about farm life." Sam looked around. "Lots of . . . open space here."

"There is that." Ty grinned. This one was even

more citified than Beth. "Beth tells me you teach philosophy."

"I do, yes," Sam said. "I only have a few days to help Beth with a—"

She elbowed her cousin and turned the full power of her smile on Ty. "Sam was worried when he heard about the sniper."

"Sniper? Yes, the sniper. Sniper?" Sam rubbed his ribs. "This should be interesting. By the way, Beth, I love the hair." He gave a tight smile. "Well, it's been a long trip, and I wonder if you'd mind if I use the facilities before we visit further."

Facilities? Ty arched a brow. "Sure. No problem. There's a half bath just off the foyer, inside the front door there."

Sam gave him a mock salute and Beth a look that told Ty he definitely wasn't in on their little secret. Beth returned to hold his hand and watched her cousin enter the front door. Of course, she didn't go near it.

Sam looked back and gave her a thumbs-up sign. Ty chuckled. "What the hell kinda game are you two playing?" he asked. "I may be a farmer, but I'm not stupid, Beth. You're scared shitless of my foyer, and he made a beeline for it. Give."

She sighed. "I was trying to explain inside, when Sam arrived."

"I'm still listening."

The front door opened again and Sam came down the porch steps. "You're not worried about any more snipers out here?" he asked, looking around at all the openness.

"I'm not sure the shooter will try the same method

twice," Beth said, and she looked toward the barn, thinking again about Ruby. "Instinct."

"Interesting thing, instinct," Sam said. "I had sort of a . . . feeling about the foyer of your house, Ty."

"Imagine that." He folded his arms across his abdomen. "You two really oughta consider taking this act on the road."

Beth's cheeks actually reddened. "Did she engage you, Sam?"

"Yes, but not in the way she wants to engage *you*." It was Sam's turn to feign innocence.

"Criminy. Why don't you two just spill the beans here?" Ty held his hands out, palms up, in surrender. "You're confusing the hell out of me. Who's engaging whom and for what? Pearl's the only person in the house right now."

Beth faced him and took both his hands in hers. "This is what I was trying to explain to you when Sam arrived, Ty."

"Then explain it now." He shot a look at Sam, who shook his head. "Your cousin says it's your show, Beth."

"Sam and I share a genetic gift."

"You do look a lot alike," Ty admitted. "What gift, besides brains and good looks?" He jabbed a finger at Sam. "Don't get any ideas."

Sam laughed. "Not to worry, cowboy. I don't swing that way."

"I am *not* a cowboy."

"Touchy, aren't we?"

"Beth!" Ty gave her hands a hard squeeze. "Now, please."

"We're empathic, Ty. Some would call it psychic,

and that's true to a certain extent, especially for Sam, but—"

"Whoa, hold on a minute here." Ty removed his hat and raked his fingers through his hair. Maybe the sun was hotter than he'd realized. "I don't buy into this metaphysical nonsense. Try again."

"It's not metaphysical. It's genetic."

"Genetic. Like in your DNA? Like having blue eyes or brown hair?" Ty rolled his eyes. "Sure. Right. I really buy that happy horseshit."

Beth gave his hands a squeeze. "You read the articles about me online, Ty. How do you think I solved all those murders?"

He thought back to the "Distinguished Detective" article and the mention of "unorthodox methods." He really wanted to believe her. Trust her. He needed to, because . . . well, just because.

"I'm not sure, Beth," he said in complete honesty. "Tell me."

"Do you remember the first day we came here together?"

He nodded. "I'll never forget. You almost keeled over and kept asking me if anybody'd ever . . . died in this house."

She nodded vigorously.

Ty looked at Sam, whose expression told him he was on the right track. "Okay, so you're telling me that you used some kind of psychic mumbo jumbo to solve all those murders back in Chicago?"

"After a fashion," Sam said when Beth remained silent. He reached out and put a hand on his cousin's shoulder. "It was much more . . . dramatic for her than that, I'm afraid. And far more personal."

"Personal? What does that mean?" Ty didn't understand at all. He shoved his hat back on his head. He wished Beth would reach for his hands again, but she didn't.

"I told you I'd have to show you." Her expression was stricken. Pained. "You won't believe me unless you see for yourself."

"I—I'm sorry, Beth, but this is just too weird for me." He reached for her hands, but she pulled back.

Sam kept his hand on her shoulder. It was clear the cousins were as close as brother and sister.

"Sam, tell me what you think you—what's the right word?—sensed in my house just now. Please?"

The big man's expression grew solemn, his hazel eyes—the same shade as Beth's—held sadness. "I'm not sure either of you are ready to hear this."

"I am," Beth said. "Please, Sam. I begged you to come here for this."

The cousins held each other's gaze for several seconds, then faced Ty again. Sam took her hand and pressed it into Ty's.

"You're going to need each other while you hear this."

Beth bit her lower lip and looked up at Ty, meeting his gaze directly for the first time in several minutes. "I think I know what he's going to tell us."

"My God," Ty said, his grip tightening. "It's Lorilee."

Sam nodded. "The spirit in your foyer was known in this world as Lorilee Brubaker-Malone."

Beth swayed and Ty slid his arm around her shoulders. "So Lorilee has a message for both of us," she said. "What did she ask you to do, Sam?"

He gave her a sad smile. "Two things, actually." He looked at Ty now. "The way this gift works with me is that those who've died and left things unfinished often can't rest in peace."

Ty nodded, seeming as if he really wanted to accept this. "I'm listening." He looked at Beth. "I'm trying to understand. And . . . this means Lorilee really is dead." He squeezed his eyes shut. "Right here in our home."

Beth squeezed his hand. "Yes, that's what it means, and there's more." She sighed and gave Sam a knowing look. "You finish first, Cuz."

"Lorilee wants you, Ty, to know she's sorry about the . . . secret drinking." He shot a quick look at Beth, then turned his full attention back to Ty. "And she wants you to know that she made an appointment to have herself admitted for treatment."

Ty rubbed his eyes with the thumb and forefinger of his free hand, keeping the other around Beth's shoulders. "I knew she had a drinking problem, and I've been kicking myself all this time for not doing something about it." He sighed. "Intervention, I think it's called."

"Yes, that's what it's called," Beth said, her stomach in knots. Ty didn't deserve another woman in his life with a drinking problem. "Go on, Sam. What else did she tell you?"

"About her diary." He returned his attention to Ty. "She wants you to give it to the lady who can help her." He shook his head. "She was a little vague about where she'd left it, though."

"The lady who can help her?" Ty shook his head. "Who—?"

"Me. She means me." Beth pressed the heel of her

hand to her forehead. "I'm the one who can help her. She's been trying to engage me since I first stepped through your front door."

She felt Ty's gaze on her and drew a deep breath before meeting it. "Ty, it's time you understood *my* gift, and all its implications."

"Right now isn't the time," Sam said, looking beyond them. "Looks like a mob headed this way."

"Mob?" Ty looked over his shoulder and chuckled, though his heart couldn't have been in it. "That 'mob' is my family."

"Ah, sorry about that," Sam said. "Which reminds me that Lorilee also said how much she loves and misses her babies, and that she thinks you're doing a beautiful job raising them."

"We need to find that diary," Beth said as they all stood there waiting for the children and their grandparents. "Any ideas, Ty?"

He nodded. "My guess is the studio."

"I'll start there," she said. "I noticed something else while going over my notes this morning."

"What's that?"

"Today is the anniversary of her disappearance."

"Death," Ty corrected.

"Murder," Beth added.

Ty looked from Sam to Beth, then back again, finally settling on Beth. "I guess she didn't remove her own body from the place where she died."

"No, of course not." Beth gave his hand another squeeze. "The date of her death can be very powerful for empathic purposes." She looked at Sam for correlation, and he nodded. "And I need to have Sam here when I engage Lorilee."

"I'll ask Bill to take the kids back home with him tonight."

"Good," Beth said. "I think that's best. Can we send Pearl and Cecil on a trip or errand?"

"You don't want any witnesses?"

Beth shook her head. "This is incredibly painful for me, Ty."

Sam cleared his throat. "She wouldn't risk this for just anybody." Anger punctuated his words. "Be grateful and cooperate."

Ty met Sam's gaze, and Beth sensed the two men squaring off, the way men do. This was the proverbial male pissing contest. She finally sighed and said, "Knock it off—both of you."

"Okay, Beth," Sam said. "It's just that we both love you. That's all."

Beth couldn't look at Ty after that comment, but she also made a mental note that he hadn't denied the feelings Sam had attributed to him. Was that what she wanted?

She was terrified of the answer.

"Daddy, Daddy, Daddy!" Grace shouted as she threw herself at her father. "What a pretty pony!"

"She's not a pony, honey," he said, gathering his youngest child in his arms and squeezing his eyes tightly shut.

The man had just learned his wife was really dead, but he didn't have the proof. He needed that, so he could tell his children. Beth's resolve grew.

Sarah said, "I think we have a name, Dad."

"What?"

"Stormy," Mark answered. "She's the color of rain clouds."

"We thought Cloud at first, but Stormy is bestest," Grace said matter-of-factly.

"Well, then, Stormy it is." Ty waited until Bill and Ruby had joined them, then introduced them all to Sam Dearborn.

After all the introductions, Ruby asked, "Are you an investigator, too?"

Sam laughed. "A college professor."

Bill leaned close to Ruby and asked, "Didn't you see the earring?" He didn't bother to whisper.

Beth had a hunch Ty was working on a scheme that would send the children away overnight again. She didn't know exactly what, but having the kids around while she faced her gift and her demons would be too risky.

Finally, he said, "Bill, I seem to recall Sarah mentioning that Hannah Montana would be in Nashville tonight."

"Is that so?" Bill winked at his wife. "Who's Hannah Idaho?"

"Montana, Grandpa," Sarah and Grace both corrected, laughing.

"I forgot to get tickets." Ty shook his head. "My mind's been on this investigation. But I remember you have some connections . . ."

Beth had already discerned from Mark's birthday party that there was nothing Bill Brubaker liked better than spoiling his grandchildren, and playing the role of Daddy Warbucks while he was at it.

He puffed up and said, "Let me make a call. I'll see what I can do."

After a minute, he asked, "How many tickets?"

Ty said, "We three have to stay here for the investigation, but why not take Cecil and Pearl along? They've earned some time off, and they can help you with the kids."

"Excellent idea." Bill finalized the deal and disconnected his BlackBerry. "Well, y'all, if we're going to Nashville, we'd better get packing. Especially you, Ruby Slowpoke."

Grandma Ruby rolled her eyes and said, "Woo-hoo. Hannah Montana."

Mark grinned and said, "I think she's pretty hot."

That comment from a twelve-year-old broke the tension, for at least a few minutes. Even Beth, Ty, and Sam managed to laugh. Mark didn't seem to get the joke.

"All right, you two," Ty said when they were alone. "Let's go diary hunting."

What he really wanted to do was take Beth with the haunted eyes to bed for some long, slow massage and lots of gentle lovemaking. Though he didn't know what to make of this "empathic" stuff, he knew one thing: her cousin had been dead right when he'd said they both loved Beth. How it had happened so fast, Ty couldn't imagine, but he was in love with this woman. And he didn't want her to hurt. The pain in her eyes was eating away at him.

"Lorilee said the diary is in a decorative wooden box," Sam explained as they climbed the stairs single file to her attic studio.

"Okay," Ty said. "Did Beth tell you I haven't moved anything up here since Lorilee's death?"

Sam whistled low. "Lots of dust bunnies?"

"Not in Pearl's domain," Beth said. "It's clean

enough, but everything is where it was the day Lorilee died."

"A pity we can't convince her to just come up here and show us where it is," Sam said dryly.

"We only have until tomorrow afternoon, so let's get cracking," Ty suggested. Even though proving his wife's death had been the goal, he still wasn't comfortable with the concept, because he didn't have real *proof.* It wasn't as if he could tell anyone or put the gossips in their place.

He hadn't entered the attic since that first day he and Beth had come up here together. The children came up occasionally, but only with Pearl's permission, and for a specific purpose. So Pearl was the only person who should have had access to the room in the last few days.

Ty opened the closed door at the top of the narrow staircase and immediately knew someone had been there. Papers were scattered everywhere, drawers were pulled completely out of the files and upended.

"Holy shit," he said.

"Someone beat us here," Beth said from behind him.

"Looking for the diary?" Sam asked as they all emerged into the ransacked room.

Ty shook his head. "I don't think anyone else knew she kept one."

"Looking for *anything* I might find that could incriminate him or her," Beth said, nodding matter-of-factly. "We made it common knowledge that I intended to go through Lorilee's files up here." She held her hands out to indicate the room. "And now we have this, on top of two attempts on my life."

Ty swallowed hard. "This is getting ugly."

"Tell me about it." Beth's haunted expression gave way to something new. Fierce determination. "I've had it with this, Ty. We're going to catch this killer."

"Look out! She's baaa-aaack," Sam said with a big grin. After Beth gave him the middle-fingered salute, he cleared his throat and looked at Ty. "Who could have gotten up here since you were here last?"

He shook his head. "Beats hell out of me."

"I know the perfect time when no one would have noticed or heard," Beth said, her eyes narrowed and flashing.

Ty followed her train of thought. "Mark's party." He shook his head slowly. "Very clever. House was full of people, lots of commotion. Anyone could have slipped up here to trash the place. But *why*?"

"I think Beth already solved that mystery," Sam said as he walked around the room, touching various pieces of furniture as if he thought they might speak to him. "They were looking for anything she might use against them before she could find it. What we don't—and can't—know is if they found anything or removed it. Like the diary."

"Unless we find it."

"So let's dig," Ty said.

CHAPTER NINETEEN

Late in the afternoon, the sunlight streaming through the skylights faded, changing to an almost greenish cast. Beth watched Ty, where he sat sorting through piles of discarded paper, unused canvases, cases of paints and brushes.

"It's going to storm," he said absently.

"Always the farmer." Beth paused behind where he sat on the floor to stroke his dark hair. Something warm passed from him and into her. Wanting more—needing it to anchor her—she rested her open palm on the top of his head, pressing her fist to her heart as his warmth and strength poured through her.

She wanted to name the emotion, but fear stopped her. When she opened her eyes, she found Sam watching from across the room, a knowing look in his eyes. He obviously recognized the connection Beth had discovered with Ty. She would discuss it with him later. Was her gift evolving?

Dare she hope that anything would be better than what she'd experienced before? Or . . . could it be worse?

She would know the answer by morning. Beth

swallowed hard. If she lived that long. This encounter would either make or break Beth Dearborn.

"What have we here?" Sam had his hand on top of a tall bookcase with ornate woodwork along its front. He stepped onto an overturned drawer to bring himself to eye level with its top. "Come to papa."

"Did you find something?" Dread and anticipation shot through Beth as Sam removed a wooden box. "Ty, is that the one?"

"I think so." He scrambled to his feet and brushed dust off his jeans as he crossed the room. "Yeah, that's it. Lorilee kept her diary in that box. She said it belonged to her grandmother. It's a music box."

Lightning flashed over the house, illuminating the room through the skylights. Thunder rumbled.

"Definitely going to storm." Ty looked up at the darkening sky. "Let's take this downstairs. I'll make some coffee. It's going to be a long night."

"That's for sure," Beth said. The longest night of her life. Thunder rumbled louder this time, and she cringed.

Sam put his steadying hand on her shoulder. "The storm?"

She nodded and patted his hand. Ty was already heading down the stairs. She looked back over her shoulder. "Thank you for coming."

"I told you I would."

She smiled. "I know, but you came early and just in time."

"I always do, Cuz." He kissed the top of her head. "Interesting thing about storms, though. That's what you have to thank for me being here early."

"I was going to ask you about that."

"So maybe they aren't so bad, after all?"

"Speak for yourself, Sam." She started down the stairs as the first drops of rain struck the skylights and the wind howled overhead. "Speak for yourself."

With every step down the narrow staircase, Beth felt every pulse of lightning, every gust of wind, every bellow of thunder. Her senses were heightened, and she knew why. Her gift was making an encore performance.

Tonight.

In the kitchen, the storm didn't seem as threatening. Yet. Beth and Sam made sandwiches while Ty put on a pot of coffee.

The phone on the kitchen wall rang, and he answered it. "Ty Malone speaking." He frowned first, then nodded and said, "Sure, Bill. That's fine."

"What's fine?" Beth asked after he hung up the receiver.

"The tickets will be for tomorrow's show, so they aren't leaving until tomorrow afternoon, but he's keeping the kids anyway because of the weather."

"Good." Beth sighed in relief. "That's good."

"Monday's a school holiday for some unknown reason." He glanced out the window. "I should've checked on Cissy before this storm hit," he said over the coffee grinder.

Beth wiggled the mouse to wake up the monitor and clicked on Barncam. "They look fine, Ty. See? There's Cissy and her aptly named filly, Stormy."

He joined her there and slipped his arm around her waist. "They do. I'll sneak out there once the rain stops."

"As the only surviving male member of the Dearborn family," Sam said loftily and cleared his throat, "I should probably ask your intentions toward my cousin." He grinned at Beth's gasp when she whirled around to glower. "Alas, I place life and limb at a greater value than my honor, so what the hell?"

Ty laughed, and even Beth had to roll her eyes in exasperation. "You're lucky I'm not armed, Sammy."

"Ouch."

Ty took Beth's hand. "If it's all right with you, Professor, we'll discuss my intentions after we finish this evening's business." His words were for Sam, but he looked straight at Beth as he spoke.

"Um, certainly." Sam set the plate of sandwiches on the table. "Sustenance, then the diary."

Beth's stomach lurched. She wasn't sure she could keep anything down, but she would need her strength to get through this. So she took a seat at the table between her two favorite men and ate a sandwich and sipped coffee while they chatted about the weather as if it were any ordinary day.

The storm intensified. It seemed to have no end. Finally, she said, "Let's get started reading. I'll begin, and we can take turns if my voice wears out." She hoped yet feared this diary would give them the answers.

The dated entries began shortly after Sarah's birth. By mutual consent, they agreed to move forward to the month of Lorilee's death. They could always go back if they thought they'd missed something important.

"I know it's wrong," Beth read, "but sipping rum

calms me." Her voice trembled. She knew exactly how Lorilee had felt.

"I don't always drink at home. Sometimes I go to a motel bar over toward Marysville. I slip in wearing a hat, drink my fill, then make it home before the school bus."

Ty sighed, his chin in his hands. "I should have tried to stop her. To help her."

"It's not your fault, Ty. None of this—"

Lightning struck what sounded like the tree behind the house. Beth screamed. Her heart leapt into her throat. Sweat poured down her face, her neck, between her breasts.

"It's all right, Beth. Only a storm," Ty said, pulling his chair close enough that he could drape his arm around her shoulders and press his thigh against hers. "Do you want one of us to read now?"

"Not yet. I—I think I need to do this." She looked around the table. "That Lorilee wants me to do it."

Sam nodded. "Yes. That was her message. She was pretty specific." He refilled her coffee. "Hang in there, Cuz."

Beth took a long swallow of the bracing coffee, trying to ignore the high-pitched keen of the wind. After clearing her throat, she resumed where she'd left off reading.

"I'm careful not to drink so much that I can't drive home in time to meet the bus. Even so, with every day that passes, I realize more and more that I need help.

"I started checking on treatment centers—clinics, I guess they're called—for ladies like me, who have problems with alcohol or drugs. Even though I know I need help, I can't quite bring myself to get it yet."

"I should've—"

"Shh." Beth patted Ty's arm. "This is the last day. It may be important."

"I don't think she would have asked me to give it to you if it weren't important," Sam added.

"Point taken." Ty nodded. Thunder boomed. Rain fell. Wind howled.

"I saw Ruby with Gary at the motel bar today. Even worse, they saw *me*. I'm in a terrible pickle. If I tell Daddy about his young bride's affair, how will I explain my presence in that terrible place?"

"Gary? Do you know this Gary?" Sam asked when both Beth and Ty fell silent.

"You could say that," Ty said quietly. "My half brother."

"Oh." Sam appeared thoughtful. "Interesting."

"And he was here the day of the party."

Ty straightened. "Yeah. Uninvited."

Later that same day, Lorilee made another entry. "I can't live like this anymore. I made an appointment at the Frobisher Clinic in Marysville."

Ty confirmed it was an actual treatment clinic, as he'd seen their ads in the newspaper. "All this is starting to make sense. Sorta," he said.

Beth's cell phone rang just as another clap of thunder boomed. "Shit." She pulled the phone from her pocket and flipped it open. "Dearborn here."

She listened, her eyes widening, then a smile spread across her face. "Thanks. Make sure Sheriff Bailey gets a copy of that report, too." She disconnected and looked around the table. "The signature on the letter was *not* Lorilee's."

Ty rested his forehead on the wooden table, then

met Beth's gaze. "Is that enough proof, or do you still . . . ?"

She smiled sadly, feeling stronger and more determined than ever. "She was murdered, Ty." She held the diary up for emphasis. "I still have to prove that for you, for your kids, and for Avery Mutual. *And* I have to solve it." She looked from Ty to Sam, then back to Ty. "For Lorilee, and for me."

The diary implicating Ruby and Gary and the forged signature were definitely enough evidence to reopen the case. But Beth figured she could solve the whole thing tonight by engaging Lorilee once and for all.

"I believe in you," Ty said.

"Thank you." She smiled sadly, hoping he meant that. "But you need to hear the rest of it before you say that." She glanced at Sam for support and found it.

"I'm listening."

"Okay." Beth drained her coffee and set the diary aside. "My empathic gift allows those who've died violently—especially murder victims—to reenact their deaths through my senses."

Confusion, quickly followed by horror, flashed across Ty's face. "No. Are you saying you actually re-live—experience—someone's murder in order to solve it?"

Sam went to the refrigerator and brought her back a bottle of cool water. "Thanks, Sam." She took a drink, then returned her attention to Ty. "Yes. That's what I'm saying."

"Beth . . . that's like being murdered yourself." He shook his head. "I can't stand by and watch you—"

"I don't remember asking for permission." She

smiled and patted his hand, then pushed back from the table and stood.

Ty rose and grasped her shoulders. "Beth, is that why you quit the police force?"

She hesitated. "Partly." She covered his hand with hers. "Let's get this show on the road, boys."

Beth walked purposefully from the kitchen into the parlor, and toward the foyer. Lightning continued to flash, but the thunder and wind were diminished now. At least that was something.

"Beth?" Sam called. "Do you want me to go with you?"

She hesitated, then shook her head. "Just be here to pick up the pieces, Cuz. Like old times."

She took a few more steps toward the archway leading into the foyer, then turned to face Ty. Her throat clogged with unspoken emotions. He came to her, gathered her against him, and kissed her long and hard.

"I love you, Beth."

She didn't want to leave the warmth of his embrace. His protection. His love pouring into her through their empathic connection. But she must. For him. For his children. For her employer. For herself.

And for Lorilee.

Beth eventually pulled back just enough to hold his hand for several seconds, loath to break that precious contact. "I know," she whispered. "I know, Ty." Her voice broke. "I feel it here." She pressed his hand to her heart. She swallowed convulsively, unable to say more. Not yet.

Then, before she could change her mind, she tore her hand from his grasp and launched herself through the portal. Ty and Sam both stayed in the doorway, watching, worry etched into their faces.

Beth drew a deep breath and said, "Okay, Lorilee. Come and get me. I'm all yours."

The dead woman came at Beth like a locomotive. Her possession was fast and powerful and complete.

"I've been waiting so long," she said. *"Why did you make me wait?"*

It didn't matter. She was here now. Why were they having this conversation? In her earlier encounters, the spirits had merely reenacted their deaths through Beth, then moved on to the other side. End of story. But Lorilee wanted to chat. Next thing you knew, they'd be exchanging recipes.

Or notes about Ty?

Don't go there, Dearborn.

Now they were back to when Lorilee had been alive. Beth sensed the shift. Oh, she hadn't bargained on feeling drunk, yet she did. Lorilee had clearly been plastered the day she died.

She sprayed her mouth with breath freshener on her way to answer the front door that long-ago day. A younger version of Ruby Brubaker with her over-dyed hair and heavily made-up face waited on the other side.

Lorilee did not like her mother-in-law much in the first place, and after seeing her with Gary yesterday, she liked her even less. She tried to close the door, but a man's boot blocked her effort. Gary Harlan shoved through the door, past Ruby and Lorilee.

Ruby shouted at him not to hurt Lorilee, just to scare her a little so she'd keep her mouth shut. But Gary proceeded to pummel Lorilee with crushing blows to the face. Pain. Fear. Lorilee tried to shield herself, but to no avail. She fell, but the punishing blows continued—bone shattered, teeth broke, blood spurted from Lorilee's nose—until there was nothing.

Beth came out of Lorilee's grip with a strangled scream. Ty gathered her in his arms and carried her to the sofa in the parlor, where Sam bathed her face with a damp cloth.

"Beth? Can you hear me? Beth?" Sam kept stroking her face. "Talk to us. Talk to us."

"I—I'm okay." She sat up weakly, and Ty steadied her. "Look."

A transparent figure took shape a few feet away. It was Lorilee. Beth didn't understand. This had never happened before.

Lorilee's eyes were filled with resignation as she approached Ty. She touched his cheek, then turned to Beth.

"I wanted to be like you—sober, and strong enough to stay that way." Lorilee's smile was sad but resigned. "I'm finished here now. Thank you."

And she vanished.

"Holy shit," Ty said, holding Beth's hand in a death grip. "Holy shit."

"Correct me if I'm wrong, Cuz," Sam said with a nervous laugh, "but isn't this something new and rather amazing?" He looked at her. "I mean, even for you?"

"This is the first time I've had personal interaction with the spirit afterward," she said, still in awe. "It seems somehow . . . more complete."

Then tough, stubborn, strong Beth Dearborn col-

lapsed into Ty's arms again and wept—for Lorilee
and in thanks for the gift she'd welcomed back into
her life.

Sarah Malone couldn't sleep. Her grandfather's big
old house was pretty cool, but Grandma Ruby gave
her the creeps. The woman watched her with those
false eyelashes half-closed over her eyes all the time.
She was just . . . *weird.*

So Sarah snuck up to the attic to explore. Momma
had shown it to her when she'd been a little girl. It
was a big dusty storage room filled with treasures,
where girls could explore and pretend and play
dress-up. Tonight, it was an escape for Sarah.

While rummaging through a trunk, she fondled
old dresses from decades past, admired a lace handkerchief and wondered which of her ancestors had
carried it. Then she found a small jewelry box that
had belonged to her grandmother. When Grandpa
married Ruby, all his first wife's things were moved
to the attic. One ring looked familiar. A shiver raced
up Sarah's spine as she read the engraving inside the
yellow-gold band.

Her parents' wedding date.

Why was her momma's wedding ring here? She
had to show her daddy and Ms. Dearborn. She
slipped out the back door and across the field, with
nothing but moonlight to guide her. The fastest
way home was across the footbridge north of Rick
Heppel's place. Even in the dark, Sarah knew her
way around the countryside as well as her own
room.

Near the River Road, her step-grandmother's red

Jeep pulled to a stop beside her. "What are you doing out here, Sarah? Your Grandpa will be worried sick."

Wearing her mother's wedding band, Sarah clutched that hand behind her back when she noticed who was driving the Jeep. Gary Harlan was not a nice man. She didn't know what, but she knew there was something bad between her dad and him.

"What are you hidin', Sarah?" Gary asked, and jumped down from the Jeep.

Before Sarah could react, Gary wrenched the ring from her finger. He asked her what it was.

She didn't answer, so he shoved it in Grandma Ruby's face. "Didn't I tell you not to hold onto this damned ring?"

He turned toward the river again and flung the ring as far as he could into the water. Sarah screamed and started toward the river, but he grabbed her wrist and dragged her toward the Jeep.

"You aren't telling anyone about that ring, you little brat."

"Don't hurt her, Gary!" Grandma Ruby shouted. "Don't hurt her, too."

Beth noticed a definite change in the way Ty looked at her. It frightened her almost as much as facing her gift again had.

"I'm going out to check on Cissy and her foal," he said. "Sam, there's a spare room down here off the kitchen. Bed's made."

"Thanks, Ty. It's been a long day."

Ty kissed Beth's cheek. "I won't be long," he whispered. "Wait up for me?"

Beth nodded. They had a lot to talk about, and he

still didn't realize she was a drunk. She and Sam had left out that part of her walk down memory lane. Knowing about Lorilee's drinking problem and her own, how could she risk sticking Ty with another woman addicted to alcohol?

And his children certainly deserved better.

The back door closed and Sam said, "He loves you."

"I know."

"And you love him."

"I know."

"That should be enough."

Beth hugged herself against the evening chill. The air still felt strange, even though the brunt of the storm had moved east.

"Lorilee was a practicing alcoholic, Sam," she said. "I'm a recovering alcoholic." She shook her head. "He deserves better."

Sam crossed the room and looked into her eyes. "He's a big boy, Beth." He sighed and pursed his lips, then added, "You asked him to trust you. Maybe you should return the favor."

" 'Night, Sam."

He shook his head. "I'll just grab my bag from the car. You're hopeless, kiddo."

"I love you, too, Cuz." She gave him a big hug. "Now get your bag before it gets any later. We're all zonked."

"Tell me about it." A huge yawn spread across his face as he headed out the front door. "Oh, I think you can use the front door now."

"Ha. Ha."

Beth was in deep shit. She'd fallen deep and hard

and fast for Ty Malone, and it looked as if he was willing to reciprocate.

What about her safe, nomadic life? What about his three children? What if she fell off the wagon? She couldn't burden anyone else with her problems. She was accustomed to taking care of herself, and things had to stay that way. Then if she blew it, no one got hurt but Beth Dearborn—not Ty or his innocent children.

What could she do? What should she do? Did she stay and risk it all, or did she run away and turn her back on her only chance at love?

The phone in the kitchen rang, shattering Beth's thoughts. It was just as well. She wasn't making much progress.

"Malone residence, Dearborn speaking," she answered.

"It's Bill Brubaker, Ms. Dearborn," he said. "Sarah's missing. She said she was going up to the attic right after dinner. It was a spot where she and Lorilee spent a lot of time, so I didn't think anything of it. Now she's gone."

"Gone?" Beth squeezed her eyes closed, sensing there was more. "What do you mean by *gone*, Mr. Brubaker?"

"Not here. We've looked everywhere." He sighed. "What's really strange, though, is . . ."

"What?"

"My wife is missing, too."

Your wife, the murderess? Beth's internal alarms went into overdrive. "When did you last see either of them, and where?"

He'd seen Ruby about twenty minutes later than

he remembered having seen Sarah. Beth made a few notes on a message pad Pearl kept near the phone. Remembering what Lorilee's spirit had revealed to her earlier, Beth had to ask one more question.

"Do you know if Gary Harlan is there, Mr. Brubaker?"

The old man put her on hold and called the bunkhouse to check. Gary wasn't in his bed either. With deceptive calm, Beth asked the man to let Ty know the minute any of them returned.

How was Beth going to find Sarah? Her empathy couldn't help her now. Sam walked in the front door with his bag and found her pacing in the kitchen.

"What's wrong?" he asked. "I can tell something's happened."

She explained and Sam slumped into a kitchen chair. "Shit."

Ty came in the back door. "Everything's okay in the barn." He stopped walking and stared at them both. "What is it?"

Beth went to him, placed her hands on his shoulders, and said, "Ruby and Harlan have Sarah."

"No." He looked at the phone on the wall, his expression one of pure terror. "No, they can't have my Sarah—not my little girl."

"Do you have any idea where he might take her?"

Ty dragged his hand through his hair, his eyes wild with worry. "Yes." He swallowed hard. "Our mother's house."

"Where is it?" Beth kept her hands on him, absorbing his fear, his pain.

"Edge of Brubaker. Fairly isolated. Empty. He inherited it after she died."

"Then they can't get there either." She shook her head. "The bridge."

"He has a boat." Ty was already moving through the house toward the front door. "Can you drive that Chevy while I call Heppel?"

"I'll drive the Chevy," Sam said. "I've always wanted to drive the getaway car, and it's on my credit card."

All Ty wanted was to see his daughter's smiling face again. And he wanted to tell her she'd been right about her mother.

Please, God—don't take her, too.

Once they explained it all to Rick Heppel—excluding the empathic, woo-woo stuff—and he understood he was being asked to play a role in hunting down Lorilee's killers, nothing would stop him from firing up his chopper. There was just enough room, he said, for all of them. He had headsets and a communication system, so they could talk in the chopper, despite the noise.

"I gather there's never been any love lost between you and your half brother," Sam commented as they flew toward Brubaker.

"He's always hated me." Ty sighed. "And when I married Lorilee, that clinched it."

"She told me he was sweet on her before you came here," Rick confirmed. "Said you were her love at first sight."

Beth checked the Colt again, just to make sure. "We learned to fire a forty-five at the academy, but this one's a little older."

Rick glanced back at it. "Well, that brings back memories I'd rather forget."

"I'll bet it does," Ty said. "My father carried it in Nam."

Rick looked up sharply from checking the instruments. "Your father?"

Ty nodded. Rick faced forward and concentrated on night flying. "Where do you want me to put this bird down, Ty?"

"On Gary Harlan's head."

"Look!" Beth pointed at an old pickup stopped by the neglected ranch house.

"Gary's old truck. He keeps it here," Ty said. "Rick, put your bird down on the sittin' ducks."

"With pleasure." He started lowering his chopper into the front lawn of Ty's mother's old house.

Gary dragged Sarah toward the woods as the chopper descended. Ty saw Ruby standing there with her jaw dropped. "I don't think we were expected."

A bullet ricocheted off the runners. "You son of a bitch. I'll teach you to shoot at my bird." Rick stopped short of landing and resumed forward momentum, chasing down Gary, Ruby, and Sarah.

"Put her down, Rick," Ty said quietly. "I need to get out there with my daughter."

"Suit yourself." He landed the chopper and another bullet ricocheted off the propeller. "Son of a bitch."

"Stay in here with Rick," Beth said to Sam.

"Maybe," he said. "We'll see."

"Dad!" Sarah shouted as they emerged from the noisy chopper, but Gary smothered her cry with his hand.

"I tried to tell him not to hurt her like he—"

Gary put a bullet right through Ruby's back. Her

eyes rolled into the back of her head and she plunged facedown into the mud.

"My God," Ty said. "Beth?"

"Ruby's dead." She stayed next to him while they both watched Gary back toward the woods with his gun pressed to Sarah's temple.

"Beth, I know it hurts you, and I wouldn't ask if it weren't for Sarah." His voice sounded wretched. "Can you talk to her? Will she tell us where he's taking her?"

Beth was silent for several moments. "A hunting cabin?" She looked at Ty. "She said you know the place."

"I do." He squeezed her hand. "Where the hell's the sheriff?"

"Ruby said Gary left his keys in the truck. It'll be faster."

"This is damned strange," Ty said. "Getting directions from a dead woman."

Beth and Ty drove the old pickup to the hunting cabin, leaving Rick and Sam with instructions to send the sheriff there as soon as he arrived. Since Gary and Sarah were on foot, Beth and Ty reached the cabin first.

Beth slipped into the cabin pantry, since she was armed. Ty waited outside, behind a tree, with instructions to give a bird call when he saw them.

Beth heard the call and also Sarah's weeping. Poor kid. It was all she could do to stop herself from rushing to the girl's rescue too soon. Instead, she prepared the Colt and waited. It didn't take long for Gary to swing open that pantry door, and the bastard was faster than she'd anticipated. She was exhausted, but she still managed to lunge at him.

They ended up on the floor, fighting. The wiry son of a bitch wrested the Colt from her grasp and flung it across the floor. Sarah was tied to a chair and unable to help.

Where the hell was Ty?

Harlan managed to get his hands around Beth's throat, his thumbs pressed against her windpipe. Her pulse pounded and the world darkened.

She had experienced dozens of deaths in her life, but never her own. Beth was slipping away. She knew the signs.

Sarah screamed. "You're killing her! Stop! Please stop!"

Beth Dearborn was not ready to die. She wasn't finished yet. Mustering the dwindling shreds of her strength, she brought her knee sharply into Harlan's groin.

He howled and jerked back just as the wood splintered on the cabin door. "Lock me out, you bastard," Ty shouted as he continued kicking.

The door was solid and sturdy, but Beth knew the power of adrenalin. Ty would break through and at least save his daughter, if not Beth.

Though her throat was on fire and her body weakened, she was determined to fight Harlan long enough. Ty needed time, and she would give it to him.

Gary lowered his head and came toward her like a battering ram. Beth stepped aside and he slammed into a log post. The man's rage and insanity kept him going. He shook his head and turned to face her.

"You're dead, bitch," he said.

He came at her again, but Beth was ready. She positioned herself and allowed his own momentum and her training to maneuver the throw. He hit the floor hard. She heard bones crack. He groaned, but didn't move.

Beth retrieved the Colt just as Ty squeezed through the broken boards and into the cabin. "You okay?" he asked as he untied Sarah, his gaze on Beth.

"Daddy!" Sarah threw herself into her father's arms.

Beth watched father and daughter as she kept the Colt aimed at the groaning son of a bitch on the floor. Her job was almost finished here. Everything would be all right now.

"I want you to wait outside, Sarah," Ty said. "Go to the truck. When the sheriff gets here, send him in. Okay?"

She sniffled and nodded. "Ms. Dearborn was amazing."

"Yes, she is," Ty said as Sarah obeyed him and left the cabin.

Beth felt his gaze on her. He didn't speak as he walked across the room and picked up his brother's handgun.

"Only years practicing restraint are keeping me from using this on my murdering half brother." His voice was barely more than a whisper. He stood staring at the weapon, turning it slowly in his hands.

When he met her gaze, Beth saw his pain and her heart ached. She wanted to go to him, to hold him in her arms, to offer him comfort. Instead, her sense of duty and training—and fear?—kept her right where she was, with an antique gun aimed at a man with broken bones. "You broke my fucking leg," Harlan mumbled, slowly rolling onto his back.

"If you move another inch, you won't have to worry about pain anymore," Beth warned.

Harlan's gaze drifted toward Ty. "Well, if it isn't my loving baby brother."

"Don't mess with me, Gary," Ty warned.

"I think the bitch broke my ribs, too."

"Good, and she's not a bitch."

Harlan sneered, despite the blood still oozing from his nose. "So it's like that. She your new whore, Tyrone?"

Ty took a quick step toward the bastard on the floor, but Beth shook her head. "No, Ty. He's not worth it."

Harlan turned his gaze toward Beth again. "How the hell'd you know where to find me?"

"Ruby told me," she said with the nastiest smile she could manage.

He appeared confused. "You can't prove a fucking thing," he taunted.

"Try us, you bast—"

"Allow me, Ty. Allow me." So Beth gave him an agonizingly detailed accounting of Lorilee's murder just as Sheriff Dan Bailey arrived to listen from the doorway.

And, rather than deny it, Gary turned to gloat at his half brother. "Yeah, just that way, baby brother."

Sheriff Bailey, weapon drawn, said from the doorway, "Good work, Dearborn. Heard every word."

Realizing he'd just confessed to Lorilee's murder, Gary bolted to his feet, lunging toward Bailey with a hideous cracking sound from his broken leg. He ignored multiple commands to halt.

More than one bullet stopped Gary Harlan's flight from justice.

Beth turned to Ty just as Gary's spirit left his body

and tried to engage her. He expected her to relive his death, but she told him no. In the past, she'd been unable to prevent spirits who needed her help from making themselves welcome, whether she wanted them there or not. She was stronger now. Plus, Gary didn't deserve her help. After all, he hadn't been murdered. On the contrary, *he* was the murderer.

"I blocked him," she said. For the first time, Beth Dearborn had *control* of her empathic gift. "I don't believe it . . ."

Ty hugged her, and she wound her arms around his waist, breathing in his scent. *He* had given her another gift—control.

Back at the sheriff's office in Brubaker, Sarah told them about the ring she'd found and where it was now. Grandma Ruby had tearfully confessed to her where Gary had buried her momma, and how she'd managed to hide the ring, thinking she'd somehow give it to Sarah one day to appease her own guilt.

A search along the creek revealed Lorilee's seven-year-old grave and Lorilee's remains. They had Gary's confession, Lorilee's diary, and enough evidence to close the case.

Now maybe Lorilee Brubaker-Malone could rest in peace. And it was way past time to restore her reputation. After a quiet discussion with Sarah, Ty vowed to use Lorilee's insurance policy to fund an alcohol-rehabilitation program.

"Lorilee would have liked that," Beth said.

It took nearly all night, but finally Bill Brubaker had been informed of everything that happened. It would take time for the man to overcome his feelings of guilt that his bride had been responsible for his daughter's murder.

The children were all safe. When Bill asked that they be allowed to stay the remainder of the night, Ty couldn't refuse. The old man's expression appeared stricken. He needed his family. Even Sarah said she wanted to stay with him. After all, in the end, Grandma Ruby redeemed herself by trying to save Sarah, and she actually had tried to save Lorilee, too.

Beth, Sam, and Ty returned to the farm. Pearl and Cecil were back in their little house, so Ty wouldn't have to worry about taking care of things.

Alone in the parlor, Ty took Beth by the hand and led her up the stairs, where they made love until the first streaks of dawn shown on the eastern horizon. Long after he'd fallen asleep, she lay staring into the darkness, savoring the steady rhythm of his heart, the warmth of his breath. In the dimness, Beth looked down at Ty's sleeping face and tried to memorize it. How had she fallen in love so fast? So completely?

She already had orders to report to Memphis for her next assignment. Or maybe she'd go back to Chicago with Sam—quit the insurance game and try to get back on the force. Maybe . . .

She left Ty's room, packed her bags, left the Colt in its box on her bed, and headed downstairs to meet Sam. She saw him leaning against his rental car, waiting for her. And she already knew he would try to talk her out of going.

She opened the front door—the same one she'd avoided for so long—and stood frozen. Paralyzed. She couldn't move another step. It was as if an invisible barrier had formed across the threshold and wouldn't let her pass. Tears scalded her eyes. She wanted out of here. She had to go now.

"Stay," Lorilee whispered. *"I waited to see if you would stay. You're needed here. Don't leave him."*

"Don't . . ." Beth pushed on the screen again, and it swung open. Lorilee was gone, and Beth knew it was for good this time.

She stopped on the porch to look out across the pasture, the fields, the trees along the creek. She'd grown to love more than Ty. She'd also grown to love this place.

She faced Sam—her beloved Sam. Disapproval oozed from his every pore, but he would keep his opinion to himself for now, at least until he was sure she was all right. Then he'd give her hell.

"Running away, Beth?" Ty asked from behind her. "Kinda early for a city girl."

"Ty, don't . . ."

"No, *you* listen." He placed one hand on each side of her face. "You just hush and listen."

Beth tried to speak, but couldn't. She bit her lip and nodded.

"I, Ty Malone, love you, Beth Dearborn. Get that straight." He smiled and kissed her. "You're the bravest woman I've ever known." He kissed her again. "Will you give this small town, this farm life, and me a try?"

"Ty . . . I'm—I'm an alcoholic."

His brow furrowed. "I reckon Lorilee's ghost said as much, but you don't drink now."

"I'm a *recovering* alcoholic."

"You don't drink," he repeated. "How long have you been sober, Beth?"

"Three years and some."

"That's a hell of an accomplishment. You're brave." He kissed her again. "It just shows you have the kind of strength this family needs."

"You . . . think I'm brave?" He thought she was brave? It was crazy, but Beth couldn't imagine a life anywhere without Ty and his kids. Lorilee's kids. Beth realized that Ty thought she deserved to be loved, to have a chance to raise his children. Staying sober so long told him she was a strong woman, one who might even be a good influence on everyone.

"I'm not cut out to be a farmer, Ty—not full-time, anyway." She shook her head slowly. "Now that I'm finally learning to control my gift, I want—need—to use it."

Sam cleared his throat. "Ever think of doing some consulting work, Cuz?"

"Consulting?" she echoed.

"I happen to know a certain chief of police who would sell his left nut to have you available even by phone once in a while."

Ty chuckled. "Come to think of it, a certain small-town sheriff would appreciate your services, too." He sighed and gripped her upper arms. "Stay."

She nodded, her throat clogged with unshed tears. "I think," she finally said, "that Lorilee left a little part of herself with me."

Ty didn't argue. "I carried a boatload of guilt for not getting her help when I knew in my gut she needed it." He drew a deep breath and released it slowly. "You've allowed me to do that."

"Well, kids," Sam said, "I don't think I'm needed here anymore." He applauded, waved, blew her a kiss, and drove away in his rented Chevrolet.

"I believe in miracles again, Beth," Ty said, holding her in his arms. "And now, because of you, I believe in love again."

He kissed her again—a kiss filled with promises. When Beth pulled away, she gazed into his eyes, and into her future.

"I'm not going anywhere, cowboy."

"A thrill ride." —LISA JACKSON on *Ice*

Stephanie Rowe

A MAN WITH NO PAST

Luke Webber thinks he's erased his entire history. New name, new life, no paper trail. He thinks that up in the wilds of Alaska no one will find him. He's wrong.

A WOMAN WITH NO FUTURE

When Isabella shows up on his doorstep, she's got a bullet in her shoulder and all that Luke's been trying to avoid is hot on her trail. Without his help, she'll die. But helping her will mean surrendering everything—his body, his heart . . . and quite possibly his life.

CHILL

"Pulse-pounding chills and hot romance."
—JoAnn Ross on *Ice*

ISBN 13: 978-0-505-52776-9

✂ ☐ **YES!**

Sign me up for the Love Spell Book Club and send my
FREE BOOKS! If I choose to stay in the club, I will pay
only $8.50* each month, a savings of $6.48!

NAME: _____

ADDRESS: _____

TELEPHONE: _____

EMAIL: _____

☐ I want to pay by credit card.

☐ **VISA**   ☐ **MasterCard.**   ☐ **DISCOVER**

ACCOUNT #: _____

EXPIRATION DATE: _____

SIGNATURE: _____

Mail this page along with $2.00 shipping and handling to:
Love Spell Book Club
PO Box 6640
Wayne, PA 19087
Or fax (must include credit card information) to:
610-995-9274
You can also sign up online at **www.dorchesterpub.com**.
*Plus $2.00 for shipping. Offer open to residents of the U.S. and Canada only.
Canadian residents please call 1-800-481-9191 for pricing information.
If under 18, a parent or guardian must sign. Terms, prices and conditions subject to
change. Subscription subject to acceptance. Dorchester Publishing reserves the right
to reject any order or cancel any subscription.